Original Syn

Iron Wraiths MC

Book I

A.J. Downey

Copyright

~

Edited and book design by Maggie Kern at Ms.K Edits

Cover art by Dar Albert at Wicket Art Designs

Dedication

To Josh, and the Savannah trip in June of 2023. For making it so memorable and letting me prattle on about all things spooky, history, and this book without making me feel dumb or boring in the slightest.

Chapter One

Madisyn...

"Dammit, Zeke," I swore under my breath as I eyed the biker standing outside the riverfront doorway. He was leaned back against the side of the building, flipping through one of those little notepads, a lit cigarette dangling from his lips, bobbing as he counted under his breath. Ash fell into his light brown beard as he flipped and counted pages like it was cash. I had a sinking feeling in the pit of my stomach.

I was looking for my older brother, Zeke, but honestly, the way our dynamic was working lately? I might as well have been the older sibling for all he was acting like a wayward teenage boy.

I sniffed and raised my chin defiantly. I wasn't about to let this foolishness continue, so I squared my shoulders, kept my chin up, and marched resolutely forward. I mean, I'm sure I wasn't exactly imposing, but I tried for what all five foot two of my frame would convey.

I would be lying if I said I wasn't scared, but there was only one thing that scared me more than the Iron Wraiths motorcycle gang of Savannah, and that was losing my brother.

I stopped in front of the biker and said clearly, "I'm here for my brother, Zeke. I know he's in there gambling."

The man slowly raised his deep brown eyes from his hands and the notebook in them and fixed them on mine. His eyebrows went up into a look of surprise, and his eyes widened in disbelief. He looked both this way and that, up the cobblestone street, and then around the corner and up the alleyway back behind the building.

"You talking to me?" he asked and he gave me a wolfish grin.

"Do you see anyone else?" I asked archly, crossing my arms over my chest, which just made his eyes drop from my face to my not insubstantial breasts.

I snapped my fingers at him and all but barked, "Eyes up here!"

He barked back, only not with words. No, he laughed. He took his cigarette out of his mouth between his fingers and laughed and laughed – until he didn't. Stopping abruptly, he stuck the cancer stick back between his lips, sucked on it, and blew out a plume of smoke. Completely deadpan and completely serious, he said to me, "Fuck off, little girl."

"I'm twenty-three goddamned years old, you rotten fuck, and I'm not leaving without my brother!" I practically screamed in his face, my frustration and anger boiling over.

He pushed off the building sharply at the insult and his hand flashed out faster than should be possible for a man of his size to move. He seized my arm above the elbow, his fingers digging in painfully. I reared back, throwing my weight backward and away from him, but he held onto me easily. He plucked his cigarette out of his mouth with his other hand and flicked the burning butt off his thumb out into the gutter with his middle finger.

"We don't use names around here," he said, giving me a vicious shake for emphasis and to make sure he had my attention. "Mine sure as fuck ain't 'rotten' or 'fuck,' but you've got my attention now. I want to know just who you fucking belong to."

I felt my mouth drop open at the implication that I was *owned* by anyone, like a-a-a *cow* or something. His much taller six-foot frame was dragging me through the door behind him before I could do much more than sputter in indignation.

Of course, once my panicked brain caught up to the fact that he was dragging me where I wanted to go, I stopped resisting *as* hard, but I didn't give up the fight completely.

"I can *walk*. Get your hand off me!" I snapped. He unhanded me at a poker table in the dimly lit and sparsely furnished concrete basement of the building, and I set eyes on my brother just in front of me.

"Come on, Zeke. Let's go," I demanded coldly.

"Madi? What the fuck?" my brother demanded indignantly.

"I mean it, Zeke. Get off your fucking ass and *let's go*, right now!" I didn't have to force the venom into my tone. It was naturally occurring by this point. I had so fucking had it with my brother and the fact that he was here right now. With the *Iron* fucking *Wraiths!*

"Madi, get the fuck out of here. What are you even doing right now? Are you *crazy*?" Zeke demanded. He had gotten up, replacing the biker's hand on my arm with his own.

"Specter?" a strong voice asked – a deep baritone with a rich timber that seeped out of the shadows at the side of the room. I almost didn't see the man until he slipped off the top of the low cabinets against the wall. He'd been half-sitting on them, and observing the poker game. Where I hadn't been super afraid at Specter of the heavy hand, this man made me freeze like a deer in the headlights, my heart stuttering harder than my voice had outside. Only there wasn't anything indignant about this stutter. No, this stutter was one of fear.

Something about the way this new man moved, the way he glided in all that heavy black leather with barely a creak or a whisper, at how his heavy soled black boots barely made a sound against the raw concrete floor, and at how *everyone*, my brother included, froze at the sound of his voice, turning their attention to this man... well, it screamed that *he was in charge*. Not only did it scream that he was in charge, it telegraphed as clearly as a neon flashing sign that he was the thing in the room to be afraid of. Especially with how *no one*, and I do mean not a one of them, would make eye contact with him.

3

I swallowed hard and found my equilibrium as fast as I could as he stepped into the light. *If we were going down, we'd go down together... idiot,* I thought at my brother.

"Who's this?" the man demanded, and his dark eyes fixed on mine. I steeled myself and gave as good as I got, meeting his gaze, and not backing down despite how my heart quavered craven in my chest.

"Madisyn, you've got to *go,*" Zeke demanded. My brother's voice was tight with fear. I felt my mouth go dry, but I wasn't about to give any of these idiot males the satisfaction of seeing me sweat.

"Madisyn," I said. "Madisyn Reyn—"

"I just told you we don't do names," the first man, Specter, said, his shoulders shaking with silent laughter and drawing my attention away from the dark man from the shadows.

I snapped my eyes from him to the second man, the man in charge, as he took a further step into the light. My prey instinct told me to stay rooted to the spot, and not just that, but to not take my eyes off him. That taking my eyes off him could prove to be fatal.

Of course, with my fight-or-flight reflexes kicking in, gluing my gaze onto him, I had nothing to do now but look at him, and look at him, I did. He was older than me. Older than Zeke, too, but not so old any of his jet-black hair had started to thread with any silver.

He rasped a hand along the dark stubble coating his chin, his deep, dark, poisonous eyes flicking from Specter, to my brother, to me.

"Syn, I'm sorry. I don't know what she's doing here," Zeke said, dropping his hand from just above my elbow and taking a step back. My rage at my brother went up a notch as he took that step away from me. Like, *seriously? I come in here to save your ass from yourself, and at the first hint of any actual trouble, you just drop me like a bad habit? Just like that?* God, he was being an asshole.

Specter clapped his hands onto my brother's shoulders and dragged him back away from me, pushing him back down into the seat he'd vacated right in front of us at the table. My anger wavered, my fear and empathy nudging it out of the way at the spill of cards and poker chips atop the maroon felt.

With a bravery I didn't feel, and worry that I did, I flicked my eyes to Specter's.

"Will you quit manhandling people?" I demanded coldly, my vision once again distracted, returning immediately to the dark man, the man in charge, as he took another step in my direction and barked a laugh.

"I see something I'd like to manhandle," he said, eyeing me. I snorted, taking a reflexive step back. "Maybe there's a deal we could come to." His grin was wolfish.

"Real original," I said sarcastically, rolling my eyes.

"Madisyn..." Zeke's voice was tinged with a mix of desperation and exasperation. It had me shutting my mouth with an almost audible clack of teeth at the sound of it. I looked into my brother's blue eyes, a match for mine. They looked *desperate* for me to shut my mouth, shining out from under his messy mop of sandy-blond hair just a shade or two darker than my own. It looked as though he'd been gripping it with his hands and the realization of his disarray hit me like a ton of bricks.

I immediately felt an answering fear to his own swell in my chest as the man in charge rolled my name around in his mouth like he was tasting it.

"Madisyn..." he practically purred, and I felt queasy. I'd be damned if I would show it, though.

"And you are?" I demanded archly.

"Synister." Specter was grinning, but it wasn't friendly. "President of the Iron Wraiths. Put some respect on his name."

"Oh, for Christ's sake!" I snapped. "Zeke, come on. Let's go," I said and couldn't help the note of pleading that had entered my voice at my last words. All sense of bravado was fleeing the quieter the rest of the men around the table got and the longer this went on.

Zeke made to stand up, but Specter clapped his hands onto his shoulders and forced him back down to sit heavily in his chair.

"He ain't finished losing his ass, sweet – is it little or big sister?" Synister asked. His smile was a slow spreading of lips, showing very even and white teeth. His canines were naturally pronounced and it gave him this feral, if cunning, sort of vibe. The misgivings that'd been stirring in my breast finally crumbled completely into fear, my heart rate growing in intensity with the sheer unabashed audacity and intensity of the look that the man called Synister was giving me.

He'd been aptly named. He did give out a sinister vibe.

It was something raw and primal. He didn't even bother to hide the naked desire in it, and if I hadn't felt like some kind of prey animal in his crosshairs the moment before, I absolutely and for certain did now. I swallowed hard and tried my best to put on one hell of a convincing act.

"No, he's more than done," I said coldly and felt a slight surge of pride that my voice didn't tremble or shake.

"Not until I say he is, and he ain't leaving without paying *something* of what he owes me."

"Zeke, get up. Let's *go*," I said and I put some steel in my voice.

"I'm good for it, Syn. I promise you. Just let me get Madi out of here. She doesn't—"

My brother's panicked pleading fell silent as Synister tore his gaze from mine and fixed it on Zeke. The expression on his face, which I didn't find particularly attractive, but I didn't precisely find him *unattractive* either, slipped from something resembling amused, to cold and unimpressed. My brother shut right up, which Zeke *never* did. Fear lanced me through the chest again, a javelin through my heart and out my back, pinning me to the floor where I stood. What Synister said next chilled me to the bone.

"You're going to pay me *something*. What's to keep me from holding little sister here as collateral until you do?" Synister demanded.

Specter was rubbing my brother's shoulders, digging in painfully, and Zeke's panicked look crumbled into downright terrified as his eyes flew to my face. I felt my shoulders knot.

Goddammit, Zeke, I thought dispassionately, sick of his bullshit, which had sailed right on past *beyond the pale* by this point and was rapidly plunging into the depths of insanity.

Fear ran an icy finger up and down my spine. I fought not to shiver in front of this pack of hungry jackals who were all but licking their chops like I was some prime cut of beef left unattended.

"How much does he owe you?" I asked tiredly. I didn't know what I expected, but the figure Synister listed off so casually? That certainly wasn't it.

"A hundred and eighty grand," he said coolly, his expression growing bored. I closed my eyes and tried very hard to find a way to breathe around such a large figure.

A hundred and eighty grand? What the fuck, Zeke? How could you? And with them...

I prayed the thoughts stayed in my head and weren't telegraphed on my face.

"Tell you what," Synister said, and I opened my eyes to stare at my brother, whose eyes bounced back and forth, taking in my reddening face. "I'll make you a deal, little sister."

I flicked my eyes to Synister's and didn't blink or flinch. I didn't say anything, either. I simply waited him out.

"I'll let him walk out of here whole and take you as a down payment on his debt."

"Madi don't," Zeke warned, sounding desperate.

"And just what is *that* supposed to mean?" I demanded.

Synister's eyes flicked from the crown of my head to the soles of my feet and back again, his gaze settling back onto mine.

"You agree to fuck me and I'll knock five grand off his debt and let him go right now to find me the rest of what he owes me."

I barked a laugh and shook my head.

"You're insane," I said bitterly. Or I was... I couldn't decide which, because I didn't want to lose my brother, but at the same time... *shit, are you seriously even considering this Madisyn Jayne?* I thought to myself incredulously.

Synister's lips twitched in amusement as he saw my resolve begin to weaken and I knew it. I was really bad at this. My fucking face might as well have been the bouncing ball above a goddamn sing-along of my every thought.

"There's more than one kind of currency in the underworld, sweet baby sister," Synister declared, his grin wolfish once more.

The better to eat you with, I thought.

Chuckling swept through the room, seeping out of the dark and the cracks, swirling about the table in little eddies of terrible amusement at my expense, as I had to wonder if I had just said that out loud.

"If it makes you feel better, I'll buy you dinner first," Synister said, his grin growing into something that very nearly made hysterical laughter bubble up and out of my throat.

I felt my mouth drop open and I barely turned that hysterical giggle into a scoffing laugh as I said incredulously, "You're actually fucking serious."

"Madisyn Jayne, don't even think about it," Zeke warned, and again, lightning fast, Specter's hand flew out and he grabbed my brother by the chin, ratcheting his head back at a painful and scary angle.

"Don't!" I took a half-step forward like I could actually do anything, and my voice faltered as I finished my sentence. That icy finger of fear was now a hand wrapped resolutely around my spine and was gripping it tight, all the muscles in my back tense and aching. "Don't hurt him."

I turned on Synister and with all the strength I didn't feel, said, "Five K is insulting. Do better than that."

"So that's a yes then?" he asked slyly, and I shifted on my feet.

"It's not a no," I said uncomfortably, very aware every eye in the place was on me. "Do better than that, and it might move the needle off the narrow maybe it's sitting on."

"Ten."

"Get real."

His grin was back and there was a spirit of a challenge in his dark eyes.

"Fifteen," he said, arching a brow, and I gave him an exasperated look.

"Your chances are dropping, not gaining like you want them to. Get fucking serious already," I said.

"Ooo, she has a dirty mouth," Specter said, and he was smiling this creepy misogynistic smile that made my stomach queasy.

"Fine, all seriousness," Synister said. "Fifty thousand off his debt, if you agree to let me hit that."

I rolled my eyes. "And I suppose you want to do it now in front of these yahoos?" I demanded. I wanted to do better than fifty, but by the sound of his voice, I knew he was going to be firm. I didn't know if I could push my luck any further... I mean, I had to think that at least he was *willing* to bargain and I wasn't staked out on the fucking poker table with them all taking turns while I screamed... so yeah. I would much rather not push my luck any harder than was safe – which yeah, *none of this was safe* – holy fuck.

"No, I said I'd buy you dinner first," he said, and thank God, the amusement was back in his eyes.

"And what if I said there was something to sweeten the pot?" I countered, swallowing hard, thinking that if I was going to do this to save my worthless brother's skin, then by God, I was going to make it count.

"Ha!" He barked a laugh. "I doubt you have anything that'd take it up a notch," he said.

"Just for that? Eighty," I said, balling my hands into fists as laughter erupted around the table, echoing off the brick walls and sifting down from the rafters.

"Eighty fucking grand? You're awfully sure of yourself there, little sister. What's your big secret?" he asked. "Your pussy made out of gold?" His eyebrows went up, and he seemed genuinely curious.

I raised my chin and narrowed my eyes. Taking a deep breath, I decided that if he wanted to be crude about it, then I could be crude

9

too. I couldn't possibly be any more embarrassed or humiliated at this point, and if I was seriously entertaining this ludicrous idea of his in the first place...

"Madisyn." My brother's voice was tight with pain and his tone full of urging that I not do this. I couldn't even look at him by this point.

"Virgin pussy has to be worth more, right?" I asked. I couldn't even look Synister in the eye by this point... but by God, if I was going to leverage my body to save my brother's hide, I might as well leverage it for all it was fucking worth – right?

My question was met with a silence so profound it practically rang in my ears. I flicked my gaze to the man of the hour, and Synister's eyebrows went up like I had finally done or said something that really interested him. He swept me with his gaze and said, "Dinner, Friday night, be ready at six. Dress for it. We'll continue these negotiations someplace a little more private."

I nodded, my shoulders easing down some from where I was wearing them for earrings.

"It's a date," I said, and he barked a laugh.

"Specter, let him up and show them both out," Syn said. He melted back into the shadows and retook his seat on the cabinets, hoisting himself up more fully to lean his back against the wall.

We were dismissed, thoroughly and completely.

Specter let my brother up out of his seat and gestured grandly that we may go. I turned and met my brother's eyes, and he looked something akin to devastated. I felt the anger and indignance flash in my own gaze and thrust my chin that he'd better *march*.

I turned to follow Zeke as Synister called from the shadows of his alcove, "See you Friday, Madi."

I felt sick, but we were walking out and we were both walking out in one piece... which was a win for now.

Still, *what had I just done?*

Chapter Two

Synister...

"Are you fucking serious?" Corvus, my second-in-command, ran a hand through his hair, slicking it back from his face. He ran his other hand over his beard as he looked at me from his place at my right hand.

"As a heart attack," Specter, our road captain, said, laughing. He was looking at his hands and had thought Corvus was talking to him, when in reality? Corvus's whiskey-brown eyes bored into mine. I stared back and gave no quarter, unrelenting, not giving so much as a centimeter in my resolve.

The reality of the situation was that the kid didn't have it. There was no way he could come up with the kind of money we were talking. Was his family a rich one?

One of Savannah's most affluent.

Were they going to give it to him?

Not only no, but hell no. He'd tapped out the good graces of his rich parents. They'd cut him off a while ago. Little sister didn't have the cash, either, but I hadn't been lying when I'd said there was more than one type of currency in the underworld and cash, ass, or grass? She certainly had the second one.

She hit all the right places for me – small, petite even, curvy in the right places with ample tits and a cute little ass, and those *hips*! I could grab onto 'em and *mm*.

Looks weren't everything, though. She was also going to be a bit of a challenge, that one. She had just the right amount of spice to her. I liked that... and a *virgin?*

At first, I hadn't believed her, but then those cheeks had pinked up so beautifully. And when she wouldn't look at me?

Not *wouldn't. Couldn't*, I reminded myself... Well, I could tell the difference. She stood there all false bravado, but her hands and the way she'd balled them into fists to hide their shaking had given her away. The more the conversation had gone on, that fine tremble in her hands had turned into a tremor, and then that tremor had migrated until she was full-on shaking. She stood there like a leaf in a fuckin' hurricane and thought she'd had me convinced. I found that kind of fuckin' adorable on her little five-foot-nothing frame.

She'd been all long blonde hair and wide blue eyes and I couldn't fucking resist toying with her just a little... but when she'd tried to give as good as she got?

Mm, I was getting hard just thinking about it. I got rock hard to the point of pain, thinking about how I would be her first, and how my cock could be the *only* one to satisfy her if she was good enough, or until I got tired of her or whatever. The possessive dick in me *really* liked the thought of having a plaything that was *all mine* from the word *go*.

Aw, yeah.

"You really think she's a virgin?" Haint asked, smoke curling from his mouth to his nose like a dragon, where he sat back in his seat. He raised his eyebrows at me, his hair dark – almost black – his beard only lightly threaded with a few strands here and there of salt.

"Fuck yeah," Specter said with a slow grin, and the table swept with a round of laughter like a wave in a whirlpool in eddies around the edges.

"We'll see," I declared. "Friday, after six."

"Jesus Christ, you depraved fuck." Torment's shoulders shook with laughter beneath his cut.

"Coming from you, I'll take that as a compliment," I said, licking the rolling paper on my joint and rolling it the rest of the way, tightening it down with my fingers.

More laughter came from around the long table.

"I still think it's bullshit," Corvus glowered.

I smirked and said, "You want me to spell it out for you?"

He snorted. "Yes, please," he said, unfolding his arms and reaching for his whiskey. He took a sip and stared me down, waiting.

"He'll never be able to pay us. Kid is in way too deep," I said and stuck the joint between my lips, feeling it bob and weave in the air as I sparked up my lighter and spoke around it. "I figured he might be worth keeping in our hip pocket until we could find a use for him, but he's too fuckin' weak. He would have crumbled – been useless for anything other than maybe a patsy at some point. That sister of his, though? She was interesting. She might be worth something someday."

"You still should have brought it to the table," Corvus declared.

"Yeah, well, you're maybe not wrong about that, but what's done is done," I said. "Besides that, who all is really offended that I capitalized on this?"

All hands went up and I chuckled as they all went back down.

"Now a show of hands... how many of you, is that offense taken because you weren't the lucky bastard in the right place at the right time to capitalize on it *first*?"

Every hand around the table shot up except Corvus's, but eventually, he knuckled under to the peer pressure and his hand went up too.

I leaned back in my seat and laughed with him.

"You had me going for a minute there, brother."

He shook his head, grinning, and said, "Ah, yeah, I do believe I did." I knew better. Knew each of my men like the back of my own hand. Corvus liked to test the waters every once in a while, and I truthfully preferred it that way. It not just kept me on my toes, but it kept a lot of these other fuckers in check from doing it themselves.

I shook my head, grinning ruefully, and asked, "So, what other business we got to attend to?"

We finished up and I called out to my sergeant-at-arms, Requiem.

"Req! Gimme a minute?" He threw chin at me and came over.

"What's up, Syn?" he asked me.

"Need you to track down big brother. Get little sister's number and address from him."

"Think he'll give it up?"

I raised an eyebrow and he grinned at me.

"Copy that," he said. "Just didn't know how far you wanted me to go."

"His pussy ass is letting his little sister pay his debts with her body and he's still out there running up those debts last I heard. He's earned some fucking karma."

"Earned some karma or are we sending a message that nobody else better get the bright idea that they should get to have a turn?" Requiem asked me.

I just raised an eyebrow and looked at him.

"That's what I thought," he said, laughing a little to himself and nodding.

He scraped his bottom lip between his teeth thoughtfully and called out, "Hey, yo, Torment!"

Tor looked up from whatever he was reading that he had in his hands, and Requiem jerked his head like they should head out.

Tor nodded, set the papers aside, and strode for the door to go handle business.

"Allocating club resources now?" Corvus asked, but his grin belied that there was any real argument that he was trying to make here.

"Like Requiem and Torment would pass up on the opportunity to put the hurt on a man," I said, scoffing.

Corvus barked a laugh, a braying caw of a thing that had partially been to blame for his road name.

He shook his head and wandered away from our table, and I sighed. I rapped knuckles against the metal edged surface and got up.

"Where you headed, boss?" Specter called out.

"For a ride," I declared.

"Not without at least two of us," he reminded me, and I felt my smile grow a little unfriendly.

"Then you better pick who and you'd better keep your asses up," I called back over my shoulder.

I heard the rattle of buckle and chain and the swish of denim behind me as a couple of the guys peeled off from the knot of them at the bar to follow me, and I smiled to myself.

Sometimes, it was good to be King. Sometimes, it was a pain in the ass. Most of the time, like now, it was neither here nor there... but one thing was for sure. When the rest of these boys got a load of Madi Reynolds, it was for sure going to be a great time to be king. I loved making these other fuckers lowkey jealous.

Chapter Three

Madisyn...

"What the fuck? Don't these weirdoes have any *grown-up* nicknames?" Valory, my roommate, asked as I sat heavily on the edge of my bed.

I was in my favorite pair of paint-stained overalls, staring at the text message that had come through on my phone.

Be ready in one hour. I'll pick you up outside your dorm. -Synister

He knew where I lived. He knew my phone number... but *how?* It made my blood run cold just thinking about it. Still... an hour... I looked down at myself and back to Valory.

"Help?" I asked meekly.

"Get in the shower, shave your legs, pits, exfoliate – girl, do your thing. I'll go through your clothes."

"Okay," I said.

The shower was probably the worst place for me to be. I always did a crazy amount of thinking in the shower... but Jesus... now?

I guess I had put the encounter out of my mind. When he hadn't asked for any real identifying information, I thought that maybe he was just trying to scare me, and by default, Zeke, who was firmly in the throes of his crazy obsession and addiction with playing the odds.

I should have known better than that.

I should have expected that this was going to happen. I absolutely cursed myself for telling a roomful of men that I was a fucking virgin and using it like some kind of–of–of *bargaining chip*. Like one of those plastic chips on their fucking table, raising the stakes beyond reason.

Shit, the reason I *was* still a virgin at *twenty-three* was straight up because men were such *dogs* anymore.

I didn't believe in the rampant hookup culture surrounding us, and I longed for something old-fashioned. Like out of one of the classic regency novels I liked to read... which I guess I'd gotten myself into one of *those* a little too on the nose.

I snorted at my unintentional rhyme in my head.

I mean, wasn't what I was doing entirely too close to an Austen novel? A young woman trading away herself for marriage to better her family's circumstances? Damn the consequences of the rapscallion she wound up with so long as her family was saved and her future, no matter how terrible, could be negated with time alone with her books and needlepoint.

I wasn't looking at *marriage* here, though... but I was sure feeling like a hooker. Not a cheap one, by any means... and not that there was anything wrong with sex work. I mean, I didn't think so or that it was for me, but if our parents found out? *Oh, the hell and the shame that would rain down like the motherfucking apocalypse...*

I pressed my hands over my face in the hot shower spray and took several deep breaths.

Well, there was no going back now. No matter how awful this was going to be, the only way through it was *through it*. Honestly, I didn't know that it was the *best* thing for Zeke, but I loved my brother and I had to do *something* or they were going to hurt him, possibly even kill him, and God, honestly, *our parents...* I had to think of our parents, too. Except this felt like some kind of ultimate betrayal to them. The *scandal* if this ever got out in my mother's circle of sharks, I mean friends; this kind of gossip would be like chum in the waters and would be an absolute feeding frenzy among the aging socialites. My mother would never live it down.

Shit.

This sucked. I was scared, like *really* scared... but I was going to do it anyway because I couldn't and wouldn't go back on my word. That's not how my father raised either of his children.

Plus, I would be lying if I said I wasn't at least curious about Synister and what the heat in his dark eyes could mean. The way his gaze had pressed against my skin and traveled over it like I always pictured a lover's hands doing was something. I'd never felt the weight of someone's gaze so keenly, and it caused me to shiver under the hot shower spray, the water suddenly feeling lukewarm.

I sighed and got out of the shower and dried off. I blow dried my hair and went back to my room with my shower caddy in my robe and found Valory at her desk. She spun in her chair and looked over at my bed and lifted a shoulder in a shrug.

"Like, the choices that didn't have paint on them weren't *awesome*, but I think this'll work."

She had out a pair of light skinny jeans with a pair of tan Chelsea boots and a cream blouse that was light and fluttery. She had also put out some of my gold chains and costume jewelry and my brown felt hat. She'd laid my tawny golden wrap nearby. It was very "bohemian modern art student" but also pretty versatile and elegant. I turned to her, grateful, and said, "Oh, my God – you rock! Thank you *so much!*"

She looked at me with apprehension, nodded, and said, "For someone from a rich family, you're severely lacking in a wardrobe."

I snorted and said, "Yeah, well, none of that debutante shit was ever really important to me. My family isn't exactly *old* rich, if you know what I mean."

"No, yeah, I get that but..." She turned around fully in her chair and rested her plump hands on top of her thighs and sighed. "I don't like this. I mean, are you *sure?*"

I bit my bottom lip, looked back up at her, and said, "No, but I'm going to do it anyway. Zeke is in trouble, and this was the only language I could think of that these Neanderthals could possibly understand. I don't have that kind of cash, and neither does Zeke. And our parents? They cut him off a long time ago."

"Shouldn't you be sorta following their cues on that?" she asked.

"I thought about that, I really did... but..." I let out a harsh sigh. "Zeke is messed up. There's no denying that, but he needs some kind of rehab, not to just be tossed into the deep end of the pool to sink or swim on his own. Not with the Iron fucking Wraiths in the water circling like sharks."

I thought back to my shower thoughts, about my mother's aging socialite friends, and I had come to the conclusion that yeah, they and the Iron Wraiths were both sharks. Maybe not cut from the same exact cloth but maybe similar materials. Different breeds, same species, you know? Something about absolute power and corrupting absolutely. If it was one thing I knew, money definitely equaled power, and the rich of Savannah and the Iron Wraiths both had *money.*

"...or dementors," Valory muttered, snapping me out of my thoughts on the subject.

"I'm sorry, what?" I asked, giving her a blank stare as she looked back to her table where she had a fashion drawing.

"You said the Iron Wraiths were circling like sharks. I was saying they were more like dementors. You know, the black ghosty things from Harry Potter that like to suck the joy out of literally everything to the point you literally *die.*"

She rolled her eyes and turned back to her drawings, settling herself on her chair, which squeaked in protest.

Valory was plus-sized and it wasn't all her fault. Like, it wasn't laziness or overeating or eating unhealthily or *any* of that. She had a slew of medical complications that had helped her along in putting the weight on. She'd ended up with a bunch of eating disorders and a really big uphill battle with getting doctors to take her seriously that something was up and it wasn't just she was fat and needed to lose weight.

I couldn't fathom everything she'd been through, but I'd had my own different struggles with the healthcare field in the past. I could certainly understand it, but the thing I loved most about Valory? She was here and not about to take anybody's bullshit. She was in the art school's fashion design courses, working on an entire line for plus-sized bodies, and I thought that was beyond fabulous.

She was smart and spot on with her alliterations, too. I mean, even the veil-draped skull thing on their back patches gave dementor vibes.

Ugh.

I sighed in a bit of defeat as I pulled my clothes on and looked around our dorm room.

I was here for a degree in fine art and happened to work best with oil paints as my preferred medium of choice. Still, despite our differing fields of degree, Valory and I had collaborated on a fun project or two when she'd made a dress out of canvas strips that I'd helped paint for a doll. The focus was designing something worthy of the Met Gala for one of her courses, and we'd brainstormed all night and worked like dogs on it.

The whole thing had paid off, though. She'd gotten an 'A' and a 4.2 GPA overall for that one course.

Hence, whenever I did have a date or something to dress for when it came to my parents, she was my go-to. It kept me from having a whole lot of anxiety about it, that's for sure.

Anyway, we were as close as close could be as far as college dorm mates went, and we told each other *everything*. This whole thing with Zeke and the Iron Wraiths was no exception.

"Dementors..." I trailed off thoughtfully, going back to what she'd just said. She rolled her eyes and nodded.

"Have you seen their back patches? Also, they seem to be pretty good at sucking the life out of people. Look at Zeke, and now I really have to worry about *you*."

I didn't laugh. I mean, she wasn't wrong… but I understood a few things about higher circles or whatever… the upper echelon of society. I swear I'm thinking that in such a tone that I couldn't roll my eyes any harder.

To Valory I joked, "Get out of my head. I was literally just thinking that and you're right. Dementors makes much better sense than sharks for the Iron Wraiths."

"They're more terrifying than sharks," she said with a sniff. "Sharks are just sharks doing shark things… dementors?" She shuddered in her seat. "Yeah, so, you can see why I worry, I hope?"

"People sharks are worse than shark-sharks," I said. "The rich bitches my mom and dad run with are definitely people sharks… totally different animal."

"You know, to anyone else, I think they would think you're crazy and not making any sense with the whole sharks versus people sharks. I'm not sure what that says about me, that what came out of your mouth just made perfect sense to me."

I had to laugh at that.

To me, people were just people, but as was evidenced with my brother, money certainly changed them. Most of the time, not for any better or whatever. Again, with the money is power thing and the corruption of power and all that vicious cycle bullshit.

Valory was right, though… the Iron Wraiths had money, but their power didn't necessarily come from it. The Iron Wraiths were untouchable around here, in part because the majority of them came from Savannah's old money but the reality of it was, they were more powerful through *fear*. I mean, they were feared around here for good reason – most of which was because they could literally do anything they wanted to. They made people disappear, and nothing ever seemed to happen to them. It was like they walked a different plane of existence from the rest of us, and even from the rich bitches that'd spawned them in the first place or whatever.

21

It was weird, too, though, at the same time. Like, I mean, no one would *ever* say anything to one of their faces, but it was heavily implied behind hands and in whispers that they weren't *real* bikers because most of them had come from money. I didn't know about that. They seemed awfully real to me, having seen them up close and personal.

Again, though, it traced right back around to how they were just kind of next level, and I'd made a deal with their literal devil – bargaining my body if not my soul.

I fought not to shudder and finished getting dressed in the nicest things I pretty much owned outside of my parents' house and a shopping trip with my mother.

I felt like the hat would have looked better with my hair curled, but I didn't have time for that.

I slung my purse on its gold chain across my body, over my head, with my arm through the strap and let my housemate fluff and tug and adjust and do all the things a fashion designer – but in all reality, a super nervous friend – would do before I took myself out into the wild.

She didn't like it. I didn't either. But in for a penny, in for a pound or whatever.

I went downstairs and out the glass double doors of the dorm's lobby and stopped dead in my tracks.

Synister leaned against a sleek, black, glossy Mercedes, his hands deep in his suit pants pockets. He looked up, sunglasses covering his eyes and rendering them unreadable, but the downturn to his generous mouth told me he didn't approve of how I'd dressed. I couldn't exactly blame him. He unbuttoned his suit jacket. I realized it had been perfectly tailored to his form, and his form was very nice in this vest that had busks in the front like a corset. As I slowly drew nearer, I realized it had boning to it too – thanks to my roommate being a fashion major and having watched her assemble her own corsets before.

"I told you to dress for dinner," he said. His voice held every bit of disapproval his look had telegraphed and then some.

"I did," I murmured and he opened the door to the car.

"Get in," he ordered and I looked up at him.

"Hello to you, too," I said, trying to lighten the mood any which way I could.

"Get in the car, Madisyn," he said coldly.

I took a deep breath and slid into the leather seat. I felt a whole lot like I'd just slid into a parallel dimension or the unknown.

This was off to a *great* start.

Fuck my life.

Chapter Four

S **ynister...**
       I held the door open for her, irritated. I wondered if her family came from money, how the fuck did she not know what *"dress for dinner"* meant. Still, there was nothing for it but to fucking fix it.

She was underdressed, and I wouldn't have it.

She slid into the passenger seat of my SL 63 Roadster and I shut her inside. I went around the back of the car and got into the driver's seat, immediately punching buttons on the nav screen to make some calls to fix this mess.

The first call I made was to the restaurant to see about pushing our reservation a couple of hours. I figured it would take at least that long to get her presentable, adding to it with where we had to go and what we had to do to get her there.

She sat in silence, stiff in her seat, staring fixedly out the window. The next call I made I kept it in French as that was the stylist's preferred language. As far as languages went, I knew seven. I had a proficiency for them, always had. I didn't show my hand on that often, as it was a useful skill and had served me well in several back-alley and backwater dealings in the past. Especially with the fucking Russians. They liked to undercut a bitch at every turn and it never failed they leaned heavily on the dumb American not knowing any Russian to do it right in front of them.

The look on their faces were priceless when I finally let the cat out of the bag on that one.

My mother had always told me I was an old soul, and old souls always remembered with their hearts even if they couldn't remember with their new minds. She'd said the whole language thing was a heart over mind thing, and while I didn't believe in all of that bullshit, I had loved my mother. It didn't hurt to let her believe what she wanted on that score. My father, however, didn't mind – what did they call it now? Dulling her sparkle or shine?

I gripped the wheel in irritation, the leather creaking under my hands as I strangled it and piloted us carefully through the Savannah evening traffic and around the squares of the historic district. I kept my eyes on the road as I weaved us through the shitshow of tourists looking to get their drink on and locals just trying to get wherever the hell they were going. I finally pulled up to our first destination, after ten or fifteen minutes that during a weekday without traffic would have taken all but three to arrive at.

Antoinette and her assistant were waiting on the curb out front for us. For the type of cash I was about to drop in her establishment, I pretty much expected nothing less.

I pulled up into the loading zone smoothly and her skinny male assistant opened Madisyn's door for her.

Antoinette fussed over her, leading her by the hands and speaking exuberantly in broken English with a smattering of French in her thick accent that she poured on here in America for the "experience" and so that she could pretty much charge more. But she was good at what she did, so I just let her go.

I handed the fob to my car over to the assistant and said, "You scratch it, you die."

He paled, bobbed his head and shoulders in this awkward half-nod, half-bow thing and fucked off to park the car.

My phone rang as I went to head inside after the girls. I picked up without looking at who was calling and growled into it, "Yeah, this is Syn."

"Oh-ho!" Corvus, my second-in-command crowed into the microphone on his end. "Going that good already?" he asked.

"Are you calling for something specific or are you just trying to gossip with me about what you perceive as a date rather than the business transaction that I don't want her to think it is?" I asked coolly. I knew my tone was as my road name implied – sinister.

Corvus just chuckled, unfazed, which served to irritate me just that little bit more. I hated being inconvenienced.

"What'd she go and do to piss you off already?" he asked.

"I'm not pissed off, merely irritated," I corrected him.

"Oh, well that's not so bad then." I could hear his grin over the line and I shook my head, pausing outside the doors to Antoinette's boutique. They were classic, and timeless, just like the French woman inside... for all that, she'd not been my type.

"I told her to dress for dinner and she came out in jeans," I said.

Corvus's laughter was raucous and once again reminded me of the language of the birds I had so partially named him for. It did every time, without fail.

I gritted my teeth.

"Did you have something important to tell me?" I demanded, putting my hand into the pocket of my slacks, and balling it into a fist, my nails biting into the heel of my hand, a sharp and welcome reminder to keep my temper.

"A little problem with the venue for the next fight night," he said to me. "Nothing to worry about. I've already got it sorted and things moved."

"Oh?" I asked.

"Enjoy your dinner and especially enjoy your fuckin' dessert," he said. "Just wanted you to know a problem came up but the solution is already in play so it's nothing to fucking worry about. The details are unimportant."

I extracted my hand from my pocket and pinched the bridge of my nose, letting out a harsh breath.

"The details are *always* important," I grated and Corvus chuckled.

"Not tonight they aren't. Do you trust me?"

No, I thought. I didn't trust anyone but myself – but on this...

"Yes, of course," I told him.

"Liar," he said. "But I know what you mean. You can trust me on this one. It's handled, and when you *do* get the details, I think you'll be pleased. Now, go enjoy that pussy."

I glanced through the detail work where the oval of glass wasn't frosted at its edges and exhaled. Antoinette had several dresses over her arm and was holding them up in front of Madisyn who was leaning back, her blue eyes wide, her expression painted with dismay. The petite young woman had her hands up as though Antoinette was some sort of boogeyman advancing on her with a weapon.

I liked the look. Madisyn wore it well. I just preferred she wore it looking at *me*.

"Bet," I told Corvus and I ended the call. I put my phone on silent so there would be no further disruptions and tucked it into the inside pocket of my suit jacket. I ran my hand down the busks of my corset vest and opened the door, sweeping in and heading for the little lounge area Antoinette had set up with its two winged-back chairs and low table between them.

A round dais was set up on the big area rug that housed it all in front of an ornate triple mirror for whoever was trying things on to get a good look at themselves and to show off for whoever was with them.

I took a seat on one of the opulent chairs and settled back in it.

Antoinette did her thing, holding up a dress to which Madisyn waved her hands and warded her off like some fiend. Before she could say a thing, I asked, "What's the problem?"

Madi turned to me and said, "I can't afford any of this!"

I arched a brow and turned to Antoinette, ignoring Madi's proclamation completely, and said, "Dark, something backless. Maybe with a little sparkle, but don't go overboard."

Antoinette's lips curved into an appreciative smile and gave a nod. She went among her racks and started looking as Madisyn stared at me open-mouthed like I was insane.

"Did you not hear me?" she demanded.

I felt my own lips curve into a wicked smile and gave a nod. "I heard you... but you aren't buying, I am. Now, be a good girl and try these on for me." I jerked my head in Antoinette's direction and she held out an armload of dresses.

Madisyn scoffed and we were at an impasse for a moment, her blue eyes boring into mine until I finally tilted my head and reminded her gently, "Time is money."

Her eyes widened and with a huff, she rolled her eyes and headed for the changing booth to the side and behind those mirrors.

"A little spirited for your tastes, isn't she?" Antoinette asked with a throaty chuckle as she lifted the crystal top to a decanter by the register. She poured me a drink, but not one for herself... never while working. I waved her off when she went to bring it to me and she raised an eyebrow. With an indifferent shrug, she came around the counter just as her assistant came in, striding breathlessly to me to hand me my key fob.

The thick red velvet curtain rasped against the brass curtain rod it hung from and Madisyn strode out and lifted her hands in exasperation, putting them on her hips.

I looked from her to the dais and rolling her eyes again, she marched petulantly to it and stepped up. I tilted my head, sweeping her from her feet, still in their socks, to the crown of her head, lingering on those hips and the curve of her breasts as my gaze went.

I twirled a finger and she turned around for me. The shape of the dress wasn't to my liking. Too modest. When I had her on my arm tonight, I wanted every man in the room to turn their head. I wanted them to wish they were me.

"Try another," I said, fixing her eyes with mine. She stared back at me and lost some of her bravado. Stepping down, casting a lingering glance back at me, she slunk back into the changing booth to do as I bid.

She *was* spirited, just as Antoinette observed, but she was also beautiful. And when she submitted? Incredibly sexy... and that was the crux of it. She was spirited, and loyal to the bitter end. That's honestly what'd captured my attention. But whether that could translate to anything long term? That remained yet to be seen.

I highly doubted it, but it would be fun to find out.

Plus, the appeal of being her first and only?

Mm...

It was strong for a possessive bastard like me.

Again, we would see. No sense in putting the cart before the horse. She was brave, and I liked that. Didn't seem to realize or care that she was beautiful... I liked that, too.

She whisked the curtain aside and I immediately said, "No."

She jumped slightly at the terse word and immediately whisked the curtain back shut and didn't even bother coming out.

Antoinette laughed, and I felt my lips twitch in a smirk.

"How many of these am I going to have to try on?" Madisyn called from the dressing room.

"As many as it takes to find the perfect one," I told her. She whisked the curtain back again and I let my eyes rove her lovely figure. I tilted my head in the direction of the dais and she wandered out to it with all the awkwardness of a baby giraffe, which I found adorable.

I didn't even have to twirl my finger this time. She just slowly and reluctantly spun for me. I sighed and shook my head.

"No," I said with far less bite this time.

She swallowed and went back to the dressing room. Antoinette crossed her arms and raised an eyebrow at me, and I lifted one of mine in return. She wandered over to the racks and slid garments to one side, contemplating them carefully and picking some things that were shorter.

I settled back to watch the rest of the show that was sure to come my way.

Chapter Five

Madisyn...

I went back into the changing booth, whisked the curtain closed and stared at myself in the mirror. He'd rejected every dress I'd put on and there was only one left now. I stared at it like the sparkly pewter cloth was there specifically to betray me.

I put it on, but *yikes*.

It was... *holy shit*.

I swallowed hard and stared into the mirror. It was a draped front halter that accentuated my breasts, but there was no wearing a bra with it. It was backless as most halters were, but this was like barely above my ass crack low. The only thing worse about it was how *short* it was, and not just short, but how it was slit up both thighs to the point I had to get *really* creative if I wanted to keep my panties on.

I hitched the strings of them as high as I could up on my hips, but *mm*, it was dangerous.

I turned this way and that, and faltered on going out there when he intoned my name.

"Madisyn..."

I felt like an errant child when he said it like that, but shit, shit, *shit!*

I raised my chin defiantly at myself in the mirror over being such a coward and turned around. I whisked the curtain aside for something like the sixtieth damn time and marched my ass out there. I stepped up on the little round platform and crossed my arms over my chest, but shouldn't have. It just pushed my tits together and up for a better look at them.

Synister's look was impassive as he looked at me and then past me into the mirrors. He crooked a finger at me to come to him. I hesitated but did.

"Closer," he ordered, and reluctantly I drifted up to him. He eased forward onto the edge of his seat and put his hands on my hips, looking up at me. He tilted his head as I stared down into his eyes from barely a foot away. I felt his fingers slip into the slits at my hips. He quickly and elegantly hooked his fingers into the waistband of my panties and, in front of God and everyone, slipped them down my legs.

"Step out," he ordered. I swallowed hard and did as he commanded, stepping back and away from him but out of my panties as my face burned with humiliation.

My gaze flitted from his to the French woman and her assistant standing by the counter. The woman looked amused in a cruel sort of way, while the assistant was as wide-eyed as I was, looking as shell-shocked as I felt.

"Hair and makeup," Synister called out to them. "I'll look for her shoes."

"Yes, of course," the woman purred and her assistant came up to me. Taking my hand and arm as though he was afraid that I was going to faint, he said, "Come right along with me, sweetie. I'll get you taken care of."

"Curl her hair," Synister called out. "Gentle curls, not too tight."

I looked back over my shoulder at him as the assistant nodded and towed me forward, but Synister wasn't looking at us at all. He was bending over the rack of shoes against the wall, his hand on his chin as he checked what I presumed were sizes.

The assistant tugged on my arm gently and I went with him, rattled to the core. Not just because of *what* Synister had just done but how he'd looked at me when he'd done it... how... *Jesus.*

"Can I get you some water, baby?" the assistant asked and I looked up at him.

"I'm sorry, what's your name?" I asked.

"It's Jeromy," he said, a reassuring hand on my shoulder. He had one of those accents. The kindly one that was also considered effeminate and *deeply* Georgian born and bred. Like he was a true Southern belle trapped in a man's body.

I tried to pull myself together and said, "Thank you, Jeromy. Water would be lovely."

"One second, sweetheart." He scurried off and I looked at myself in the lighted vanity mirror, keenly aware that in sitting in the stylist's chair, I was sitting on nothing. There wasn't enough skirt to this dress to be able to. I hadn't even remembered sitting down.

Holy fuck, what was *wrong* with me?

I didn't like how wide-eyed the woman staring back at me was. I didn't like how her light tan seemed to float on top of her pallor like oil on water. I didn't like how her heart thundered against the inside of her ribs and how I replayed in my mind over and over Synister sitting on the edge of that chair. How he might as well have been on his knees with the way he looked up at me. How gentle his touch had been as he'd skimmed my panties down my legs – but mostly, at that *look.*

How his gaze had caressed my face like-like-like he was worshipping at some altar, sending benediction with his gaze into mine.

I swallowed hard at my reflection and I was so *afraid.* Not afraid of having sex with him or even that it would be my first time... afraid that – afraid of how much – *oh God.*

I didn't even want to think about it. About how it might be *good.* I realized I hadn't honestly thought about it at all... about how much it could or would hurt, about how much it might not. Excitement mixed with a heavy dose of fear swirled through my veins and I couldn't decide what I was more afraid of now.

That he would hurt me or how much I might actually *like* being with him. It was like with that one small act, the reality of what I was actually doing had set in full force, penetrating to my very bones.

I took even shallow breaths and listened to the low thrum of indistinct conversation from the front of the shop between Synister and the woman.

They had a history. I could tell...

So why would he bring me here?

To say I was in a state of confusion was an understatement. All of a sudden, there was just too much happening all at once and I was overwhelmed. Like, *really* overwhelmed.

Jeromy came back with a tall glass of cold water. The condensation on the outside of the glass was cool to the touch and felt good when I pressed it to the flushed skin of my neck and chest.

"There you go," Jeromy said encouragingly, as I drank deeply from the glass, suddenly thirsty. He was standing behind the seat and smiling from behind his spectacles – which was the only way I had to describe the wire-framed round glasses he wore.

He smiled at me over my head and said, "Now, what shall we do to match this pretty dress? Because, honey," he fanned himself, "you are *smokin'* and I hardly know what to do with myself!"

I laughed and he grinned. I said, "I feel both over and under-dressed at the same time. Is that even possible?"

"Honey, baby, sweetie pie – in that dress? *All things* are possible."

I laughed and Synister's voice from behind us wiped the smile right off my face. "Keep her fairly natural. A smokey eye would be alright but don't go overboard. I don't want her tarted up."

Jeromy turned sideways, revealing the man who stood in the doorway, his hands in his pockets, looking some kind of otherworldly in that corset vest thing in his suit. Like... *wow.*

34

"Definitely don't want to look like more of a tart," I whispered. "The dress does more than enough of that."

Synister smirked at the jab and pulled a hand from his pocket, twisting his wrist to look at his watch face. I realized the band was the same pewter as the dress.

Whether he knew it or not, he'd made me an accessory... *how nice.*

I dropped my eyes when he raised his to mine in the reflection of the mirror.

"You have forty-five minutes. Get your socks off, Madisyn. I don't want them to dent your lovely skin. I picked out a pair of sandals for you."

He turned and walked back down the short hall, out into the boutique, and I met Jeromy's eyes in the mirror. He lifted a shoulder in a shrug and went to get a drape as I took off my socks.

He took them and walked them out front. When he came back, he started right to work on me, redoing my makeup and styling my hair just as Synister had ordered. I tried not to feel sick at that. At being made to order. Like I was a steak not a human. But the way Synister looked at me, I knew there was quite a bit more to it than that. At least, I hoped there was.

What are you thinking? I silently demanded of myself. *Of course, you don't! This is a onetime thing, girl. You shouldn't read too far into it and make up stories in your mind, Madisyn. It just leads to heartbreak.*

This was a business transaction. Not a date. This was a deal to get my dumbass brother out of trouble. God, did that fact both break my heart and fill its cracked pieces with bitterness.

I needed to remember all of this, because *my God, today...* it was an awful mess I'd put myself into.

Jeromy was a whizz and very skilled at what he did. He took less than forty-five minutes and then it felt like it was time to face the music.

I went out behind him and he presented me to Antoinette. It

turned out, Jeromy was a wealth of information – but frustratingly closed mouthed about Syn. I'd told him the deal I'd made and he'd simply looked at me with sympathy and compassion. He had told me, "Girl, you made a deal with Savannah's very own devil," echoing my thoughts of earlier a little too thoroughly but with none of the glib that I'd thought them with.

Shit.

He'd steered the conversation pointedly left of center after that, and I'd let him. I wasn't at all sure what he'd meant by that comment, but I suppose I was about to find out.

"Very nice." Synister complimented Jeromy's work, then he crooked a finger at me and said, "Come here, Madisyn."

I went over to him, and he patted his knee. I awkwardly raised my foot but put it right back down when I realized I was going to flash him and the whole room if I did that. He smirked. Jeromy took pity on me and brought over a low footstool to preserve my modesty.

I mean, Syn couldn't rightly bend at the waist too much with that corset vest thing on – and I had to admit, he was damn fine in it... but still. When he did what bending he could to take up my heel to slip the first sandal on my foot, his jacket gaped enough for me to see the butt of the matte black gun in its expensive-looking leather holster up under his arm.

I faltered, standing on one foot like I was and balancing. Synister looked up sharply, his dark eyes catching mine. I stilled under that stormy predator's gaze and swallowed hard.

His hands were warm against my skin and gentle as all get out, as he slipped the high sandal on my foot and zipped it into place at the heel.

It matched the dress, perfectly.

He repeated the process with the other shoe and then stood, accepting a bag with the clothes I'd arrived in from Jeromy.

"A pleasure as always," Antoinette said with a warm smile at Synister. One that didn't quite reach her eyes.

He said something in French that made her laugh in delight, but the laugh sounded forced.

He turned to me.

"Now, you're dressed for dinner," he said. It was like the expectation had been set and I didn't quite know what to do with that because in that moment, it was as though he'd already decided that this was just the *first* dinner and that there would be more.

I didn't know if I wanted there to be more. I mean...

"Shall I get the car?" Jeromy asked, interrupting my silent panic. Synister held out the fob without taking his eyes off me.

Jeromy took it and Syn handed over the bag of my clothes. "Put this in the back seat," he ordered, and Jeromy hurried off to fetch the Mercedes.

Synister steered me toward the boutique's door as Antoinette looked on, and we went out front.

"Why do all of this?" I asked.

"Because," he said, slipping on a pair of sunglasses. "I can."

Where did those even come from? I asked myself. I mean, he'd been wearing them when he'd picked me up but I hadn't even realized he'd hidden them away, nor did I have the first clue *where* he'd hidden them that didn't ruin the line of his suit. Especially with how sleek everything had to be with that corset thing on that did so many things for me. Oh my *God*.

Thankfully, I didn't have long to think about it, or to try and pointedly look *anywhere* but at Synister.

Jeromy took less than half as long to pull up with the car than it had taken him to park and come back the first time. I was grateful for that. Grateful still that traffic was a lot less and that there weren't that many people out here to gawk at me standing half-naked on the curb.

When Jeromy pulled up to the curb, Syn opened my door for me.

He smirked down at me and said, "Knees together. Sit first, then put your legs in."

I stared up at him as my mouth dropped open. He laughed,

placing the pad of his index finger beneath my chin, and closing my mouth for me with a teasing nudge.

I tried not to shudder at the touch.

"Keep that up, you'll catch a fly or something."

"You're confusing as hell," I said, and he arched an eyebrow over his mirrored aviators.

"Oh?"

"If you care so much about me flashing the world, why'd you dress me like a hooker?" I demanded.

His expression lost its amusement.

"Get in the car, Madisyn," he said and the coldness of it made me want to shiver. I got into the car as he'd instructed, grateful for the instruction because I didn't know how to do it otherwise. I mean, I hadn't thought about it.

He went around the front of the car, my eyes following him, as Jeromy handed off the key fob and went around to stand up on the curb where I'd just been. I checked the back seat and found the luxury paper bag with its twisted paper handles there just as Synister had instructed.

He slid into the driver's seat smoothly and I looked at him.

"Don't you ever call yourself that again," he said and I blinked bewildered. He looked at me and I could collect nothing from his expression.

He simply stared at me, burning a hole right through me until I muttered, "Okay..."

After the verbal acknowledgment, he put the car into gear and pulled smoothly away from the curb.

I stared out the window, pointedly not looking at him as my cheeks burned with shame and humiliation because...

"Isn't that what I am, though? I mean, isn't that what this is?"

"No," he stated tersely, and I turned to take in his profile which was like chiseled stone.

"I agreed to have sex with you for money," I said, rolling my eyes.

"I'm pretty sure that's the definition of what a hooker is. Like a *textbook* definition at that."

"We'll talk about it over dinner," he said. He sounded irritated if not angry. I didn't know why, but I felt a little bit of self-satisfaction about that. It was nice to know I could get under his skin as much as he had gotten under mine with all this... I don't know. Whatever it was.

Chapter Six

Synister...

Apparently, along with loyal to a fault and stunningly beautiful, Madisyn Jayne Reynolds was tenacious and stubborn. Two qualities I could appreciate within the right applications, but her insistence on remaining steadfast in feeling like a whore wasn't what I wanted out of this. On its face value, certainly, I understood how she would think so, being that money was involved, but money was an inconsequential thing for me. The amount her brother owed me, I could make in minutes or less with the right trades. No, I didn't see it so much as a transaction. The reason my desire for her had been kicked into high gear was her *sacrifice*.

There was something so incredibly sexy and appealing to me about it. The fact she would be so willing to sacrifice her purity in favor of her cad of a brother intrigued me. It made me wonder, when the negotiations truly began over dinner, just how much she'd be willing to give... or *take*.

I was curious about that last part. The fact that she'd protested at Antoinette's had both surprised me and pleased me. She'd not been greedy. Quite the opposite, and something that intrigued me further.

I didn't know many rich kids from rich stock with an attitude like hers, and I found it refreshing. Refreshing and curious.

She was an interesting game to me, and I admit my penchant for playing for keeps was going to be hard to keep in check. I had a certain fondness for conquests, but found I grew bored quickly once the prize was mine for the taking.

Still, as far as conquests went, she ticked a lot of boxes for me.

Petite, yet curvaceous. Blonde and blue eyed. Strong willed, yet sweetly submissive. Pure of heart in a way you just didn't see any more except on television and in some novels. A rare beauty... not just on the outside, but on the inside, too. Also sweetly naïve which usually I found annoying, but from Madisyn? I found the quality adorable, and almost endearing.

I'd found myself growing hard half a dozen times already just within our scant contact so far.

I prided myself on maintaining control at all times, but something about Madisyn was robbing me of it. I wasn't sure I liked that, but as I thought back to my mother and my own father... Shit.

Shit. Fuck. Goddamn. Motherfucker.

I slammed the door on any and all thoughts of that fucking cad and tried not to miss my mom. She'd died from cancer. I don't think she'd fought it all that hard, to be honest. Mostly because other than me, what the hell did she have to live for? By the time she'd gone, I'd been an adult. A young one, no more than Madisyn's age, but an adult nonetheless.

Hell, I still wasn't much of an adult in some ways, but I was certainly more of one now. Enough of one that I'd been steadily and carefully dismantling my father's power ever since, by way of buying up shares of his most prized endeavors until I was the majority shareholder.

I took great pleasure in eroding his power base. The man would never retire. I would make certain that when he was forced to, that it would be in disgrace and, if at all possible, that he would be destitute when I made him do it.

I pulled up smoothly in front of one of Savannah's most popular dining establishments – The Olde Pink House – and shifted smoothly into "park" at the curb.

"Wait until I get your door," I told her, and Madisyn turned from the window and looked at me.

"We're ridiculously overdressed for this place," she tried to protest, and I just smirked.

"Good," I said. "That means all eyes will be right where they should be."

I got out of the luxury cage to her little scoffing sound of protest and tossed the fob to the man I'd paid to be on standby to park it. The Olde Pink House didn't have valet parking, so I'd made my own.

I opened Madisyn's door and she kept her knees together, a light blush creeping across her tits on display and up her chest and neck. She swung her legs out first and planted her feet primly together and firmly on the ground. I held down a hand which she took, the flush painting across her nose and cheeks like a sunset painted the sky behind First Presbyterian off Chippewa Square in the summer evenings.

A lovely sight that I didn't think anyone could or would ever get tired of looking at. I had to wonder at myself and what the hell was getting into me.

She used my hand as leverage to get herself up out of her seat, and her other hand rushed to sweep down her backside to make sure the short dress was in place and covering her shapely ass. I chuckled and wheeled her around by her hand to step up and past me on the curb.

She kept her eyes downcast from the men and women around us who were staring. I put my hand to her back to guide her to the door and to the hostess station parked right outside it under the restaurant's awning. I didn't miss that she jumped at the light touch. I fought to suppress my amused smile at that and lost.

Come later in the evening, I would be doing a whole lot more than lightly touch her back, and if I had my way, she'd do a whole lot more than jump at the touches I'd be giving her.

We didn't even make it to the little podium they had set up for the hostess before the manager swept out the door and said, "Ah, Mr. Devlin, there you are. Your private table is waiting. Right this way, please."

I pressed my hand just a little bit more into Madisyn's soft flesh and propelled her ahead of me. She went without protest. I hung back just enough as she took the stairs behind the manager to one of the private dining rooms on one of the top floors.

Hell yes, I enjoyed every moment of the glimpses of the under curve of her ass cheeks and even more the slight flashes of her sweet pink pussy lips as we ascended the staircase.

The manager was in front of her, and there was no one behind us as we made our climb, so this was a private showing all for me.

I paid handsomely ahead of time for this experience and I was going to enjoy every minute of it.

We were escorted into what may have once been a small bedroom in the home, but now was a very secluded, dimly lit dining room with a table easily large enough to seat four but set for just us two.

The flatware was silver, the table settings bone china, and the glassware crystal. Overall, the opulence and magic of the small space was satisfactory to me, and I gave the manager a nod of approval. He broke out into a pleased and serene smile and said, "I'll fetch your wine and starters."

"Thank you," Madisyn murmured, as I pushed her chair in beneath her and she settled at the table.

I went around to my seat and took it.

"So, uh, do they have menus?" she asked, and I smiled at how flustered she was by the whole experience thus far.

"No need," I said. "This dining experience isn't like that. We are at the chef's mercy for all seven courses. Just relax and try to enjoy yourself."

She stared at me through the candle flames of the lit tapers between us, all wide blue eyes and soft neutrally glossed lips as her mouth hung slightly open. I could discern just the barest hint of her soft pink tongue and pictured it a little too keenly; those blue eyes looking up at me in adoration, that soft pink tongue of hers laving my dick.

Mm...

She looked flustered and more than a little disappointed that there would be no menu for her to hide behind. The time for hiding was over and the time to lay all the cards on the table was nigh.

I cocked my head and took her in and led with, "So, a virgin?"

She colored deeply and turned her head to stare mortified at the wall.

"Yes," she said evenly yet tonelessly.

"Saving yourself for marriage?" I asked lightly.

"No." She shifted uncomfortably in her seat and wouldn't elaborate beyond that.

"I see. So was it always your intent to sell it to the highest bidder then?"

Her eyes flashed angrily as she turned in my direction and speared me with an angry gaze.

Ah... that certainly got her attention, I thought. I had to admit, I quite liked how responsive she was to my little barbs. Her nostrils flared as she sat up straighter and took a deep breath, no doubt to dress me down but stopped at my chuckle.

"You don't honestly believe for one minute that I want to do this or that I want to be here, do you?" she demanded. There was no ire or venom in her tone – rather only a certain... vulnerability.

I cocked my head curiously and considered her.

"You're the one who offered," I reminded her. "In fact, the whole topic of your virginity you offered up wholeheartedly if I recall."

"It wasn't like that!" she snapped and her eyes sparkled, filling with tears of silent rage.

"It's not worth ruining your makeup, Madisyn," I told her,

shaking out my handkerchief from my trouser pocket and passing it to her across the table.

She took it, and wrapped it around her index finger, expertly patting at her waterline first one, then the other, to keep the tears from spilling and streaking her mascara.

"Would you have hurt him otherwise?" she asked.

I answered her honestly, "Yes."

"Killed him?" she asked, staring at me in silent and well-kept outrage.

I chuckled at that and said, "Dead men don't pay their debts." I adjusted the flatware at its place before me and flicked my gaze from the softly gleaming silver to her wide blue eyes and said precisely how I felt on the matter of her brother. "Only cads let their baby sister pay their debts with her body. I, for one, appreciate the fact that your brother is a cad."

I let my gaze move in a long, slow, sweep of her appearance, letting it linger on her greatest assets that were above the table, which weren't only her tits but her eyes.

She stared into mine for long moments and said, "Does he really owe you one hundred and eighty or were you making that up?"

"I never lie about those things," I told her evenly.

"You're going to have to do a lot better than fifty for this," she said. She gripped the edge of the table, her fingertips blanching white under her shapely nails which were clear coat polished and nothing more.

"Fifty to fuck you, another thirty because you're a virgin. If you're lucky, I might want to fuck you again. If I do, and that's a mighty big 'if' I'll consider taking off more. It's my final offer, Madisyn. Take it or leave it. If you leave it, I'll call one of my men right here, right now, to go break your brother's knees."

"I'm not backing down," she said quickly. "But I need one more thing."

"I said that was my final offer," I told her, arching a brow. I confess my curiosity got the better of me and so I asked, "But what would you have of me?"

She raised her chin defiantly and said, "You ban him from ever gambling in one of your... your... *establishments* ever again."

I barked a laugh at that and how delicately she tried to put it, and just had to keep on laughing.

"You are bold as brass, aren't you, woman?" I asked, knuckling a tear out from under my own eye as my laughter subsided. "Shit, with how bad he plays and as much of a loser he is – bet, bet, I'll ban him. But that won't stop him from finding another game in town. Ours isn't the only one."

"No, I know that but—" She made a sound somewhere between desperation and exasperation.

"He's sick," she said finally after a moment of silence, in which she wouldn't look at me. When she turned those eyes on me again, they were glassy but not with anger this time. No, this time it was closer to despair.

"Sick?" I echoed.

"Addiction is a sickness," she murmured.

Ah...

"Not sick," I said, shaking my head. "He just lacks self-control."

"He needs rehab, and therapy – not to pick himself up by the bootstraps!" she protested.

"Agree to disagree," I said.

She made a troubled sound and sighed.

"Whatever. You wouldn't care. You've got what you came for."

I nodded and didn't even try to spare her feelings or deny it.

"That's right," I said. "I always get what I want in the end. You should know that about me," I told her.

"What's that supposed to mean?" she asked.

I smirked.

"It means that some things are priceless and better than money, and that I am about to have one *very* good evening."

It was impressive, watching her color and yet her face drain of color simultaneously. I didn't quite know how she pulled off that feat, but I did know I liked it. She was so responsive and in some very interesting ways. She certainly wasn't boring so far.

We stared at each other from across the table when the manager returned with our wine. He uncorked the bottle, an impressive vintage and a white, which told me that whatever the chef had in store, it was likely to be chicken or fish. Delightful, even though I was partial to red meat like any other red-blooded American carnivore.

He poured us each a glass and retreated respectfully, promising the feast would commence shortly, that the starter for this evening was just undergoing some finishing touches.

"We have all the time in the world," I assured him, and fixed Madisyn with my gaze. "Some things should be savored and can't be rushed."

Her humiliation was clearly written all over her lovely face and I gave her a wicked smile. Her responses were fantastic to my little bit of ribbing and double entendre, and I delighted in them.

I loved making her squirm and keeping her off center. This was turning into a sincere form of foreplay for me and the clothes hadn't even started coming off yet.

As soon as we were alone again, I just had to ask, my curiosity piquing, "Have you any questions of me?"

Chapter Seven

Madisyn...

"Questions?" I echoed. I guess I hadn't really thought that I could ask anything. Truthfully, I said, "I didn't exactly picture you as forthcoming or that you, I don't know, actually cared."

"Ouch." He put his hands to his chest as though he'd been shot. "If I didn't care, would I be going to such great lengths?" he asked and he gestured at the grand, if small, private dining room we were in.

I felt thoroughly put in my place. Like, for real... I was more than a little ashamed because he was right about that one.

"Sorry," I murmured. I couldn't look across the table at him, instead fixing my gaze on a twinkle of candlelight sparkling from the butt of my butter knife.

"Contrary to our crude introduction, Madisyn, I like for the women I'm with to enjoy themselves, too. Sex is always more fun when it's between two consenting adults and she's not lying there like a dead fish or basically acting as a masturbatory aide."

I stared at him, speechless. I just couldn't seem to make my brain make sense of him. It was like he was this upper-crust gentleman, perfectly refined one moment, and crude beyond words the next. Just when you thought one was what you'd get, the other came out of his mouth and the whiplash from it was extraordinary.

"I don't know what to say," I said, picking up my glass and sipping at the crisp, cool, white wine in it.

It was good. Very good. However, I only took the tiniest of sips. I didn't think it would be a good idea to get drunk or even so much as tipsy around Synister, which led me to think of a good starting question.

"What's your name?" I asked.

He snorted a laugh and asked me, "Of all the things to ask, that's what you want to know?"

I gave a slight shrug with one shoulder and said, "It seemed like a good starting point."

His dark eyes were inscrutable where they searched my face.

"I heard the manager call you Mr. Devlin. I hardly think your mother named you Synister Devlin, but I could be wrong," I attempted to joke.

"Don't speak about my mother in any capacity, Madisyn. This will be your only warning on the matter."

I looked up from where I set my glass back down after another infinitesimal sip, and I froze at the look on his face. Tempestuous didn't even begin to cover it.

I took my hand back slowly, the appendage shaking as I withdrew it from my glass and put it back in my lap. Like I was afraid any sudden movement would have the man across the table snapping his jaws like some sort of savage and with that one wrong move, he would bite me like a rabid dog. I don't know why I felt that way when he was honestly as still as the grave and always seemed to be in perfect control.

Maybe that was it. Maybe it was that stillness, like a snake in the grass coiled and waiting. That stillness tripped my prey drive something awful, knowing that the next logical step was to strike, although

I didn't think he ever would. He was in far, far, too much control for that.

He rested his hands on the table and tilted his head to the side quickly, his neck giving an audible pop that made me jump slightly.

So, he has mommy issues, I thought to myself. Out loud I said, "I'm sorry."

He simply nodded once to acknowledge the apology, though he said nothing by way of accepting or rejecting it, so I had to guess that nod was the closest thing I would get.

"Micah," he said after a lingering miasma of silence.

"Micah?" I asked.

"Micah James Devlin is what my mother named me," he said. "Now, pick a different subject."

I sat in uncomfortable silence, almost afraid to say anything else with how mercurial he was being. Like, *what did I say?* I mean, what the hell topic was safe?

Well, fortune favored the brave or some shit like that, so I took a deep breath, held it for a moment, and letting it out slowly, made the admission out loud, "You scare me."

His gaze held mine and I took the opportunity to search his face, and I mean really search it. His generous lips parted and his rugged features remained unreadable otherwise. His dark eyes bored into mine, however; as though willing me silently – but willing me to *what*, I didn't know. The silent compulsion was there, though, like a weight against my skin. Like rain from the sky when it was wet and how it caused your clothes to cling and settle against your skin.

"You're right to be scared," he said softly. "I'm not a good man, Madisyn. I won't even pretend to be. Not for you and not for anyone. What you see is what you get."

I swallowed hard, my mouth suddenly dry, and whispered, "Does that mean you'll hurt me tonight? I mean, is... is that what you're into? I know that some people are and—"

"We'll see," he said evenly, his face giving nothing away. "I can't promise that we're compatible sexually. What's fun for me might not be fun for you, but if you're asking me if I like to beat women to get off? No, I won't hit you. That's not... that's not my style," he said.

I think it was the closest thing to reassuring I was going to get and I couldn't honestly tell you if it was or wasn't. I mean, *what the fuck?*

"Any more questions?" he asked as the first course was set before us.

"Too many to count," I confessed. "But none that I'm brave enough to ask right now," I said, glancing at the manager who continued to serve us and did so with a polite smile that practically screamed his discretion, but not only "no" but "hell no." It wasn't that I didn't trust his discretion. I'm sure Synister had paid more than enough for this dinner to maintain the man's silence. I just didn't want Synister angry with me. Irritated and annoyed honestly scared me enough – sending my skin to crawling. But then I would catch him looking at me, like he was right now, as we quietly chewed our canapé to start our meal with. The way his face softened when he didn't think I was looking or that I saw intrigued me.

He wouldn't promise not to hurt me, but he all but promised not to hit me – which was interesting and confusing at the same time. I guess when you were a man who called himself Synister, and who was pretty much known by and large as such, pain took on a whole new meaning and various different shapes.

"You're awfully thoughtful," he remarked as the second course arrived at the table.

"I suppose I have a lot to think about," I said softly.

"Penny for your thoughts?" he asked.

"Afraid they'll cost a lot more than that," I countered and he chuckled at that.

"Looking to clear your brother's debt completely?" he asked.

"In for a penny, in for a pound," I responded.

"Interesting chosen turn of phrase," he remarked.

"I like to read," I said.

"Oh? What?" he asked, and I figured it was a safe enough topic of conversation.

"The classics, mostly. Austen, Brontë." At his blank look I went with titles to try and ring a bell for him. "*Pride and Prejudice, Wuthering Heights.* Shit like that."

"I know who Jane Austen and Emily Brontë are," he said and almost sounded defensive. "I just didn't peg you for the sort."

I felt my eyebrows go up. "The sort?" I echoed. I think I was vaguely insulted somehow.

"I don't honestly know what to expect when it comes to you, Miss Reynolds, but I find myself increasingly intrigued and surprised the longer we talk."

"Should I be insulted?" I asked, smiling. "Or is that an actual net positive from the great Synister, King of the Iron Wraiths' big bad motorcycle gang."

He laughed at that, dropping his fork with a clack, and putting his hand over his stomach as he leaned back in his straight-backed and opulent chair under the softly glimmering crystal of the dimly lit chandelier above us. He laughed so hard and completely that the very flames on the candles flickered as though dancing to the song of his amusement.

I smiled, finally feeling like I'd gotten something human out of him.

"King – oh, that's great. The guys are going to love that," he said, trying to catch his breath and not bothering to deny the rest. At least not right away.

"First of all, it's *President,* not *King—*" he started.

"Tomato, To-mah-to," I said with a slight shrug.

He smiled at me and shook his head, continuing on as though I hadn't spoken with, "Second of all, it's a *club*, not a *gang*."

"Potato, Po-tah-to," I replied and he laughed again and shook his head.

"The distinctions are *very* important."

"Oh, alright," I said, not understanding. But some things you didn't really need to. As long as they were important to the person you were talking to, that was oftentimes enough. King versus President, Gang versus Club, neither really honestly and truly mattered in their distinctions. To me, they were practically the same thing.

He watched me for several moments and said to me, "I don't particularly care that *you* don't care. Just do me a favor and don't make the mistake in front of some of the other men of the club. There are some who wouldn't like it."

I cocked my head curiously and nodded finally, unsure how or why I would encounter any of them again and honestly not really wanting to.

"Okay," I murmured.

He stared at me over the... I didn't even know what course at this point, but I did know the meal was light, looked good, and from what I remembered, tasted good. I found myself both wishing it were over and that it would last forever simultaneously. I was tired from a full day of classwork and the stress of this whole thing.

"What are you thinking?" he asked me again sometime later as the plates were cleared from in front of us.

"That the meal has been lovely so far. Thank you for that," I said.

"You were thinking awfully hard for that to be it," he declared. "Nerves settling in?"

I stayed silent, because what could I say? I simply nodded and couldn't look at him.

"Ah, well," he said after a moment. "I suppose that's to be expected."

"Mm," was my noncommittal response as I finished the wine in my glass. It was still my first and when the manager came around to refill it, I put my hand over it and said as politely as could be, "Oh, no, thank you."

He smiled and set it aside and left the room. I caught Synister watching me again, as though I was the most interesting thing in the opulent room.

Chapter Eight

Synister...

She was trying not to let her nerves show, but the longer the meal dragged on, the more impossible it became for her.

I couldn't say I minded her discomfiture all that much. There wasn't anything that came to my mind on how to fix it. Sure, I probably could have said any number of things to placate her, but why? More importantly, what if they wound up being lies? I didn't know her well enough to know what she liked or didn't. I could guess, but that wasn't my style. Besides, I wasn't one to pay lip service. Why talk the talk when walking the walk was what mattered. No amount of talking would do in a situation like this. Would it make things easier? For me, probably. For her? Maybe, but maybe not at the same time.

No, this was a situation of hurry up and wait and see. I would be lying if I said that it didn't please me, to watch her wonder and worry a bit.

Some of the latter was honestly for her own good. A lesson in making deals with the devil... as in, you shouldn't do it.

As far as devils of Savannah went, I was one of the worst – just not in the way you would necessarily think. I had a certain amount of respect for women. Not all women, mind you, but certainly for women of Madisyn's caliber.

She'd proven herself loyal – which is something I couldn't say for a lot of women these days. She'd also proven she'd been willing to sacrifice it all for someone she loved... and I didn't think her brother realized how lucky he was to have a sister who loved him so unconditionally.

While her sacrifice was a dirty one, debasing herself for my pleasure, it was no less a strangely noble one in my eyes. Probably because I was the one on the receiving end of that sacrifice. I couldn't guarantee I would be as kind in my way of thinking if it had been one of the other guys in my place. I would probably see her as less a Madonna and far more the Whore if it'd been anyone else getting their dick wet in her virginal pussy.

Which reminded me...

"A point of earlier that needs to be made," I said as I cut into the sublime lemon cheesecake that had been put before us as dessert.

She looked up from hers and gave me her rapt attention, which I appreciated.

"You don't get to feel like a whore," I said gently. "I'll not have you think of yourself in such base terms. Not for the sacrifice you're willing to make out of love – however misplaced it might be – for your family."

"Why do you care?" she asked and her voice was breathy as though stolen.

"I don't know, but I do," I said. "Is what you're doing dirty?" I turned my mouth down and tilted my head to acknowledge that yes, yes it was. "Yes, but there's a few different levels of filth and I think it's incredibly sexy."

"How?" she asked. "*Why?*"

I gave her a wicked grin.

"You're a young woman coming into her own power, and that's incredibly hot," I told her with a shrug. I savored a bite of the cool, lemony cheesecake. The subtly sweet burst of citrus flavor a welcome one, cooling my mouth from the slight spice of the whitefish meal.

"I don't feel that way," she said.

"Perception is everything," I told her. "Perhaps you need to change yours."

She looked thoughtful and that was good. To be perfectly honest, I'm not sure why it mattered to me what she thought, but then a memory flashed through my mind of my mother sitting at her vanity, carefully applying makeup to cover the bruising, and I confessed to myself that bruises went more than skin deep.

I heaved a silent sigh and watched her pick at her dessert. She tried a few bites, but she didn't seem particularly enamored with it, and I could completely understand why. Her face was more than just pretty to look at. It was expressive in a way that was entirely new to me. I could almost read every thought and emotion on it as easily as I could read the fluctuating markets.

I could tell that she found me attractive almost as much as she feared me and what I would do. I was very much so looking forward to seeing what responses I could bring out of her once we were back at my place.

When she set down her fork and folded her hands in her lap, I set aside my own fork and rested my hands atop the table, smoothing over the crisp white table linens.

"How are you in heels?" I asked.

"What?" she asked, looking up sharply.

"How do you handle walking in heels?" I asked.

"Fine, why?" she asked.

"I can either have the cage brought around, or it's about a fifteen to twenty-minute walk. I find I often prefer a walk after dinner. I thought you might like one, too."

She stared at me, searching my face, and finally said, "A walk would be nice."

I smiled, nodded, and pulled out my phone. I called down to my man and he answered on the first ring.

"What's up, boss?"

"Take the car back to the house and the bag in the back seat up to my room. We're going to walk. Stand by in case she gets tired and we need a pick up."

"You got it," he said and I ended the call.

As far as prospects went, Spooky was a good one. I felt as though he would make it someday. I also felt as though it would be a long while before he did. He was young and had quite a bit of experience to gain before earning his colors.

I lifted the napkin from my lap and wiped my mouth, and she lifted hers and set it aside on the table. I rose and went to her side, holding out a hand to her and leveraging her chair back from the table with her in it as she rose. She was a very compact woman, robust in the places I liked, but still very diminutive in stature and as such, she hardly weighed anything at all.

I held out my arm and she looked up at me, cocking her head as she threaded hers through it and rested her hand on my wrist. Her tense posture easing some with the small, old-fashioned gesture on my part.

We left the dining room and went down the hall, slipping down the stairs and passing the manager with a polite nod as we slipped out the door. Everything had been paid well ahead of time, including a handsome gratuity to keep things above board and the place amenable to a return visit in the future from me should I want it.

All eyes were on me and Madisyn as we slipped across Abercorn and into Reynold's Square. Past John Wesley's monument and beneath the Spanish moss-draped trees, I steered us gently in the direction of Congress, where we crossed and continued along Abercorn.

She was quiet and tense beside me. I let her have her silence and let her stay within her thoughts. I'm sure it was a lot and I didn't begrudge her any of her feelings on the matter. I myself couldn't really decide my mood. I had so many choices before me in what I would do to her and the fantasies multiplied and shifted like the shadows on the walk as the sun began to set behind us.

"You're quiet," I remarked, as we passed Colonial Park Cemetery. The gates were shut tight as the light failed and shadows shifted and moved at the corners of your vision as you passed by the thinned-out gravestones and burial vaults.

Madisyn stuttered to a bit of a stop and asked aloud, "Did someone get locked in?"

I chuckled.

"No. You're seeing the wraiths."

"Wraiths?" she asked.

"Ghosts," I said. "The shadows moving among the graves and vaults are one of Colonial Park's most common paranormal sightings."

"You believe in ghosts?" she asked, peering up at me in the deepening shadows reaching for the sky.

"I do. You?"

She peered past me where we'd stopped by the wrought iron fence and said quietly, "I didn't use to... but... I know I just saw something."

"You did, but it's no one that's alive. I promise you."

I started walking and she lingered a half-step behind me before reluctantly catching up.

"I've never seen anything like that before," she said.

"A night of many firsts, then," I said and she looked up at me sharply.

"That's not funny," she said unhappily and I smiled.

"It wasn't meant to be a joke at your expense, Madi. I promise. I wasn't poking fun."

Around three blocks beyond the last of Colonial Park, I took us into Lafayette Square, skirting past another of Savannah's more famously haunted houses – The Andrew Low house. Madisyn looked on at the grand old house and sighed.

"I love these old places," she murmured. "It's one of my very favorite things about Savannah. All the old and beautiful historical houses."

"Mine too, actually," I said.

"Yeah?" she asked, drawing her attention from the Low house back to me.

"Does that surprise you?" I asked.

"It does," she said.

"Then it might surprise you more that I live in one," I said with an inconsequential shrug.

"You do?" she asked.

"Me and several of the guys. I've never quite liked living alone, so I bought a place big enough that several of us could live there."

"Oh..." she sounded dismayed.

I chuckled and put a hand to her back to steer her in the direction we needed to go.

"Not to worry, they've made themselves scarce tonight. No one will be home. No walk of shame required in the morning."

"Oh! I didn't – I mean—" Her stuttering and stammering and discomfiture made my evening.

I threw back my head, laughed and said, "Woman, sometimes you're just a hair too easy."

She scoffed and punched me lightly in the arm and I laughed again, genuinely, and well-pleased. *That* was the obstinance and fire that'd caught my attention in the first place.

"Now that's the spirit," I praised, putting my arm around her and drawing her into my side. She was colored so beautifully, a match for the skies of earlier, before the pink had withdrawn to the purples and dusky hues of the gloaming.

I admit that I was enjoying our walk enough that I hopped historical squares and pointed out architectural points that I found interesting among the houses and mansions we passed along the way. She stopped a time or two and held out her hands as though to frame up a place or two. I saw her looking at square signs and even street signs as though taking copious mental notes, which I found curious.

"Tell me," I said. "What's your passion, so to speak?"

"What do you mean?" she asked as we wandered from Calhoun to Lafayette Square. Sure, the route we were taking was indirect but again, I was enjoying this which was a rare thing. Usually, I was in a rush and didn't take the time, but Madisyn was worth the effort to me for so many reasons I didn't think I even fully understood yet.

I had an instinct for people and she'd piqued mine in all the right ways – that hadn't happened with anyone, let alone a woman, in a very long time. Before I ravished her and potentially scared her off for good, I'd like to know more.

"My mother likes to say I was born in the wrong century," she said cautiously after a minute in which I'd let her gather her thoughts.

"Why is that?" I asked.

"I like the classics, like I already told you. Um, not just Regency, but Victorian era. I paint, actually. Um, I prefer oils and am studying at the School of Art and Design – but considering you picked me up outside my dorm, I assume you already knew that last part. Sorry."

"Nothing to be sorry about. I know some things but not everything. The rest I'd like to hear from you."

"Why?" she asked softly. "I mean, it's not like we're trying to date or whatever, here. I'm just trying to help my brother."

"I know," I said.

"So why all of the window dressing and wanting to know about me all of a sudden?" she asked, stopping. We were in Monterey Square, stopped beside the towering white Pulaski monument, the glow from the windows of the Mercer-Williams House overlooking the square, cutting through the draped and swaying Spanish moss from the trees. I looked back down to her and put my hands in my pockets, squaring up with her and facing her.

"The sacrifice and loyalty you're showing to your brother intrigues me," I told her honestly.

"You were threatening to hurt him," she said, as though that meant anything at all in the grand scheme of things.

"He knowingly took out debts with me with no intention or honest means of paying," I told her. "He deserves an ass kicking."

She made an exasperated sound and I cocked my head.

"I told you, he's sick—"

I shook my head.

"And I told you agree to disagree. He lacks self-control."

She sighed and looked to the Mercer-Williams house, her eyes unfocused and looking far, far, away, her voice defeated when she said, "That too. I mean, they aren't mutually exclusive, you know."

I nodded slowly.

"I can concede that point," I said.

"Then can't you concede that it's just made-up money anyway and just let it go? Let *him* go, just this once?" she pleaded.

"Let him go, or let you go?" I asked.

She looked up at me with wide blue eyes and I reached out and cupped her cheek, ghosting a thumb along her so-soft skin.

She didn't say anything. I tipped my head and said, "If you're trying to appeal to my better nature, Madisyn, I don't have one. Your brother made his choices, you made yours. There's no backing down and there's no changing your mind. You're too far in, girl, and I like what I see."

She swallowed hard and said, "Please..."

I smirked. "I like the sound of that," I said, stepping in. "Say it again."

"Please," she whispered. I closed the gap between us and put my lips against hers, carefully, softly. She gasped against my lips and I pressed my mouth to hers savagely, forcing my tongue past her lips and teeth, lashing it against hers and the inside of her mouth. She raised her hands and pressed against my chest, and I captured her slim body up against my own, hauling her tight against me, trapping her with my arm at her back.

She made a panicked whimper into my mouth, and I rolled it against our warring tongues like tasting a piece of candy. I kissed her fiercely in the shadows of the oaks of the square, and I didn't let up on the punishing kiss until she yielded against me, her body going languid with her capitulation against me.

I hummed against her mouth in purest satisfaction and tore my mouth from hers, my hand sliding into her hair, my fingers playing against the back of her neck and the base of her skull. She whimpered and rested her forehead against my chest, and I let her catch her breath.

"The deal stands," I said roughly and she nodded against me. "Come on," I said.

I steered her out of the square and onto Gordon, past the Mercer-Williams house and its carriage house shop behind it, before finally turning down my street of Whitaker.

Chapter Nine

Madisyn...

I could barely keep up with his stride as we made our way along Whitaker, bracketed by historic mansions on one side, and the street and Forsyth Park with its towering Greek Revival fountain on the other. He stopped short outside the gate of an almost ridiculously large Greek Revival mansion and opened up his phone. Using some kind of an app, the gate across the driveway's lock disengaged and swung open.

"You live here?" I asked and stared up at the grand house incredulously.

"Yes," he said, taking my hand and towing me through the gate. He took me up the steps to the front door and entered a code on the keypad of the lock.

Inside was just as lush and rich as the outside. I stopped short inside the door and looked up, my mouth agape at the classic wood carvings that were clearly original to the house and left me absolutely speechless.

"It's better in the light of day," he said, towing me with an insistent tug of my hand toward the sweeping staircase.

"Up you go," he said, insisting I go in front of him. I flushed when I realized it was for the view up the back of my skirt. Humiliation flooded my veins when I realized he'd likely gotten a preview of coming attractions as we'd gone up the staircase at the restaurant and I tried really hard not to think about that.

I felt as though I was a prisoner being marched to their execution, but that wasn't quite right. I still shook, confusion swirling behind my breastbone, as I stopped at the top of the stairs and pressed my thighs together, lips still swollen from the rough and powerful kiss he'd put on me in the square.

I was still reeling from it. Shocked and turned on, though I knew I shouldn't be. I should have been any number of things, but *excited* somehow felt entirely wrong.

Synister crested the top of the stairs and led me down the hall. He stopped outside a door and twisting the knob, pushed it open.

I stared up at him a long moment and he smiled down at me, an almost cruel twist to his lips.

"Go on, Madi. Nothing to bite you except me," he said, and I felt my breath catch and my cheeks heat. I stepped through the door and into another world. Synister's world...

I didn't honestly know what to expect. The rest of the house had been furnished with a tasteful eye toward echoing the bygone era the home had been constructed in. In here was a completely different vibe – the feel entirely modern in crisp black and white.

I pressed my lips together and surveyed the room. It had its own fireplace, the wood stained dark, almost lacquered black in appearance. It had a black marble surround and a white marble tile set in the floor at the hearth. Above the fireplace hung a black-and-white photograph. A tasteful nude of an unknown woman, her flank sleek, the curve of her ass and hip lovely. Her arm up to cover her nipples but the curve of her breasts apparent.

I dropped my eyes to the dark loveseat across from two wing-backed chairs in front of the fireplace, the table between them low and boxy and matching the iron frame about the king-sized bed.

It was iron and sturdy, raised high toward the ceiling and draped in white gauzy curtains, the bedding black from the sheets to the comforter and well made, piled with pillows, the smaller of them accented in white.

I turned slowly in place, taking in the windows beyond the bed and the white slatted blinds covering them, the black curtains hanging to either side, and the set of double doors that I imagine led out onto one of the balcony's I'd seen as we walked up.

There were two doors beside each other in the wall before the jut of the fireplace at the foot of the bed. One, I imagined, was to a closet, and the one closest to the wall we'd entered at was open, the soft gleam of polished stone hinting at a bathroom beyond.

I turned slowly in place in the expanse of room just inside the door leading out to the hall and simply took it all in as Synister shut it behind us.

"I'm glad you like what you see," he said.

"What makes you say that?" I asked quietly. I didn't know why I spoke in such a hushed tone, as though we stood in a library or church. Perhaps it was the dark of the hour outside, or the fact that he'd said he lived with others here... but something about this space called for quiet... no, *peace*.

"Your face tells me everything I need to know," he said, and I huffed a bitter laugh.

"I've always said it's not my mouth that gets me in trouble, it's my face that needs deliverance," I said sighing.

"It's an honest face," he said, slipping off his jacket. I swallowed hard. He laid it over the back of a chair at a small desk, just inside the door and to the right as you entered.

I felt frozen as he worked his cufflinks, first one then the next out of his sleeves, his eyes fixed on me.

I turned to take in the room once more and spotted the bag from the boutique with my belongings in it between the two chairs in the little living room space. I tried very valiantly to not look like I was running away as he very deliberately rolled back his sleeves over his muscular forearms.

I let my leaden feet carry me past the foot of the bed, rounding the black box-like footing table, or whatever it was, carefully, so as not to bang a knee or thigh against its sharp-looking corner.

I stopped at the doors leading onto the balcony and looked between the slats of the white blinds, the black carpet beneath the new heels plush. After the walk that had to be at least a mile in them, oh how my feet had begun to ache.

I stared out the window and between the gnarled oak trees across the way at the fountain of Forsyth Park, gleaming soft and white in the park's lamplight, and I sighed.

It was a beautiful sight, a lovely view, and one I felt may be wholly underappreciated. I sucked in a sharp breath when Synister's big hands fell lightly onto my bare shoulders, his thumbs digging carefully in between my shoulders.

"Moment of truth," he said, and his voice was dropped low in a thrum I swear I could feel to my very soul. I shuddered and closed my eyes. He stepped up, putting himself right at my back, his hands sliding carefully down my arms and skipping from them to my waist. He smoothed them around my front and drew me back into his chest. The brocade fabric of his corset vest thing was both rough and slick against my back.

"I've never done this before," I whispered. "Afraid I don't know what to do."

"That's fair," he said, and pressed his lips against my shoulder. I let my eyes slip shut and my breath escape me in a shuddering sigh.

"Uncomfortable?" he asked.

"Very," I answered.

"Hmm," he hummed thoughtfully and was silent a moment.

His arms disappeared from around me and I turned my head a little, listening more than seeing. There was the slick sound of fabric against fabric as he took something from his pocket and shook it out.

"Trust me to make it good for you, baby," he murmured darkly and I swallowed, my throat nearly closing up. I nodded, barely remembering to breathe as the soft silk of *something* covered my eyes.

I gasped and my hands flew up to touch the band of cloth as he secured it behind my head.

"Not too tight?" he asked, working fingers between it and my hair.

"No," I said truthfully.

"Can you see?" he asked.

"No," I replied, and it too was the truth.

"Good, step back for me," he said. With his hands to my hips, I let him carefully guide me back a step, then two, then three. We turned in a direction in the midst of them, but having my sight taken from me was disorienting to say the least. I couldn't say for certain what part of the room he stood me in.

He turned me around to face him and there was more of that slick sound of fabric against fabric, this time with pauses and stutters in between as he really had to work whatever it was free. I had to imagine it was his tie.

"Put your hands together like you're praying, for me," he ordered but his tone was velvet-wrapped-steel, gentle yet unyielding. Certainly not a request, but not terrifying in its demand like what typically issued forth out of his mouth.

I licked my lips, uncertain, and put my hands together in front of me like he asked.

"Lace your fingers," he told me and I complied, the hair raising on my arms and the back of my neck.

He laid the cloth of his tie over the top of my wrists, and quickly and efficiently, bound them together.

I must have made a frightened sound or a sound of protest because he shushed me.

"Shhh, you're good," he said. "Oh, you're *very* good, goddamn..." he practically growled and his hands were back on my hips, guiding me by touch.

He backed me against the bed, the height of it hitting me in the butt and the backs of my thighs. I put my hands into its plush top.

"Hold it," he said tersely, but not sharply. I froze. "Just hold it, right there, don't move."

His voice, roughened with desire like it was, caused my heart to thunder in my chest, thrashing against the inside of my ribs like a caged bird. It felt tight, constraining, hard to breathe. I listened to more material slip and shush against itself, the slide of cord through eyelets and loops, the thrash of it against the brocade-wrapped boning and busks as he loosened things at the back and finally, the clack of the busks eyelets coming loose from the pins holding the garment closed at the front.

Without my sight, it was as though my hearing was ten times as keen. And yet it was muted as the blood rushed through my veins and roared in them with every scrap of fabric I knew was less between our skins.

I felt my own breathing deepen and turn into a light pant as I drew shallow breaths, a mixture of fear and anticipation swirling in my veins as I listened to him take another step forward. I was keenly aware, even without benefit of my sight, that he was back within my space, a mere hair's breadth between us. His hands found my hips once more and I felt him kneel, heard his knees crackle slightly with the motion, his hands sliding first over the rough fabric of the pewter dress and then causing me to jump as they left the short garment behind to smooth down my legs.

The zipper at the back of my right heel lowered and his insistent hand held me steady at my calf as he slipped the shoe off my foot.

I very nearly groaned in pleasure as my foot went flat, buried in the plush carpeting beneath us.

Synister chuckled darkly and my breath caught once more at his warm hands upon my skin as he repeated the process with my left foot.

"Mm," he murmured and I heard him rise. "Now, that's much

better, isn't it?" he asked, again his voice low in that sexy and intimate pitch.

"Yes." The word escaped my lips breathy and he chuckled again, this time in satisfaction.

My breath hitched as his hands fell softly on my shoulders and I tilted my chin up out of instinct. His lips fell softly onto mine as they had in Monterey Square, but unlike last time, this time, they stayed gentle.

I felt my own lips part eagerly as he sucked my bottom lip between his own and he bit down gently on it.

A slight moan escaped my throat and he made a satisfied sound, his hands finding my ass, moving up slowly and kneading my bare back as he kissed me.

Our tongues tangled in an explorative dance, and this time, the kiss was sweet rather than punishing or demanding as it'd been before.

It barely registered to my mind when the gentle tug came at the straps holding up my dress. I reflexively tried to pull my hands apart but they were stuck fast together, the bindings at my wrists holding true.

I felt my heart leap into my throat and swell as the material peeled down my front under its own weight and Synister's soft "Shhh," lulled me back down a few steps, away from panic.

"Oh, fuck yes," he whispered as his hands shoved the satin-lined rough material off my hips. It whispered down my legs and puddled atop my feet, warming them from where they'd cooled from the modern air conditioning of the room.

"You're so fucking beautiful," he murmured into my ear, and I was frozen with uncertainty.

It took a couple of attempts to get my mouth to work and when it did, all I could really croak out was a feeble, "Thank you."

"Hmm." He hummed an approving sound and with his arms around me, and so very warm, drew me against him. My hands raised and bound between us, my arms pressed against his naked chest. I felt my heart leap at the sudden skin-on-skin contact. He kissed me once more and stepped that half-step closer and I realized *oh, thank God, he still has his pants on.*

He pressed his hands to my elbows as we kissed, breaking the contact of our lips, and ducking to put my arms around his neck. He bent and pressed his mouth to mine again and it was nice... so very nice to just be warm and close like this, accepting and returning his kisses as we stood beside his bed.

I caught my body loosening and melding into his. The longer the kiss went on, the more relaxed I became, until his hands found my ass and he lifted me with a grunt, putting me back and up onto the bed behind me.

He ducked out from beneath my arms and pressed his lips to my neck, to my collarbone, to the hollow of my throat. I gasped as he continued with those firm presses of his lips against my skin, soft kisses to my chest, a light brush of teeth against my breasts that left me gasping and writhing where he pinned me beneath him.

His hand on my ribs, trailing to my hip, he bit carefully and gently around one of my nipples.

"Ah!" The sound was a surprised one, but throaty at the same time. I panted as he paid careful attention to my nipple, capturing it between his teeth, teasing it with the warm, wet, tip of his tongue until I panted deeper and writhed unbidden beneath him.

I cried out once more as he sucked me, his hands smoothing over my body. Then he was suddenly gone, his arms going beneath my knees and at my back, as he lifted me, shrieking and laughing, to deposit me in the middle of his large bed.

I lay back and found pillows beneath my head and shoulders and then his hand was suddenly there, wrapped around my own and pulling them up, raising them above my head. I heard the rattle of metal and then the click of what could only be a carabiner clip, and his hands were suddenly gone. I tried to bring my hands down and couldn't. They jerked and stopped at the end of a short chain fastened to the headboard somewhere below the level of the mattress above my head.

I made an inarticulate noise of panic and Synister's hand was suddenly over my mouth, not pressing, not frightening, just a gentle touch.

"Shhh, you're good. Just relax. It's all good," he soothed.

My breath sawed in and out of my nose, panicked, as he took his hand away and then I felt him back off the bed.

I didn't say anything, my panicked mind refusing to form words, and then there was a sound in the perpetual dark of my stolen vision.

A rattle. A click. The whisk of a zipper being lowered in a rush. I went very still, feeling incredibly vulnerable and staked out like a sacrifice before him.

The bed dipped and he got up on it, his hands gentle as they fell onto my knees which I reflexively drew up and pressed together.

"Easy," he said. "I'm not going for it yet. I'm not done playing with you," he said, and holy fuck, why was that both simultaneously terrifying and reassuring at once?

"Shit, you're even more beautiful than I imagined," he said low and intense. I felt my body lose some of its tension incrementally as he continued to speak, all of it praise, in that low, rough, and sexy-as-hell tone.

"I-I wish I could see you," I stammered, and he gave that low-and-rumbling dark-and-sexy chuckle that I was quickly growing fond of.

"Not yet," he said. "Right now, I just want you to feel."

Whoa, shit...

It was the last thought I had when he nudged my knees apart with his hands and God help me, *I let him.* He settled between my thighs, his hands delving beneath my back and he set to wrapping my body in the steel bands of his arms. He covered my body with his and his lips found mine once more. The kiss was something deep. Deep beyond anything I could ever imagine. Deeper than the Titanic, than the Marianas Trench, and just like the depths of the ocean, it was something darker than space, darker than the imagination could conjure and it just *did something to me...* Put a calm on me, a stillness in me, the likes I couldn't honestly even begin to explain the sensation of it.

I lost myself in his touch, in his kiss. I let go to the passion of it and found myself bowing willingly and gratefully to it. So focused was I on the feel of him against my body, and his mouth against mine, I almost missed it when he settled between my thighs and pressed his hot, hard, length against the outside of my pussy.

I certainly didn't miss it when he rocked his hips back and forth, his cock pressed tight up against the length of me, from the top of my sex to the opening.

I moaned against his mouth and he moaned back into mine. He kept it up, sliding himself between my pussy lips and back and forth, creating such a delicious friction between us.

I moaned into his mouth, both of our panting breaths warm against our faces as we writhed and danced against each other, our bodies doing all the talking as the front of our minds let go and everything became so – so – *primal.* Carnal. *Delightful.*

It happened so fast, I almost didn't register it'd happened at all. One moment, we were writhing and everything was feeling so *wonderful,* and then before I knew it, or was even ready for it, he slipped against me, and then he was *inside me.*

I cried out into his mouth and jumped at the suddenness of it. There was a stretching sensation, a searing almost, and a feeling as though something had given way. I felt so incredibly and impossibly *full.*

"Easy, baby," he breathed into my ear as I cringed beneath him, letting out a broken little sound that I did not want to make. "Easy, I've got you. The worst of it is over."

I felt my legs quiver to either side of him and his weight settle atop me more firmly.

I jerked against my bonds, wanting to lower my arms around him and to hold him, but they held fast, the fabric of what I presumed was his tie biting into my wrists as the metal clip held them fast above my head.

"Here." He reached up and unclipped them and I brought them down. He delved his arm back down beneath me and held me fast as I sniffed and felt the blindfold grow damp with my tears.

The deep grinding, aching hurt swelled but then started to subside as he made soothing sounds next to my ear.

"There you go," he murmured. "That's it. Just relax. I've got you. Just breathe and just relax. You're okay, I promise. Goddamn, baby, you're *better* than okay. Holy fuck, you feel so damn good. Mm."

I held onto him as best I could and he started to move again. I gasped, sucking in a sharp breath at the unexpected sensations that wafted out from my center, where our bodies met in the most intimate of places.

He stroked firmly and deeply, but so very carefully, putting a little twist into his hips as he pressed deep. His withdraw had me shuddering and my breathing picking up in its cadence.

I whimpered and held so close to him and wished I could use my hands. He leaned up and pushed the material binding my eyes shut up off them. I squeezed them tighter against the light that seeped through my eyelids and blinked a few times to clear them. His face, which I'd thought to be too harsh to be handsome the first time I'd seen it, resolved into focus. I didn't know how I could have ever thought that looking at him now. More specifically, looking at how he looked upon *me*.

"God, you're beautiful," he said in this dazed tone of voice, his body stilling over and within mine, as he drank in my features.

"Can I have my hands back, please?" I asked in a hushed-yet-pleading tone.

"Yes, of course, give them here." I looped them back over his head and he propped himself up on one arm. The other he dragged at one of the loose ends of the black satin binding of what was indeed his necktie. The whole thing came away, unraveling expertly and loosening completely. One more tug and the whole thing came away and I was free.

I captured his face between my hands and dragged his mouth to mine. He lowered himself back down over the top of me and resumed his careful thrusting.

I cried out into his mouth, and he drove a little harder and a little deeper and *oh, the sensations.*

There was a heaviness down there, a fullness that only seemed to grow, but it was a fine sensation, a welcome one. The way it felt when you were hot, too warm, and felt like you were positively *dying* and the breeze came along and subtly kissed your skin – only from within. It was as though that breeze was kissed by the sun, too. A blush of golden glow that started where our bodies met and disbursed like dandelion fluff on the wind – magical and so very sweet, flitting along every nerve and through every vein until the magic of it was all throughout your whole body... and it never left.

The feeling only grew. Subtly at first, then more forcefully, until the breeze was a stiff wind, and then a gale. It just filled you and filled you until you felt as though you couldn't hold any more. I cried out and held tightly to the man causing all the havoc and chaos within me. It was like a burst of light, only if light were a feeling, and I found myself arching and crying out and then screaming as everything became just so incredibly and insanely *overwhelming* and blasted through me until I was absolutely raw.

I lost myself completely in the maelstrom and when I came back to myself, it seemed like eons later.

I let my head fall back to the pillows and Synister looked down from above me, my body still held fixed in the cage of his arms.

He panted and searched my face. Finally, he asked me, "You good, baby?"

I didn't trust my voice. I simply nodded and felt tears slide from the corners of my eyes to leak down my temples.

"Oh, baby, oh, sweetheart." He held me tighter and his head darted down to kiss the side of my neck as my arms went around him just as tightly. He laughed as I sobbed, and he said, "You're okay. it's all good. Oh, baby, you just came so hard... I love it. I love that for you. Good job."

I sniffed, overwhelmed, and leaned my head back so I could look at him.

"Is that what that was?" I asked, and my voice cracked and I hated it. I especially hated how he laughed at me, but I didn't hate it at all when he smacked a kiss to my lips.

He slid an arm up to capture the back of my head in the mitt of one of his huge hands, and I really didn't hate at all how he cuddled me and said, "That's what that was. Looked pretty fucking good, to me."

Now that I was calming down, I had to agree.

"Ah!" I cried out as he pulled his hips back and he slid from me. I shuddered and clung to him. He hummed in appreciation and kissed my shoulder.

"Goddamn, that was good," he said, and I bit my bottom lip.

"Yeah, right up until I embarrassed myself," I complained.

"Hey, no, none of that. Your first time at anything can be scary, especially when you don't know what's going to happen or what to expect."

I stared at him and blurted out before I lost the nerve, "Thank you."

He cocked his head. "For what?" he asked.

"For being so nice to me," I said. He met my solid gaze and didn't say a word. He just clambered back off of me and off the side of the bed and held out a hand.

"Come on, let's get you on the pot and cleaned up," he said.

"What?" I asked, sitting up.

"You need to use the bathroom. Come on."

It wasn't quite the ending I expected, and the shift in him was almost palpable, I guess, I didn't know. I guess the glimpse of Micah was gone and Synister was back.

It was the only way I had to describe it, or make sense of it.

Chapter Ten

Synister…

I was sitting up in bed, the night having dragged on into the wee hours of the morning, but I didn't want to sleep. Not that I wasn't tired, I was. I just didn't want to sleep.

Madisyn was tucked into my side, her head on my chest, and I had an arm around her, my hand buried in the back of her luxurious blonde hair which was thick and impossibly soft. I massaged the back of her scalp absently as I clicked through screens on my laptop in my lap.

I'd taken out my contacts and wore my glasses, which I wasn't a fan of in the slightest. She'd reverted from relaxed and sexy to unsure and timid once I'd leaped up to get her taken care of, but I wasn't sorry for it.

I was pretty certain no one had ever told her she needed to pee after sex. She'd been true to her word about the whole virginity thing. It'd been a heady thing, pushing into her and past that barrier. The evidence of her maidenhood stained my dick as I'd washed up in the bathroom while she'd sat on the john. I wouldn't let her up until she'd gone.

I'd tried to temper the weirdness of it by gently cleaning her up after she'd taken a leak and gotten up. There was only so much toilet paper could handle post coitus.

I'd told her to get back in bed and had handled my contacts and shit. I'd brought my laptop over from the desk and set it in the pool of lamplight on the bedside table, but then I'd paid attention to her. I had held her while she'd stewed in silence and thought and felt whatever she was going to think and feel.

The head rubbing had put her out fairly quickly. Once she was out, I'd gotten to work.

I had my phone silenced but face up by my opposite leg and the screen lit up.

I scowled and picked it up, Requiem's name, number, and hard expression flashing out at me. If he was calling this late – or early in the morning – something was fucked up.

"Yeah," I answered by way of greeting.

"Sorry to wake you," he said.

"Wasn't sleeping."

"Shit, then really sorry to interrupt you—"

"Nah, we're done." Madisyn stirred and I stilled beneath her and waited a half a second. Sure she wasn't waking, I said tersely, "Get to the fuckin' point before you make me wake her."

Requiem laughed and said, "We got a shitshow out here. One that sadly requires your presence."

"Fuck," I muttered.

"How bad and what?" I demanded.

"The Columbian would like a word."

I swore.

"What the fuck does Castañeda want this time?" I demanded.

"Won't say. Says he'll only talk to you – hence why it's a shitshow. Nothing good ever comes of that kind of fuckery."

"Don't put the cart before the horse. We can't get uppity until we know what the fuck he actually wants. When's he want to meet?" I asked.

"That's the thing. He wants to meet *right now*."

"Fuck me," I grated.

"Ah, yeah, uh-huh. That's what I've been saying," Requiem said. It was as close as I would let him get to an "I told you so" and he fuckin' knew it.

"Keep your fuckin' panties on," I told him. "I'll meet you and the boys at the clubhouse. Make the arrangements. I'll be there..." I did the calculations in my head, "in twenty minutes. Thirty on the outside."

"Copy that. See you when you get here."

"Roger." I pulled the phone away from my head and looked down at Madisyn curled against me like a sleepy kitten.

I hated leaving her. The reason I didn't want to sleep was right here. I didn't want to miss a thing with her here, but that was too damn bad. Duty to my boys and my fuckin' empire called.

I pulled up the contact info for Spooky, our prospect, and dialed through.

"Ugh! Yeah? What's up?" he answered on the second ring, and I could tell I'd woken his ass up.

"Get up, get your ass to my place, and sit on it. Madisyn is sleeping in my bed, but if she gets up or tries to go anywhere, I want you to be her shadow. Don't engage, just make sure she's good. You got me?"

"Yeah, yeah! I got you. Be there in ten," he said.

"You do that," I said. I ended that call and carefully shifted my laptop out of my lap and then painstakingly slid out from under Madi, letting her down gently into the nest of pillows and plush mattress that was my bed.

She barely stirred but I was worried she'd wake. I didn't have the time or patience for explanations. I had shit to handle, apparently.

I slipped into my walk-in closet and dressed for the slide and not for the ride – jeans, heavy boots, a plain black tee, chaps, and jacket. I slid my cut over everything and stepped back out into the room. She'd turned over, but otherwise slept relatively deeply.

Good.

It spared me any drama, and with any luck, I'd be back before she had a chance to wake.

Did I really believe that last part? No. These things always took a ridiculous amount of time to handle with the politicking and negotiating and all the bullshit that came with both. I lived for these sorts of fucking games, though. I enjoyed being the smartest bastard in the room, and very rarely did I come up against a challenge big enough to satisfy me.

Madisyn hadn't been a challenge at all, but she'd still been some pretty enjoyable sport all the same.

This was a different sort of challenge that may wind up being no sort of challenge at all. I think that's what had my blood going, the mystery of it.

I rode out to the clubhouse which was out on Bonaventure Road in the old building that'd housed this stone-counter cutting warehouse. They'd had this name that was catchy and cute and hadn't wanted to sell – so I'd bought out one of their main competitors, put one of my boys with a good head for business and a degree to back it up in place, and let him run them into the ground by way of competition until they were forced to sell.

It'd taken three years. They'd still been steadfast in not selling to me, but the joke was on them. They'd sold to who they thought was someone else but it was just a shell corporation of one of my bigger companies.

They'd been pissed when the building had been painted our signature wraith blue and gray and the mural of our club colors had gone up on the outside, but they'd learned a valuable lesson that day.

When it came to the Iron Wraiths, the path of least resistance was the better way to go. They could have made bank on my initial offer, but their moral high ground in holding out against me had been the thing to destroy them. Last I'd heard, the lifelong Savannah residents had wound up fucking off to Alabama or some shit to start their business over there.

Them's the breaks.

I pulled through the wrought iron gates I'd had erected outside and around the club and into the garage that was standing open down here. I parked the bike, taking stock of who all was here – Requiem didn't surprise me in the least. Torment, either. Grim and Reaper did a little, though. Not who I expected, but they were fine. What surprised me was the lack of Corvus.

I went up the stairs to the half of the building that was the second floor. The building was two stories on its one half, which is why I'd wanted it. The bar and common areas could be up high and not at ground level in case anyone decided they were feeling froggy and wanted to shoot the fuckin' place up.

Down on the first level we had the garage in the old warehouse. Bikes parked in the low half, some restrooms in case we decided to throw a rager or a party. The half of the building down below this elevated half had some restrooms. We'd taken out a big chunk underneath to have a covered porch-like area. An outdoor bar in the back down there with axe-throwing lanes and a firepit, and a screen to project movies on or whatever.

It was a decent leisure area.

Could do all kinds of shit down there.

Up here we had a bar and open seating but it was mostly all business in the back. I found my boys sitting at the bar, Req behind it, all waiting on me.

"Where's Cor?" I demanded.

"Not here," Req said. "Got Haint on the way and Specter. I don't like the smell comin' off this and you have me in this position for a fuckin' reason."

"I know I do. I ain't forgotten why I put you in it, either. What exactly did Castañeda say to get your panties in a twist?"

I slid up onto one of the barstools and laced my fingers, folding my hands. I could hear Haint and Specter's bikes down below, pulling into the garage.

"It's what he *won't* say, man. Just says that he wants to talk to you." He held out the burner we used to talk with our Latin American friends.

I dialed out and the man himself picked up. I couldn't say that lent any comfort to the situation, quite the opposite in fact.

"Synister," Castañeda purred into the phone, his accent a little thicker 'n usual.

"Castañeda," I intoned carefully. "To what do I owe the displeasure of being called this fucking late at night? We got problems?"

I didn't beat around the bush. It was one of the things Castañeda said he appreciated about me.

"This is not a 'we' problem, it is a 'me' problem, I'm afraid," he said.

"You calling to ask me for a favor?" I asked.

"*Si*," he said.

Well, that was different.

"Alright, I need to hear it before I agree to anything—"

"Of course, of course, my friend. Can you meet me?"

"Not alone," I told him. "I'll have at minimum two of my trusted men with me."

"Of course, I shall have my man, Renaldo, with me. I assure you, this is nothing underhanded, as you may think. I genuinely wish to ask a favor and I am willing to make you very rich to do it."

"I'm already rich," I told him, "But I have no trouble hearing you out as a professional courtesy. We do good business together."

"Si, si, we do, we do. Meet us at the usual place."

"Copy that. Say in an hour?"

"Si, that will do fine."

"Alright then," I said. I hung up and said to my guys, "He's being fuckin' cagier than usual."

"See what I mean?" Requiem sniffed.

I looked him over. He wasn't the most attractive man on the planet in the face. He kept his hair short and wore a perpetual five-o'clock shadow or scruff of a beard. Mostly because he was one of those guys who could shave but the shit would be back coming in on his face within like an hour of him doing it.

Grim was the same way. Reaper was just a creepy fuck – silent for the most part and moved like a fuckin' shadow.

Haint and Specter had joined us about midway through the call and I made some decisions.

"Req, Grim, and Reaper – you three are my wrecking crew tonight. Haint, Specter, you hold down the fort. Stand by and keep an eye on us from the fuckin' sky or whatever shit it is you do. If anything looks off, call in the cavalry and fuck shit up. I mean raze and ruin – go wild. Keep Spooky out of it. He's keeping an eye on my place. I had to leave my prize sleeping and I'm low key pissed about that shit already."

Specter grinned.

"She worth the fuss?" he asked.

"Every bit of it and every fuckin' penny, too," I told him. "Pretty sure I found my new favorite thing for right now, boys."

There was some laughter and a couple reached out to clasp hands and congratulate me.

"It's going to be at least a forty-five-minute ride. Let's get where we're going, boys."

Chapter Eleven

Madisyn...
I woke, sucking in a sharp breath and pushing myself up from his bed. The birds were starting to chirp outside his windows. I twisted and reached out an arm and encountered nothing but his high thread count sheets; cool to the touch and without him in them.

I turned, sat up and looked about. It was dark in here, the lights out and the shades still drawn as they were. I reached over and fumbled at the nearest bedside table and switched on the lamp.

"Mm..." I tried again. "Micah?" I called out softly, trying his actual name because Synister honestly just felt silly. But it didn't feel right in my mouth. I cleared my throat and tried again, but I knew he wasn't here.

"Synister?"

Silence echoed back at me from the antique walls and modern furnishings.

I slipped out of bed, padded to the bag from the boutique and found my purse in it. I let out a breath and checked my phone to a slew of messages from Valory.

I texted her back even though I was sure she was sleeping.

I'm sorry! I apparently wasn't dressed to his liking and we wound up at this boutique with this bitchy French woman and her absolutely lovely gay assistant. Then my purse and phone and everything ended up in the bag and holy shit, I have so much to tell you, but I'm fine! I promise. Everything is okay and I'm coming back now. Be there before you wake up!

I set my phone aside, pulled my things out of the bag and got dressed in my own clothes. I put the dress and the shoes into it, picking them up from where they'd been discarded on the floor. I twisted my lips back and forth, contemplating the now, much lighter bag.

I left it behind.

When I checked my phone again to put in walking directions to get back to the dorms, I had a message waiting from Valory.

Bitch! I'm not asleep! Are you crazy? I was giving you until morning and then I was calling the cops. I've been watching your location on that app I made you download and nearly had a fucking heart attack when it left the restaurant after only a minute, and it's been at that house on Whitaker ever since.

Oh, damn. I texted back with thumbs of fury.

I didn't have my phone. It was in the back seat of his car, in the bag with my clothes. Like, you wouldn't believe the dress he put me in. Oh, my God!

I didn't waste any more time, either. I slipped out of his room and down the hall, winding down the sweeping staircase and slipped out the front door quietly so as not to disturb anyone who might be here.

Whatever! Just get your ass back here, pronto! I'm watching you move. Is he driving you?

I responded quickly as I went down the steps to the pathway leading to the gate to the sidewalk.

No, he's not even here. I woke up alone.

I unlatched the gate and slipped through. Closing it behind me, I looked both this way and that, up Whitaker.

It was loud out here, but it was all nature - songbirds trying to sing the sun up and into existence, and the lonely call of an owl. The insect song had even ceased.

What!? That asshole! He just left you there?

I sighed a bit exasperated and texted back.

Apparently! Now I've got to go so I can see the nav screen to make my way back to you. It says it's about a 10-minute walk, so that's not too bad.

I switched back to the navigation screen, making it full-sized again and ignored the notification that popped up that was just Valory saying – *Okay, girl. Be careful!*

I felt so guilty for not having contacted her at all last night. I'd broken the rules and she had every right to be mad at me.

We'd had this whole plan for me to contact her regularly and I just hadn't done it. I felt stupid for it too.

Synister had shown me up and thrown me for such a loop upon his arrival that I'd just sort of lost all track of the cohesive plan. I mean, he was kind of a force of nature and, like with nature, you could only plan so far. If the tornado wanted your house, then your house would be flattened and that's exactly what it'd felt like. Like he'd touched down and swept me up, and I was carried off to Oz.

Still, that didn't absolve me of my guilt in the slightest.

I swept back through Monterey Square, past the Mercer-Williams house, and tried not to shudder when I slipped over the spot that he'd first kissed me. I didn't want to linger in my flight back to my dorm. Not with Valory still awake and waiting.

I hadn't realized how ridiculously *close* he lived to my art school, and where I lived for at least the rest of this year.

I didn't really have a cohesive plan on where I would go after. I mean, I knew I was welcome back in my parents' home, or the house on Tybee Island that was our vacation home and was a vacation rental the rest of the time that we weren't there.

Mom and Dad were officially retired and traveling abroad now that both Zeke and I were out of the house. Zeke was still in school, too, but he was finishing up his studies in Marine Science at South University. He'd taken a year and a half off between high school and college to travel. He had gone abroad and come home with his gambling addiction which we'd been fighting off and on ever since.

I hadn't taken any time off between high school and college, opting to go right into earning my degree. Painting was my passion, but I was earning my practical degree in social media management and graphic design. Still, every available credit I could take in painting, I did. I loved every minute of it.

I arrived at the dorm building and used my key card to get in the front door, opting for the stairs over the rickety, slow-moving elevator, before finally using my key to get in my room's door. No sooner had it grated in the lock than the door flew open and Valory was pulling me into a tight hug.

"I was so worried about you!" she cried, and her voice cracked toward the end.

I hugged her back tight and said, "I'm fine, really—"

"You don't look fine!" she said, and smoothed a hand over my cheek in worry. "Look at you!"

"What?" I asked bewildered. I went over to my mirror and blinked stupidly.

"Oh, yikes!" I said at the blur of makeup under my eyes and the muddy tracks at the corner from where I'd apparently cried. I didn't remember that part. Like... for reals. I didn't. *When did I cry?* I wondered, rifling through my memories and trying to recall.

"I'm fine," I said. "Really, I am. But I need to go wash my face before anyone else sees me."

"Pfft! It's like, five something in the morning. No one's gonna see you," she said. "But yeah, you should go get a shower and then you need to tell me *everything*."

86

"I will," I said. "I promise."

"Okay," she said and the solemn look on her face said I'd need to tell her every last gory little detail or I'd never be forgiven.

"You're the closest thing to a best friend I have, you know," she said, sitting on the edge of her bed, as I, wrapped in my robe and my shower caddy in my hand, reached for the room's doorknob to head down to the shower room.

I stopped, turned and said, "I am?"

"Yeah, you are," she said and she looked stressed. I stopped and went over and sat down next to her.

She looked at me with this pleading look and said, "Please don't ever do that again. You scared the life out of me."

I hugged her tight and said, "I'm so sorry. I didn't realize..." and I meant it. I'd had no clue.

She hugged me back, super tight and said, "It's okay, you're okay – this time. At least I hope you are."

I pulled back enough to look at her and nodded.

"I'm okay, physically, but I'd be lying if I said it didn't suck waking up alone like that."

She made a disgusted sound. "The asshole," she grumbled.

I shrugged a shoulder. "It wasn't all bad," I said gently.

"Well, that's good, I guess," she said and I nodded.

"Be right back," I said.

"Okay."

I took myself down to the shower and once I was inside and the hot water was hitting my face, I think it hit me. All at once. Just the magnitude of it all. Like, it came down like a ton of bricks or a piano on my head and just smashed me through the floor. I definitely would remember crying this time.

Chapter Twelve

Synister...

It was just as our boat pulled up at Bloody Point Dock and Landing in South Carolina to meet our Latin buddies that my phone vibrated in my inside jacket pocket. I let Grim and Reaper toss lines to Castañeda's boy, Renaldo, as I took a look.

It was Spooky texting me to let me know Madisyn was on the move.

Dog her every step. Don't let her know you're doing it. Make sure she gets back to her dorm.

I wasn't fucking around. He fucked this up, I'd have his nut sack as a charm to dangle from my Land Rover's rearview.

"All good?" Requiem asked low so the Columbians wouldn't hear.

I grunted. "Madisyn's on the move."

"Ah," he said. "No disrespect, but your head in the game?" he asked.

"My head's always in the game," I replied. "Don't you ever think for one minute that it's not."

He nodded and backed the fuck off where he belonged.

I wasn't some teenager or fuckin' dumb fuck who got a taste of good pussy and couldn't think of anything else. Sometimes my guys liked to forget just why I was the president of this club.

King... floated through my head unbidden and I dipped my chin under the guise of watching my step, as I climbed up out of the boat and onto the dock, to hide my smirk at the thought.

When I looked up, no one was the wiser that I'd thought anything was even remotely funny.

"Castañeda," I intoned.

"Señor Synister," he greeted me, and I was instantly on guard. Only time he added the honorific to my damn name was when he was trying to butter me up for something.

"Cut the shit. What do you need?" I asked.

"I like this about you," he said, and he raised a cigar to his lips and flicked open his Zippo to light it. "Always to the point."

I gritted my teeth, and he said, "Walk with me." I planted my feet, shoulder width apart, and gripped one wrist with my opposite hand loosely, raising my chin and looking at him imperiously, trying to decide what he was fucking playing at.

He wasn't an old guy, but he was older than me – maybe early forties edging into mid. He had just a few threads of silver at his temples and kept it clean shaven and preferred a rather old-fashioned and fuckin' stereotypical way of dress. Think suits for sure, but laid back. Like tonight, he was in black slacks and a white business shirt. But rather than a tie and suit jacket, he had on a modern take on a smoking jacket. I'd say blue, but the scant moonlight from the half-moon that was out leeched the color and made it hard to tell.

"Come, this isn't business. This is a personal matter I bring you. One that I hope, you would help me with."

I stepped up to the plate, my curiosity doubling and tripling. Requiem fell into step behind me and to my right. Renaldo did the same with Castañeda, a pace back and to the man's left as we strolled a way up the dock.

Eventually, Requiem and Renaldo held back just enough to give me and Castañeda the semblance of privacy Castañeda desired.

"My daughter," he said. "She is in love with this boy," he said.

Shit, he wasn't kidding when he said *personal*.

"You don't seem happy with that," I said.

"I am not. He is an American boy, rich family on Hilton Head."

"You want us to scare him off her."

Castañeda shook his head and looked down, scratching his bottom lip with his thumbnail. Looking back up to me, he said, "I want you to kill him."

"Just for dating your daughter?" I asked, hitching an incredulous laugh. That was a bit much, even for me.

"No," he said. "For being a *pederasta pendejo*. She has no idea, and I would rather her heart be broken by his ghosting her, or breaking up with her, but they're infatuated with each other. They're talking marriage and I can't have him ruin her life."

I looked back down the dock past Requiem and Renaldo, on down to Grim and Reaper, the wheels turning.

"I ain't no fuckin' hero," I said. "I ain't about to risk offing some socialite rich kid with all the fuckin' attention on him without some fuckin' proof and a real big payday at the end of this fucked-up rainbow."

"I thought you might say that, my friend." He reached into his smoking jacket and I straightened. He held out his hand for me to calm down but slowed his movements considerably. He pulled out a sheaf of documents and put his cigar back between his teeth while he said, "Every man can be bought, but some men shouldn't. You know?"

I took the papers and tilted them into the light from the shore. They were court documents. I frowned and read over them.

"Not even going to ask how you got ahold of these," I said. "How old's this kid?"

"Now? Twenty. He was a minor when he did what he did to that boy. But once a monster, always a monster."

I flipped pages and scowled at the record. These were sealed juvenile records. I had no fucking idea how Castañeda had gotten them, but here they were, and they contained some seriously grim shit.

"How much we talking?" I demanded. Castañeda named a figure that was more than enough when I had at least two men in my ranks who would take on this kind of shit for free. Some of us never got over what was done to us when we were kids. I know I was still working out some of my own daddy issues by ruining the fuck out of my father, and he'd never put a finger on me. Certainly not with any of this sick shit on the page.

"Let me talk it over with my boys," I said. "If it's a yes, watch the headlines. If it's a no, we'll let you know the next time we meet up. I want to keep these clandestine meetings to as few as possible so as not to tempt fate."

Castañeda's mouth turned down and he nodded in that way that said these terms were more than acceptable to him.

"Between you and me," I said. "I think you're going to be drying your daughter's tears sooner rather than later."

"I am pleased to hear it, Señor," he said, and I arched an eyebrow at him.

"Don't take that shit as gospel," I told him.

"Of course, of course," he said.

"Alright." I gave him a curt nod and made the sheaf of papers disappear into the opposite side of my jacket from my phone.

I walked back down the dock and collected Requiem and gave Renaldo a quick nod of respect. He was a young buck, but stood to inherit quite the empire from Castañeda should he ever get caught up or go down. Renaldo gave a curt nod back and drifted the opposite direction we were heading back to his boss's side.

"Catch any of that?" I asked Req low and quiet when we were almost back to the boat and well outside earshot of Castañeda and his man.

"Some of it. Sounds messy."

"Maybe. When we get back to the Georgia side of things, call in the rest of the boys."

"Copy that." Requiem nodded as we got back down into the boat which Reaper was already firing up.

I checked my phone, but there were no additional texts. Just as I went to put it away, one buzzed through.

I looked.

The sparrow is back in her house.

I snorted.

Fuckin' idiot.

If it was one thing Spooky was good for, though? It was a laugh.

Chapter Thirteen

Madisyn...

I caught several more hours of sleep after staying up past dawn and filling Valory in on just about *all* of the gory details. She listened to me, rapt, and finally said, "That's so hot in some ways but most of it? That *bastard*."

I'd snorted and laughed and said, "Yeah, well, if waking up all by myself is any indication? That bastard wasn't all that impressed and I won't be seeing him again."

Famous last words and all of that.

One of the things about Saturday was that *yes* it was a day off from the school week grind, but also? It was Professor Keating and his paint group. We'd meet up every other Saturday and go someplace new, set up our easels or sit with our sketchbooks and would just *indulge* in our art. We'd meet up at this tea shop and then would follow Professor Keating up or down the street to the destination of his choice while he shouted poetry or sang Beatles' tunes loudly and badly to make us laugh.

I missed being in his classes. He was passionate about art and artwork and these Saturdays were so nice because it was the one time he liked to, as he said it, throw caution to the wind and the rules out the window because in art – there should be no rules.

I was hoping he would pick anywhere but Forsyth Park this time, but was fairly certain he would, being that was where we'd been Saturday, last we'd done this.

"Earth to Syn... You okay there?" I ratcheted up my smile a notch as I took up my tea from the counter and turned to Levi who was hugging his sketchbook to his chest. He was a year or two younger than I was, and bright and eager to break into the comic book market as an artist. Although he wanted to be a writer for them too. He'd shown me some of his original works surrounding some kind of voodoo superhero that worked from Charleston to Savannah and places in-between.

It was all very mysterious and very cool. I was hoping that he would someday be able to go somewhere with it.

"Yeah, I'm good, why?" I asked.

"You just looked sad for a minute, and it took like three tries to even get your attention. Girl..." He kind of tilted his head and looked down on me and the look said '*don't lie to me, now,*' before he said, "You sure you're okay?"

I felt my smile grow warmer and said, "Oh yeah, just... just worried about my brother, you know?"

Levi nodded. He was one of only two people I'd confided in about Zeke's problems; Valory being the other. But he didn't know anything about what I'd done. Only Valory and Zeke knew that. I was more than a little upset that Zeke hadn't called me, or even come to talk to me.

I sighed.

"Aw, is he still at it?" he asked. "I thought he was doing better."

"He was," I said. "But yeah. I pulled him out of a spot over down on River Street just earlier this week."

Levi's eyes went wide. "Really?" he asked.

"Yeah," I said and didn't even bother to keep the disappointment off my face.

"Is that why you were with that older guy yesterday? The one in that sick Mercedes?"

"You saw that?" I asked with a grimace.

"Yeah. I saw him pick you up outside your dorm entrance after I got out of my late study hall. Who was he?"

"Yeah, I uh, agreed to go out to dinner with him," I said, falling into line as Professor Keating drummed us all up, calling us all his little lemmings, which totally wasn't as rude as it sounded. Not the way he said it. It was lighthearted and hysterical and not exactly wrong with how we all followed him up the sidewalk. Levi fell into step beside me.

"Dinner?" he asked. "That's all?" I was grateful he hadn't caught that I hadn't disclosed who Synister was.

I colored and tried to look away but Levi grabbed my arm and hissed, "Synnie, Syn, Syn! Did you..."

"Shh!" I hissed.

"Holy fuck. Girl, you *did!*" His jaw dropped and I put my hand to my forehead, shading it and looking down to hide my humiliation.

"Levi!" I groaned and he drew his head back letting go of my arm, as we stepped back into line at the end, and kept marching along in the direction of... wait, where were we going?

I checked the streets at the corner and realized we were on Drayton and Liberty about to cross Drayton to continue on Liberty. I felt my shoulders ease a little, knowing that if we were going *that way*, we weren't heading to Forsyth and thus weren't going near Synister's house.

"I don't know whether to be disappointed or proud," he said, and I looked up at him horrified. He laughed at the look on my face and said, "Proud! It's definitely proud, but maybe just a little disappointed it wasn't me."

He lifted one shoulder and dusted it off and then, grinning at me, winked.

I rolled my eyes and kept walking, my artist's pack and easel an almost heavier weight on my shoulder than it was before. Or maybe it was something else entirely that was weighing me down.

"Please don't judge," I said softly and he stopped me again, a hand on my arm.

"Yo, wait, hold up – did you not want to?" he asked me.

"It's complicated," I said, wiping my sweating palm that wasn't holding my tea on my shorts.

"What's complicated?" he demanded. "Either you did, or you didn't."

He sounded like he was just starting to rev up. I so did not need sweet-and-gregarious Levi trying to white knight against Synister and the Iron Wraiths for me.

"I did," I said, assuring him... because I mean, I did. I didn't regret it one iota. Like at all. I just regretted waking up alone and that I hadn't been good enough for a second round. I don't even know why I hoped, but I guess, I had. Talk about an ego check.

"Oh, girlfriend, you're gonna have to do way better than that to convince me that you didn't just get—" I put my hand over Levi's mouth and glared up at him.

"I consented to *everything*, Levi! Don't even go there!" I stared him down. He brought his richly tan hand up and pulled mine down from over his mouth. I looked up the block and muttered, "*Shit*. Where are we even going? We lost the group."

"Come on," he said. "It's this way, but for real – you gotta tell me why the long face. What'd that guy do?"

"It's what he *didn't* do, that's the problem," I griped.

"Which is?" he demanded.

I sighed heavily and looked up at Levi, who was easily six foot three and skinny as a rail. I said, "Stay. Okay? He didn't stay. I woke up and he was gone. No note, no text, no nothing. Just left me all alone in his great big bed, in his great big house, without so much as a 'thanks' or 'see you later' and I don't know why. Like, I want to be upset, but is that fair? He's some kind of big businessman and—" I finished the rambling word vomit the same way I started it, with a heavy sigh.

"I'm probably overthinking it all," I said.

Levi looked down at me with empathy. He wasn't a rich kid. He was a *talented* one. His mommy and daddy didn't pay for him to be here. I mean, they did, but not in the way that *my* parents did for me. Levi had worked his ass off, had earned really good grades in high school, had worked summer jobs since he was *thirteen*. He had saved every penny from parents and grandparents alike from every Christmas and every birthday, and everything else in between since he was literally *five* to make it here.

It'd sadly taken his dad dying on the job to make his dream of coming to this school a reality, though.

He didn't have any siblings. His mom was a small thing like me, and his dad had been this big man. She'd had a complicated pregnancy. It was a shame, too. His mom and dad had made a beautiful baby in Levi. In fact, Levi was Levi Percy Washington, the Third – the last of his line. His mom was this beautiful petite woman with strawberry blonde hair going gray at the temples. I'd met her once. He'd shown me a picture of his dad and him at one of his basketball games his junior year of high school. He was this big robust dark-skinned man. He and his wife had been night and day personified, and their son had gotten the best of both worlds.

He was tall like his dad, his skin bronze and permanently kissed by the sun, but he had these moonlight silvery gray eyes and these short spiky twists to his hair at the top of his head, a neat and well-lined fade at the back and sides.

He still went to the same barbershop. The one his grandfather had founded and that his two uncles on his dad's side still ran.

Everything Levi had, he and his family worked to the bone and sacrificed so much for. His dad dying on his job as a road construction worker was the biggest sacrifice of all.

The city had paid out big, enough for his mom to pay off the house, make some desperately needed repairs, and to make ends meet for Levi to finish his dream education. Something his dad had been very insistent on and proud of.

"Syn," he said as we turned onto Abercorn and saw the group crossing to the other side of it way up ahead. "You have every right to feel whichever way you feel about it," he said and I smiled.

"I do believe your mother just came out of your mouth right then," I said, giving him a playful shove. He laughed.

"Shut up!" But he looked... proud. He should have been. His parents raised a damn good kid.

"It's not a bad thing!" I cried. "Seriously, it's not," I said at his look that said, *really?*

"See, that's your problem. Your hanging with the wrong dudes. Those rich-ass motherfuckers don't know how to treat a lady."

I felt myself blush furiously and said, "I mean, well... I had fun in the moment."

Levi stopped and looked at me as we reached the corner of the wrought iron fence surrounding Colonial Park Cemetery and plucked his shirt as he tooted his own horn, "Yeah, but us kids from around the block? We know how to treat a woman right before, during, *and after the fact.*"

I laughed and said, "You know, Levi, given the state of men nowadays? I'm pretty sure that's just you, and that's because your mamma raised you right."

"Shit, who you tellin'?" he said. "Legit, if I pulled some shit like that, my mamma would slap the taste right out my mouth. Hell, my daddy'd rise up from his grave and be like 'son, c'mere so I can whoop that ass!'" He put his arms out, rolled his eyes back in his head and staggered like a zombie. I couldn't help but laugh – a genuine laugh. A real one from way down in the bottom of my belly.

"Oh, my God! Stop!" I gave him another light shove and he came back and knocked his shoulder into mine and laughed with me.

"See, now that's what you need. Someone who can make you laugh. What is it they say? Find someone to ruin your lipstick, not your mascara."

"Oh, now that was *so* your mother right there."

"Guilty," he said as we rounded the corner and slipped under the arch with its eagle, to move down the pathway inside the park.

"You know, I saw a ghost in here just last night," I said.

"No shit?" he asked, as we moved along to meet up with the rest of the group that was setting up on the grass under some oaks.

"Yep," I said.

"What'd it look like?" he asked.

I shrugged. "Like a shadow. Man sized, not as tall as you, but taller than me—"

"Shorty, everything and everyone is taller than you," he said, and I laughed again and shook my head.

"Now *you* shut up!" I cried.

He grinned and said, "But no, seriously, tell me more."

"Tell you more about what?" Christine asked, looking up from where she was unpacking her easel from her backpack.

"Madisyn saw a ghost in here last night," Levi said.

"No shit?" one of the other students called, but I didn't know his name.

"Yeah," I said, and I told them all about the shadow person flitting among the graves and what Synister had told me about it not being someone stuck in here like I'd thought.

I set up along with everyone else as I told the tale. Mr. Keating listened just as rapt as anyone and he said, finally, "I think this is as good a time as any to talk about using what you see as just a guideline versus painting or drawing a landscape as it is. So, this is what I want you to do—"

While I liked Mr. Keating's lesson and his guidance, I wasn't feeling this one today. I guess I'd had enough of having to guess or create things around what was actually there in order to arrive at some safe conclusion or whatever. So, I sort of tuned him out as I let my pencil lightly sketch the back wall and draped Spanish moss before the gravestones that'd been pulled up and bracketed to the brick.

Levi sat in the grass by me and sketched furiously in his comic book style on the page, a young blue-collar worker, standing in the sun before the same back wall to the cemetery I sketched. Only the man's shadow stretched behind him and plastered itself against that wall. His shadow had the distinct lines of a top hat, and a coat with tails, and the shadow had eyes that I was sure were going to glow once he busted out his Copic markers to ink the drawing.

"I like it," I said.

"Yeah?" he asked, looking up at me where I stood at my easel beside him.

"Yeah," I said.

"What's the story?"

He smiled at the drawing and made up a story for me on the spot. I could tell he had it in mind the second Mr. Keating had started giving guidelines for the lesson of today.

I got some painting in, but not a lot. I checked the time when we were told to pack up and that our time was up. I decided as much as I would like to stay, tomorrow or another day around the same time would have to do. I wanted the light to be similar, if not the same.

I closed the doors on my easel and looped the latch over the little knobs in the front. It made a box around the painting and kept the wet paint from being disturbed in transit.

Levi and I were last to pack up just like we'd been last to unpack our stuff when we'd arrived, as we chattered about his ideas and the story surrounding his drawing. Everyone else had scattered, which was typical of these kinds of things. We were just coming out of the gate we'd entered when I looked up and felt myself pale.

Synister was there, arms crossed over his chest, butt leaned on the seat of his bike, booted feet crossed at the ankle on the sidewalk and stretched out way in front of himself.

"Oh," Levi said when I stopped abruptly, and he looked up and caught sight of Synister too.

"You weren't where I left you, Madisyn," Synister intoned. I didn't like that his eyes were unreadable, walled off behind the lenses of his black aviators like they were.

He pushed off from his motorcycle and stalked toward me. I backed up out of reflex, my back fetching up against the stone column of one side of the park gate.

Syn put a hand above me and leaned in, putting his lips beside my ear. He asked, "Want to tell me why?"

"Syn," Levi called.

"What?" Synister demanded.

"Me, he meant me," I said breathy.

"I meant *her*," Levi echoed me. "Syn, you good?"

"I'm good, Levi! I promise," I called back and I straightened up. "You *left me*. That's why I wasn't there," I said. I made to duck under his arm and walk away but his other hand came up and lightly gripped my arm.

"Uh-uh, we aren't done talking," Synister said.

"Hey, yo, man – I don't know who you are, but a lady says she's done talking she's—"

"Levi, it's cool. I'll catch up with you later," I called out to my friend. He looked a mix of uncertain and put out. I gave Synister a stern look and he nodded slowly, letting go of my arm, but I didn't move. I just wanted Levi to go and not make a scene.

I turned to look at Levi and said, "I'm serious. It's cool. I *do* need to talk to him."

Levi still looked uncertain but relented in the end, saying, "Alright, I'ma check on you later, though."

"I'd reconsider that statement," Synister said, and he turned some kind of a look on Levi that made Levi scowl. I gave Synister a shove. Synister looked back at me and his eyebrows had gone up over his aviators in surprise.

"No way! You don't get to do that, uh-uh," I said, literally wagging a finger in Synister's face. Levi's look went from a scowl to impressed. He gave Synister a grin like my attitude spelled karma and it was pronounced "ha, ha, fuck you."

Synister turned his gaze back to me at the same time I turned from Levi back to him and he growled. And I do mean *growled*. A thrill sort of went through me and I shivered, but I didn't back down.

"Get on the bike," he ordered.

"Not until you apologize for being an asshole!" I said but my bravado waned when he took his sunglasses down and looked at me with those coal dark eyes over them.

"Last chance, Syn. I'm gonna go," Levi called.

I didn't move my gaze from Synister's and called out, "I'm good, Levi. I promise." I wasn't about to lose this stubborn battle of wills with this *insufferable* biker this time and I think Levi could see it because...

"Okay then," Levi said, and he moved out of the corner of my vision but it was still a little reluctantly.

"Who's he?" Synister demanded once Levi was well enough up the block that he wouldn't hear us.

"None of your concern. That's who he is," I snapped. Synister's gaze fixed on Levi's retreating back made me relent. "He's just a friend. You're making yourself look like a whole entire ass for absolutely no reason, for one. For two, it's not like you fucking me and ditching me in the middle of the night last night is grounds for property rights or some shit. I fulfilled my end of the damn bargain so what's with this jealous boyfriend routine?"

Synister smirked this infuriating little smirk but didn't back out of my personal space. He just turned the intensity of his focus off of Levi and back onto me. It was like walking under an air conditioning unit blowing down from a doorway as you entered a store. Intense and chilled me to the bone. I swallowed hard.

"One," he said. "I *am* an asshole. Never pretended to be otherwise. And two, just because you fulfilled our bargain last night doesn't mean our business is concluded."

"What do you want?" I snapped, but I was quickly losing my bravery now that we were alone.

Synister lowered his lips to the side of my throat. He hovered

102

there for just a moment, his warm breath almost cooler than the heat and humidity of the day where it brushed my skin.

I shuddered and my knees went weak when he brushed a light kiss against my skin.

"I want some more," he whispered, and he caught me at my waist to support me when my knees tried to buckle completely. I leaned up hard against the pillar of the gate behind me.

"How did you even know I was here?" I demanded, trying to change the subject and regain my bearings.

"I had one of my men follow you," he said.

"What?" I demanded and he smirked.

I looked this way and that. He laughed at me, saying, "He's not still out there."

I glared at him.

"Since when?" I demanded, skipping over the fact he was being a jerk because I was quickly realizing it was his natural habitat.

"Since you left my place." He pushed off from the wall behind me, backing out of my personal space. I realized he wasn't wearing his vest thing. Just a simple, black tee made out of a lightweight material, that hugged his chest and arms nicely.

"And he followed me all the way here?" I asked, my voice sounding hollow.

"From the house, to your dorm, to the tea shop, and *then* all the way here," he corrected. "He was with you all the way until I got here," he said. "Then I let him fuck off and go home."

"And when did you get here?" I asked. My chest felt a little tight... like, *what was he telling me right now?* Had I really been oblivious to being followed?

"A couple hours back," he told me, and I was distracted from my thoughts all over again. Like I couldn't stay fixed on any one thing when he was near me. There was always something new and more... more outrageous than the last thing to keep my attention constantly shifting.

"And you just waited here? For what?" I demanded but that last question was really dumb, obviously... I was just trying to buy some time to *think*. It was like I couldn't comprehend what he was telling me, like he would throw so much at my wall and *none of it* was sticking. I hated how off center that made me feel.

"For you," he said and I could tell he was trying to hold on to his patience. "I already told you, our business isn't concluded." The tone in which he said the last was clearly annoyed which – *uh-uh, no way, hombre.* I wouldn't put up with it. I raised my chin defiantly.

"And what if I say it is?" I asked. I swiftly sidestepped him on the one side, lightly went down the three easy steps to the sidewalk, and started to walk away.

"Hear from your brother yet?" he called at my back and I froze. I turned slowly, ever so slowly, the whole world going still and quiet with my anger. *Oh, you're going to go there?* I thought to myself.

With a calmness I knew I shouldn't feel I demanded, "What did you just say?"

Winter seeped off of Synister where he stood stalk-still, looking down at me from the top of the lintel of Colonial Park's gate. If you were a passerby, I could swear you saw the shimmer of power between us as the struggle was on and very real, even though neither of us moved. Neither of us backed down. He could be pissed all he wanted. I was pissed too, and goddammit –

"Get on the bike, Madisyn. I'll take you to him," he said finally and those words... it was like he hurled a stone with them and the damn thing cracked through the ice I had been trying valiantly to form as a shield against him.

I stood there in the late afternoon light and seethed for what felt like a full minute but was probably only a matter of seconds, as much at myself for giving in, him for being a jerk, and yes, even Zeke for being out there doing some stupid shit and handing this psycho the leverage he knew would work on me in an instant.

Goddammit, Zeke, why the hell do you have to be my Kryptonite? I demanded silently. Out loud?

"You are *such* a fucking asshole!" I snarled. I stomped over to his bike, standing next to it and shoving my other arm through the loose strap of my artist's backpack, putting it on the rest of the way and securing the strap across my chest so it wouldn't come loose or anything stupid on the ride.

"Again," he said, bounding down the steps to the cemetery turned park's gate and striding toward me. "Never said I wasn't."

Chapter Fourteen

Synister...

She was stiff behind me, her face unreadable since I'd put her in a full facemask helmet, the visor mirrored and deeply tinted to protect her fair skin. I'd been right on the size. The brand-new helmet fit her like a dream. Like it was supposed to, to keep her safe.

I bet the moving air felt good against her skin. It did mine. She was way too fired up to enjoy much of anything, though, and I couldn't say I was upset about that. She was cute when she was angry. She was far too easy to wind up, too, but I think that she needed to open her fuckin' eyes to the reality of the situation with her fucking cad of a brother. The way she'd stiffened, her back going ramrod straight when I'd asked if he'd even bothered to contact her had told me everything I'd needed to know about him. He didn't give a fuck about anybody but himself.

The fact that his baby sister had thrown herself on my mercy for his ungrateful ass, and he'd given her radio silence in return, chapped my ass. He knew I'd fucked her last night. He knew, even if she didn't, exactly what type of man I was and he couldn't even be fucked to call and check on her?

Nice. Real fucking nice.

She deserved better than that, and for some reason, it'd become my fucking mission to make her see he wasn't worth even half the effort she was putting in on him with this whole "he was sick" bullshit. That may be, but rather than take his medicine like a man, and exert some fucking self-control like he should have, he was out here hitting yet another fucking poker game just with a whole different crew since mine wouldn't let him in to our games anymore.

I took Madisyn out to the other side of town. A rough neighborhood that she had no business being in by herself, but with me? No sweat. Everyone out here knew who the fuck I was. If not by name, then by reputation. They knew not to fuck with me or the Iron Wraiths. Fucking with me or my boys was how you disappeared, and the rumors of a slow and painful death weren't unfounded.

As for big brother, I had it on good authority he was hanging out in one of the OTG crew – or Only the Gangsta's games. They were a street gang in one of the rougher neighborhoods of Savannah and were starting to make a name for themselves. They occasionally hit us up for a handgun or two when the need arose and we were on good terms. Hence, when I put the feelers out for Madisyn's man-child of a brother, they didn't mind giving up his location. Apparently, he had been here all night and all day, losing his fuckin' ass at cards.

I pulled up at the curb and Madisyn jumped off, going for the chin strap I'd secured beneath her chin and taking a deep breath as soon as the helmet was off of her head.

"God, I *hate* that thing!" she complained. "Feels claustrophobic in there."

I grunted and thought to myself, *you better get used to it,* but out loud I said, "Best safety rating there is. You ride with me, you wear it."

"Good thing I won't be riding with you again," she said with a deep scowl and a scoffing tone. She was so fucking *cute* when she was pissed off and she could be as pissed as she wanted with me, for right now. I was sure that all would change in a minute.

She looked around as I pulled my own helmet off my head and set it down on my bike's seat. I took hers from her and did likewise with it. She looked up and down the street, which was lonely and quiet, the houses' exteriors in rough shape – paint peeling, gutters falling, vegetation growing out of some of them. The yards were over-grown with their bent and falling down chain link fences surrounding them and dripping with rust.

The sidewalks glittered with silica and broken glass being ground underfoot back into sand from all the shot out and busted out street-lights through here. Let me tell you – this was not a part of Savannah you would want to be in after dark.

One of the houses on the block had boarded-up windows and condemnation notices plastered to them yet had clear signs that somebody or somebodies were still living in it. *Not a place to be during the day, either,* I thought. Requiem would honestly have a shit fit if he knew I was out here alone. Same with Corvus. Honestly, out of all of my guys, Torment was the only one who probably wouldn't think it was a big deal, but Torment had several screws loose like me.

We navigated a world in lines drawn by power, and we followed our lines and stayed in our lanes accordingly. There weren't many lanes off-limits to me – and this certainly wasn't one of 'em – but there were always motherfucking fish in the sea, dumb e-fucking-nough to try and swallow a fish bigger than they were. While they tended to choke on the likes of me, I could still be wounded by the teeth they had and could suffocate if there wasn't anyone nearby to get my head out of their mouth.

"Are you sure Zeke is here?" Madisyn asked, interrupting my train of thoughts. She was looking around now, drinking it all in with somber blue eyes, and she was rightfully afraid. This wasn't the place or the world for her.

"I'm sure," I told her. "You're safe as long as you stick with me and don't smart off. These fools are young, dumb, full of cum, and wouldn't hesitate to come try something if you hurt their fuckin' egos."

I checked my weapon at the small of my back and made sure my shirt was covering it. I took my colors out of one of my hard-sided saddlebags and slipped them on.

"Why not wear it before?" she asked, shrewdly.

"Colonial Park is right next door to Savannah PD's Historic District's station. Why would I fuck with getting hassled by them?"

I raised an eyebrow at her silence in retort and she colored slightly, saying, "I don't know how to feel about that."

"Don't care how you feel about that one," I said and I didn't. She could have whatever existential crisis she wanted over the fact that the cops and the club weren't on good terms. It didn't change anything. I was their president and I was all in. Nothing would ever change that. I built this damn thing from the ground up.

"You are so confusing," she griped and she uncrossed her arms, her hands moving on the straps of whatever strange backpack rig thing she had on, making a loud swish against the nylon material as she held them and shifted uncomfortably on her feet. She was antsy, and that was good. It meant she had some self-preservation in her after all.

Silence hung between us, and the space and a half that separated us might as well have been a chasm.

"You'll learn," I said and jerked my head up the block. She untwined her fingers from around the straps of her backpack thing and dropped her hands, letting her arms hang to her sides as she reluctantly fell into step beside me.

"I don't know if I want to," she said honestly, and the resignation in her tone made it one of the smartest things I'd heard her say. But we both knew her curiosity would overwhelm her and she'd find out eventually. She was so very sweet in her predictability. I liked that she kept me guessing on the minutia, but on the big things? She was pretty steady, and there was no guessing whatsoever.

Other than the absolutely mind-blowing way she responded to

my every touch and manipulation of her fine-as-hell body, I think that's what had me coming back for another round. The only down-side to fucking Madisyn Reynolds was her idiot brother. That drama wasn't anything I wanted further part in, which was why this little field trip. I was trying to see if I could nip that shit in the bud right now.

I went two houses down and up to the porch and knocked. A smaller door that was set at eye level opened, and a pair of dark eyes that seemingly floated in a sea of darkness, the whites the only thing apparent, peered out at me from behind the floral bronze grate that was decoratively set in the door.

The door snapped shut with a metal clack on the other side of that grate, and a muffled voice asked a question. A moment later, the door opened.

I went in, a hand on the back of Madisyn's shoulder, awkwardly towing her in behind me. The banger, who'd looked out the grate, shut the door behind us and threw the locks.

"Synister." Wheezy, one of the three leaders of the OTG crew, looked up from where he lounged in an old recliner. He had on sweats with half his underwear above the waistline, a white wifebeater on, a leg hooked over one arm and dangling almost artfully. His Timberland's were very stark and yellow in the rest of the room which was dingy and drab.

"Wheezy," I intoned.

"Y' boy's in there." He jerked his head and smiled as the ho he had sucking him off's head rose and fell rhythmically. I glanced at Madisyn and she was pointedly staring at the floor or alternately a wall or the ceiling, just anywhere but at Wheezy and his ho.

"Thanks," I grunted and with a hand to Madisyn, I drew her to my side.

I steered her toward the archway Wheezy had nodded toward and stepped in front of her as we passed a hallway. I could hear the rattle of chips and the swish of someone raking in the pot before I cleared the next archway in front of us.

110

There was a card table and four chairs in the dining area of the kitchen back here, and Madisyn's brother looked up from where he was raking in the pot.

"Well, I'll be. Looks like you actually won a hand for a change," I told him but my tone was dispassionate, belying any actual congratulations.

"What the fuck are you doing here?" he asked me, and I turned sideways, revealing Madi behind me.

I put my hand to her back to steady her as she trembled and looked at her brother with murderous intent.

"Syn!" Zeke cried as his sister whirled, her blonde hair flying, and she marched from whence we came.

I tilted my head and said, "Do me a favor, boys. Make sure this is his last hand at your table," I said and I fixed Zeke with a look. "I'll make it worth y'all's while the next time you need something."

"Wait!" Zeke got up, leaving his winnings as he made for his sister. I turned and followed her before he could get to her. She strode right out the front door, which was standing open, the guy that'd been guarding it looking up from his phone bored at the White people's drama unfolding in front of him. I couldn't blame him. If I hadn't had a personal stake in baby sister, I wouldn't even be here, let alone participating as anything more than a spectator.

I followed Madisyn down the overgrown path and out the gate onto the sidewalk. She doubled over, her hands on her knees as she panted for breath like she was trying to hold off on being sick.

I stood nearby and watched what would happen as Zeke hit the sidewalk right behind us and said, "Madisyn, wait, come on! Now don't do that. It's not that serious!"

Madi stood up straight, and I was surprised to find a hearty mixture of desire for her and feeling like a cad myself with the tears that stained her cheeks – which was curious.

She gave her brother a hearty shove and screamed at him. "Not that serious!? Not that *serious?* I can't believe you, Ezekiel James!" She gave her brother another hearty shove that knocked him back a pace. He threw open his arms to keep himself on balance and shouted back.

"What?" he demanded. "It wasn't high stakes, and I was *winning* in there!"

"Did you forget what I was *doing* for you last night?" Madisyn snarled, and oh... oh, this was fixing to get good. I crossed my arms over my chest and just watched this shit play out from beneath my sunglasses.

"Oh, shit—" Zeke looked at me with a shocked and accusatory look. "For real?"

I grinned and nodded. "Like you think I'd pass that up?" I asked, jerking my chin in the direction of his baby sister.

He turned back to Madisyn. "Did you really?" he demanded, his tone like he was about to dress her down. The color drained from Madisyn's face.

"Don't you dare!" She breathed, and I swore she breathed fire. "Don't you *fucking* dare!" she shouted. "You don't get to look at me like that!" she snarled. "I did it for *you*, Zeke! These people are not nice people! They will *hurt* you! They would hurt *me*, and Mom, and Dad if it would get them what they wanted out of you! I can't seriously *believe* you right now! It's like you don't even care!" Her voice cracked on the last and I felt some satisfaction.

Ah, there it is, I thought to myself. *The dawning realization that big brother doesn't really give a shit about anyone but himself.* That's what I came for, and it was a mixed bag, I admit. A bit of a dangerous game I was playing here. The game was to educate Madisyn on what her brother was really like to keep her from going to these kinds of lengths for him with anyone else. At the same time, I was trying to keep her. I wanted her to myself. Especially after last night.

I couldn't stop thinking about her. She was my new favorite obsession, but curiously different in that this didn't feel like a passing fancy like the rest had. While I couldn't tell you why, what I did know was I was curious and invested enough that I wanted to find out where it all was heading.

All that aside, it was time to drive the lesson home for little Madisyn Jayne...

"You still owe me a hundred large," I reminded him as I scratched my cheek. "Baby sister only cleared up eighty k last night." I was a real bastard for what I said next, but I wanted to test him. I wanted to test them both. "Lucky for you, I liked things enough, I'm willing to negotiate further with her."

Zeke stared at me, and for the first time, he maybe looked a little green, a little scared. He sealed the deal in confirming my suspicions about him were right with what he did next.

He looked at his sister and said, "Madisyn?" His tone was... beseeching.

Fucking predictable.

The siblings stared at each other for a long time, Madisyn staring up at her brother in abject horror.

Her mouth worked in silent outrage, her brother's face crumpling into lines of confusion as she finally found her voice and choked out, "You're fucking unbelievable." She looked from her brother to me and added, "Both of you." She turned and strode up the sidewalk in the direction of my bike.

Well, fuck. I thought. *Maybe a step too far...*

"Syn, wait!" Zeke called out, and made to go after her, but I put up a hand, stopping him.

"Go home," I told him. "You're not a welcome player at my table or this one, anymore. Figure your shit out, dude. You're fucking disgusting and a pathetic case at this point." I spit on the ground and walked away from him, trailing Madisyn. "You don't deserve to have a sister like her," I called back to him, and it was true.

So often the men didn't appreciate the women in their life... be it mother, sister, wife, or girlfriend. Zeke was no exception to that rule. While I was sure it didn't look like it, I had my appreciation for Madisyn. If I didn't, I wouldn't be here. Even though it probably didn't feel like it to her right now, I did have good intentions where she was concerned. I just had my own particular way of dealing with things.

I expected her to stop at the bike, but again, she had a way of surprising me. This time, she did it by resolutely marching on up the block, like she had no intention of stopping.

"Madisyn!" I called out to her in my best commanding tone, and she surprised me again when she flipped me off over her shoulder and kept right on going. Chuckling, I took up my helmet and put it on, keeping an eye on her. She turned left at the next block. I hurried my ass up a little and got on the front of my big beast of a Harley.

Shit, she's not playing, I thought. *She's upset enough to do something stupid.*

I fired up my bike and barely had the forethought to reach around behind me and pull her helmet around the front of me and put it in my lap. I rode up and around the corner, and I caught up to her, slowing way down and walking the bike alongside her.

"Stop, Madisyn!" I called out over the chug of the engine.

She ignored me.

"Madisyn, I said stop!" I ordered more forcefully. If she wanted a fight, I would give her one. I was annoyed now. I wasn't going to beg her to get on, but I sure as fuck wasn't going to leave her in this hood, either. It would be much nicer if she would fucking cooperate, but I didn't need her cooperation. In the end, I would have my way, one way or the other.

When she didn't so much as acknowledge my existence, I'd had enough. I pulled up ahead of her and got off the bike, leaving her helmet on the seat and ripping mine off. I dropped mine in the strip of grass between the sidewalk and the curb, and stepped in front of her, catching her by the arms. She fought me, trying to pull away from me, and she did manage to slip free. When she did, she unleashed fists of fury against my chest. She punched and slapped me, shoving at me mercilessly and she *meant it*. But still, all it did was amuse me.

She was like a kitten in a rage, ineffectual but so damn cute, her small stature no match for me and my size advantage over her. I didn't lose my temper, instead, I let her go for a moment or two to wear her down.

"You son of a bitch!" she cried and her voice cracked again. I cocked my head, got a hold of her, and held her a half a pace back from me, choosing my words carefully to cut right through the bullshit.

"You can be pissed at me all you want, baby girl," I told her. "But all I did was show you the truth."

She looked up at me, stopping dead in her tracks. Her clear blue eyes showed the shattered heartbreak. I loved her eyes. They were like crystal clear windows to her soul and I think what I loved about them, about her, the most, was again, there wasn't any guessing with her. She wore her heart on her sleeve and it was just so clear in her expression. Every thought, every feeling that she had that tumbled through her head, behind those eyes, and she gave one hundred percent what you saw in them.

She really couldn't keep a damn thing off her face, and I was suddenly feeling an emotion I was wholly unused to at the expression on it now.

Guilt.

"Anyone ever tell you ignorance is bliss?" she demanded and her eyes welled. She looked like she was going to say more but then she stared off into the distance, her face contorting in pain as she faced what she'd been so unwilling to and broke down.

"I don't even know who he is anymore." Her voice cracked. Where she'd been trying to beat the shit out of me the moment before, now, she was folding into my arms like I was the last refuge she could take from that pain. She shattered against me.

"I want my best friend back," she wailed and she broke down sobbing against my chest.

Maybe too far... was the fleeting thought that I had, echoing the sentiment of guilt from the moment before.

I put my arms around her and huffed a sigh. I just held her. I didn't really know what else to do. She melded into my front and I put an arm around her back, which was bulky as fuck with her backpack on, and the other I put to the back of her head, pressing her face to my chest. I bowed my head and kissed the top of her head and breathed her fresh clean scent in. She smelled as beautiful as she looked. Like sugar and lemon, and a summer wind at the beach. Salty and pure.

She felt good in my arms, but I had to ask myself if Madisyn Reynolds was worth the work. She was more than just a base lay. Way more. I already knew that... *shit.* The way she'd looked at me as I'd moved inside her. The way she'd held me back and stared into my fucking soul from bare inches away as I'd fucked her. The way she'd looked and *hadn't flinched* when I'd let the darkness fill my eyes. The way she'd simply closed her eyes in perfect trust and had arched beneath me in supplication to my whims and desires. I'd never been so fucking turned on in my life.

The trouble wasn't in my self-control. I knew I could walk away. It'd be unpleasant, but I could. The trouble was in how much I didn't want to – and beyond that? The real trouble was her brother. I didn't need her asking me to rein him in at every fuckin' turn if we were to move forward and make this thing more than just a situationship.

I knew I was already in pretty deep, even if no one else did. With everything I had going on with the club, my businesses both above and below board, and now Castañeda and his familial bullshit? I didn't need to add her brother and his bullshit to the tab I had running. Unlike him, I knew when to fucking quit on something or someone, and he was a total loss by this point.

Still, I couldn't deny how my blood heated to a light simmer as she cried it out against me and just how much I wanted back in her pussy. Madisyn was definitely not a lost cause. Far from it. She was someone I wanted very badly and for more than just sex. I genuinely enjoyed her company and our conversations, plus, I admit, there was more to it than that.

"Come on," I said, and I actively tried to gentle the usual stern harshness out of my tone. "I'll take you someplace quiet. We can talk."

She reluctantly let me go and stepped back, wiping under her eyes with her fingertips and looking stressed and miserable.

I picked up my helmet and took her hand, giving it a squeeze, and towed her over to the waiting bike. I put mine down and took up hers to get it on her right. I got my lid on and got back on the bike. She waited until I was settled and then got on behind me.

There wasn't a whole lot of time to enjoy one of my favorite places on earth, but there was enough. Enough to hopefully calm her down, and to allow us to reach some kind of a deal.

I wasn't even close to being done pursuing Madisyn, but by the same token, I realized, and pretty easily, I'd fucked up with how I'd handled this. I hadn't realized the sibling bond went as deep as it apparently did.

It was a good thing, that if it came down to it, I still had a couple of bargaining chips left up my sleeve. I didn't like the fact that I might need them.

Chapter Fifteen

Madisyn...

I tried not to think about how hurt and angry I was as we passed under the overpass for the Harry S. Truman Parkway. We swept past a modern cemetery, Hillcrest something, and an older one marked Catholic Cemetery right next to it. I couldn't be sure, but they might have been the same thing?

All I knew, was that any time I passed those cemeteries, it was only one place we could be heading, and that made me perk up just a little.

I hadn't had a whole lot of visits to Bonaventure Cemetery. I mean, there were the field trips when we were kids, but as an adult? And especially after I'd started painting? No. After my time in Colonial Park earlier, I definitely wouldn't mind going into Bonaventure to see what treasures I could find within to capture on canvas.

At the very least, I had an extra canvas board stored beneath the one I'd started at Colonial Park just a few scant hours ago, and I could sketch a scene and maybe take pictures with my phone to finish it later. But I didn't want to do that. No, I really liked to stand there and do it. Colonial Park was easy enough to get to but Bonaventure? I mean, I could catch a rideshare, but I didn't like to make frivolous expenses like that. Even if my parents didn't mind, I minded.

My mother liked to joke that I'd had a past life in the Great Depression or something with how I pinched pennies and was so careful with my spending. It certainly hadn't been her or Daddy to instill such habits in me. They sadly seemed to have missed Zeke completely, too. I wasn't sure how I'd wound up with the lion's share, but I wished like crazy I could impart some onto my stupid brother.

My heart sank a bit when we turned left through a wrought iron gate and I blinked at the blue building with the Iron Wraith logo painted in a large mural on the front side of it. We were across the street from Bonaventure's gift shop and just a block or so short of the cemetery gates. I couldn't remember what this place was before, but now? Now it was clearly the Iron Wraith's clubhouse.

Shit.

Synister pulled us into a garage on the lower half of the sort of L-shaped building, and he rounded in front of a line of bikes already parked within. He tapped my leg and I got off. He walked his bike back into the line of them before he cut the engine.

I worked quickly to get the helmet off my head while I watched him back the bike into place. The visor didn't fog too badly, but I really didn't like the way it squished my face, and how claustrophobic it felt.

As soon as it was off, I felt like I could breathe. I took a good look around.

There was a stairwell just inside and beside the garage door we'd entered through, which wasn't much of a garage door up front. I mean, it was narrow and rolled like one, but was only big enough to fit the bike through – not a car. I looked down the length of the garage portion down here and there was a bigger door at the back that had obviously let in the few cars and trucks parked in here down closer to it. I guess you had to drive around behind the building to get to that one.

The full-sized vehicles were all new and shiny things. There was a black Range Rover, and a newer gunmetal gray RAM pickup, and finally a Porsche that was an obnoxiously bright yellow. I could picture Synister owning the Range Rover, maybe the truck, but the Porsche? No way.

"Synister. Yo, what's up?" I looked up and there was a catwalk of sorts running all along the outer perimeter of the second floor. A man stood at the railing, a beer in his hands. He leaned against the boxy iron rail and was studying me. I studied him right back until Synister's voice pulled my attention back to him.

"You need to use the bathroom or anything?" he asked me and I nodded, now that he mentioned it.

"It's through there. We're not staying, so don't get comfortable," he said to me. I followed his pointing finger and went across to the door he indicated. His words, though clipped and borderline rude, had my excitement stirring in my chest. Maybe we were going to Bonaventure after all. I hoped so.

I opened the door to a very nice bathroom with just a toilet and a sink in it and went to step inside.

"Yeah, I'm coming up," Synister called to the man who'd called out first. I couldn't see what kind of gesture he'd made to prompt Synister's verbal response to him, since I hadn't heard anything.

I went into the bathroom and leaned heavily on the door, my easel clunking against it. I pushed off of it and slid out of the straps and found a hook set on the back of the door well above my head to hang it, which I did.

The floor was epoxied, and shiny in wispy blues, grays, and white against a black background that had some sort of metal flake to it. It was nice, looked like something from outer space or maybe it was supposed to represent the beyond or something.

I took my phone out of my back pocket and had three or four texts from Valory. Looks like Levi had met up with her and told her things. I sighed and filled her in lightning fast and then used the bathroom as my phone screen flashed like lightning but made no sound with her responses.

She wasn't a happy camper but I told her I was fine and that I was safe. I absolutely *promised* I'd learned my lesson of the night before and I would do way better at keeping up with texting.

I got a stern **you'd better!** and then I washed my hands and face, drying myself off before I took my bottle of alcohol out of my artist's bag. Using another paper towel, I sprayed, and wiped down my phone because *ew* – and I thought about things like that.

Back out in the garage it was silent, but there was some noise coming from upstairs – indistinct conversation and some kind of sports game in the background.

I shrugged back into my pack and was about to make for the stairs when Synister appeared at the mouth of the catwalk and turned for the stairs himself.

"I'll catch you guys later," he called over his shoulder, and then he was lightly jogging down the steps which had metal tops and burnt wood undersides in the front. Very modern, very sturdy, very Synister, in appearance.

He stopped at the bottom of the steps, taking the last two much slower and stood a few paces from me.

I couldn't read his gaze. He'd put his sunglasses back on. We studied each other silently, me warily, and after a moment, he made a sudden movement. I jumped lightly but all he'd done was hold out a hand to me and stood still, simply staring at me.

"Where are we going?" I asked nervously, not taking it, not yet. I didn't know if I honestly wanted to. He was being such an asshole today, and I was growing tired what with all the stress.

"A walk," he said, and there was something to his tone. It was softer, as though he finally saw I was going through it and decided he needed to cut the bullshit.

"To Bonaventure?" I asked and hated that I sounded hopeful.

"Yes, but it closes at five, so our time is pretty finite if you want to go," he said evenly. I rolled my lips together and reluctantly took his hand. He towed me along and I went, slipping back out into the sunshine and humidity, through the garage door we'd entered

121

through on the bike.

"It's been years since I've gone in," I told him.

He surprised me by saying, "It's one of my favorite places in the world. Even when it's lousy with tourists."

"Yeah?" I asked, dropping his hand when we reached the street, unsure that I wanted to be that close or familiar with him, even though we'd had sex just the night before.

We walked the half a block or so down the side of Bonaventure Road in companionable silence.

"I'd like to ask you something personal," he said as we approached the gate to the cemetery.

"I'm surprised you didn't just ask and expect me to answer," I said, rolling my eyes. He bowed his head, burying his hands in his jeans' pockets.

"I made a grave error, back there with your brother," he said. "I'm trying to make up for it."

"How so?" I asked. "I mean, I didn't think you cared whose feelings you hurt. You said you were an asshole and that's kind of an asshole's whole schtick, you know?"

He chuckled and nodded. He said, "Normally I don't care whose feelings I hurt, but in this case, I really wasn't trying to hurt yours."

"Seriously? How do you figure that?" I asked, and my tone was absolutely dripping with sarcasm.

"It wasn't my choice to leave your side last night. Club business came up. It do be like that sometimes," he said with an explosive sigh as we started heading in toward the actual graves. We slowed our pace into an easy stroll along the main oak arched and Spanish moss draped – I don't know what you would call it. Drive? Boulevard? Whatever the case, it was the widest paved path that led straight into the heart of Bonaventure, and was the easiest walk but not the prettiest, in my opinion. My favorite statues usually were hidden in pockets on the periphery and edges of the cemetery. It'd been so long since I'd been here, I couldn't tell you where they were or take you right to them. No, I would have to rediscover them all over again and I kind of liked that.

"Well, I woke up and you were gone. I didn't know what it meant, so I got dressed and went home."

"You left your dress and shoes," he said.

"I mean, I - they aren't really mine," I said, shrugging lamely.

"Of course, they are. I bought them for you," he said with a chuckle.

"Are you saying I hurt your feelings?" I asked and again, I couldn't keep the sarcasm out of my tone.

"A bit, yes," he said, and I stopped abruptly and looked up at him. "Seriously?"

"I do have them from time to time," he said. "I also have a temper, which you've now encountered."

"Are you saying you're pissed at me for leaving when you weren't there?" I asked. "Is that what that was all about?" My outrage meter was climbing to the point I reached for my phone. To text Valory, or a rideshare to come get me, I didn't know which, but both thoughts were certainly crossing my mind.

"May I ask that personal question or not?" he asked, sidestepping my question altogether. I blinked at the rapid change of subject. "It has direct bearing on where this conversation is going," he promised, and I gritted my teeth.

I closed my eyes, counted silently to three and prayed for patience. I said, "Go ahead."

"Did you enjoy it?"

I felt my cheeks instantly grow hot and I looked back the way we came, that rideshare looking like the better option with every passing second.

"Madisyn?" he asked when I'd remained silent too long in my vacant staring.

"Yes," I said abruptly. I turned to face him and looked up at him. I didn't know why I was still hanging in there and I wasn't just fucking leaving, but I flashed back on last night, and the way he'd looked at me as he'd moved so carefully inside me.

His smile was... pleased at my admission.

"Enough to do it again?" he asked softly.

"I..." I wanted to say "I don't know" but the way my blood quickened in my veins and my heart throbbed painfully against the cage of my ribs would have made it a lie. I was honestly a human – I don't know what you would call it. Lie detector wasn't the right word, because I couldn't tell for shit when other people were lying to me. But whatever it was when *you* couldn't lie and everything was written all over your face...

"One more time," he said, and his tone had changed to one that was clearly trying to convince me. "I'll write off your brother's debt. I'll wine you and dine you – whatever it takes. Just give me one more time."

I looked up at him and told the truth.

"Yes, to my brother's debt being cleared, because even though he's... he's so lost right now and in the weeds with this whole thing, and even though he really hurt my feelings today, – he's still my brother, and I love him. I don't want anything bad to happen to him."

I sniffed, getting choked up at the thought of it all and just how crazy overwhelming literally *everything* had gotten for me in the last twenty-four hours or so.

"As for the stupid dress and shoes and the getting all fancy? I don't want any of that. That's not me," I said, shaking my head. "Like, I appreciate the dinner last night and even the makeover or whatever had its nice points, too – but if you want another chance, you need to actually get to know me and just plain *be nicer to me* than you were today. I don't like feeling this way. It's stressing me out and making me sick. It shouldn't be this way."

He searched my face from behind the unreadable wall of his black lenses and finally nodded slowly.

"Deal," he said. "Nothing fancy, then. We'll do something you want to do."

"And the rest?" I asked, not letting him off the hook. I started walking again.

"I'm sorry I made you feel badly today. It wasn't entirely my intention, just a nasty byproduct of what I was trying to do—"

"Which was?" I demanded archly.

"To drive home the point that your brother is..." He looked thoughtful for a second and said, "Too far gone in his gambling addiction for you to save him. He's at rock bottom. The only person that can save someone in that circumstance is themselves, and they want to have to do it."

I stared at him, stopping in my tracks again, and tried to decide how much of what he was saying was just a lie to get back into my pants. Ultimately I had to decide that this was not that. There was genuinely something more there.

"Other than something simple, nothing fancy, and clearing the rest of your brother's debt, was there anything else that you wanted?" he asked.

"Yes," I said. "I want to know about you, too – the real you. Micah Devlin, not Synister, or whatever you are as like a day job or president or whatever it is you do for a living."

"I own several companies but I'm also a day trader," he said with an amused smirk.

"Wow, really?" I asked.

"Yes. Why does that sound like it bothers you?" he asked.

"Day trading and playing the stock market is a whole lot of risk, isn't it? I mean, it's just like gambling—"

"Only for those that don't know what the fuck they're doing," he said. "Look at me."

I looked at him as we strolled along and didn't remember even moving again. "Do I look like a man who doesn't know what he's doing?" he asked.

"No, I know," I said softly. "You're always in control."

"That's right," he said... and then surprised me when he added, "Except, it seems, when it comes to you."

I blinked and looked over to him, taking my eyes off the gorgeous scenery around us. I had to ask, "What's that supposed to mean?"

"I think you know already," he shot back and I swallowed hard. I mean, I didn't, but he was looking at me so intently I didn't want to say as much out loud. Instead, I simply let it go and nodded. Maybe Valory could clue me in on this one later because, damn.

We wandered down a side path and I breathed out in appreciation as we came up on our first bit of statuary.

I stopped and looked way up at her, perched high above me – her hand outstretched and an anchor leaned up against her leg, her other hand atop it.

"Hope," he said.

"What?" I asked.

"The anchor, paired with a woman like this, usually means hope."

"Really?"

"Really. Hope anchors us." He was looking up at her and I studied his profile.

"What do you hope for?" I asked softly.

"Right now, that I'll get another opportunity to make you scream my name. I didn't quite get you to that point last round."

"Oh, my God!" I turned and walked away to a peal of his genuine laughter. I'd been hoping, since we were sort of having a deep moment together there, that he would have actually, you know, confided in me a little, but foiled again! So it would seem.

He caught up to me easily, his strides easily overtaking mine.

"What do you hope for?" he asked me. I didn't have the energy to come up with anything glib and so I had to go with the simple truth. I sighed. It was always hard confessing out loud how utterly boring I was.

"I hope that I can someday find a job or a life that will allow me to paint beautiful things all day," I said.

"Painting is your passion?" he asked, and I appreciated that he didn't make fun of me over it.

"Yeah," I said. "What about yours?"

His smile was a cold one, but he didn't hesitate to answer me. "Power."

"Why does that not surprise me?" I asked, but there wasn't any eye rolling or sarcasm put behind it. It was just a simple statement of fact.

He looked over at me.

"One of the things I like about you, Madisyn Jayne Reynolds, you're not just beautiful, you're not just loyal to a fault, you're intelligent, too. Do you run on your heart more than your head? Yes, I think you do. But when you're as pure of heart as you seem to be? I can't fault you for it, or say that it's a bad thing. It makes you sweet, maybe a little naïve, but I think that's adorable."

I sort of slowed and paused, stuttering to a stop completely as the assessment he'd just given me rang and echoed in my ears.

"Are you sure you're not just trying to tell me what you think I want to hear in order to get back into my pants?" I asked. "Because I already said I would, and I would really rather you not lie to me about things like that. I don't like it when I'm made fun of."

He reached out slowly and when I didn't jerk back, he brushed a thumb along my jaw and stepped into my space. I looked up at him and he looked down at me and said, "I mean what I say no matter what," he said. "I wouldn't lie about something like that."

Oh.

I swallowed hard.

"Then thank you," I whispered. "I think that has to be one of the nicest things anyone has ever said to me."

"Including your boy toy at Colonial Park?" he asked with just the barest hint of a smile that made me want to shiver.

"Stop it," I admonished him. "Levi is just a friend. And whatever this is?" I said, waffling my hands back and forth between us. "You don't *ever* get to dictate who my friends are."

"I like it when you're feisty," he murmured and then his lips were on mine.

I both loved and loathed in equal measure how my body responded to his. Which was to say, I *melted*. This kiss was gentler than any we'd shared in previously. I could almost believe that he was really sorry the way he tasted my bottom lip and waited, patiently, for my own tongue to taste his before he deepened things, taking it up a notch. I realized pretty quickly that he really was sorry with how sweet he was being to me right now with his gentle touch and careful kissing.

It had none of the unbridled lust and passion of the night before, but a sweet and careful consideration that hadn't existed until right up to this point.

"I don't make it a habit of saying 'I'm sorry' very often," he told me, drawing back to raise his sunglasses so that he could look at me. I swallowed hard and waited for what he would say next. "I'm sorry I hurt you today."

"Apology accepted," I whispered.

"Our situation is a complicated one," he acknowledged. "I like complicated. Maybe a little too much."

I nodded. "Somehow I get that about you," I said. "I'm quite the opposite. I don't really like complicated. I like peace and... and quietude."

He smiled at the last of what I said.

"That beautiful big brain of yours spitting out the vocabulary on me," he said with a gently teasing smile.

"You've been a bit of a brute and a neanderthal today," I said, gently teasing back. "Maybe I'm hoping it'll rub off on you and lead you back to being a little more civilized."

He threw back his head and laughed, then towed me into his arms wrapping me up into a tight hug.

"Just when I think you're predictable," he said.

"Me?" I asked. "Oh, I'm very predictable." I knew that about me.

"I know," he said. "It's one of the things I like about you. But then you go and speak your mind like that, and suddenly I'm not so sure anymore."

I grinned, tickled that he would think me other than just plain, ordinary, and *boring*. All the things I had always been teased for, growing up by Zeke and his friends. No, my brother was definitely the wild child of the two of us and I was alright with that. I had tried to offset it my whole life by being easier on my parents.

I didn't think anyone noticed, let alone would ever *like me* for it.

We stopped in front of a grave that had a woman sitting atop it, a wreath at her feet, her head propped on her hand as she looked pensive, the Spanish moss draped just *so* around her and I stopped.

"How much time do we have left?" I asked.

Synister looked at his watch.

"About an hour, maybe an hour and fifteen," he said.

I shrugged out of my backpack. "Would you mind helping me by taking pictures?" I asked as I hurriedly set to unboxing everything and setting up.

"Sure," he said. "Just every angle... or?"

"Yes, please," I said.

"Alright."

I switched out canvas boards and carefully stowed the one still wet from Colonial Park. I said, "I guess I'm operating on a theme today."

"Oh yeah?" he said distracted as he raised his phone to frame her up and snap some pictures.

"Apparently," I said as I let my pencil's lead scratch along the surface of my canvas board.

He walked out behind me, took a picture and called out, "Your ass looks good in those shorts."

I snorted, giggled and asked, "Are you taking pictures?"

"Abso-fucking-lutely, they'll last longer. Give me something to look at and think about tonight."

I burst out in a peal of laughter and it felt good, my foul mood and temper beginning to lift.

I sent a picture or two to Valory to reassure her that all was well and ignored the missed calls from my brother. I was determined not to let him and his problems ruin this for me, and eager to hold on to this bright and shining moment from today. You know, silver linings and all of that.

Chapter Sixteen

Synister...

We wound up wandering back toward the clubhouse when one of the golf cart tours stopped by us and said the gates were closing and that they'd give us a ride so we didn't get shut in.

It didn't matter if they did or not. I knew a guy.

I wasn't stupid. I would never share with Madisyn just *why* Bonaventure was one of my favorite places on the planet. Not just because of its beauty or serenity, like the feeling I got when looking at her. It wasn't just because my mother was buried here, either. She was located just past one of the rows Madisyn and I found ourselves in while she painted. She was buried in one of the family plots, dating all the way back to one of the original families of Savannah, and the bloodline from which she was descended. It wasn't that I would likely be buried here, too, when I was gone, in that very same plot.

No, it was because along with those other things, Bonaventure was the real seat of my power, in several ways.

There were a lot more bodies buried here than what was on the cemetery's rolls. More than a couple I'd put here myself. Several more planted here by the rest of the boys in the club. Bonaventure held a shit-ton of secrets, and it was so brilliant because no one would *ever* suspect.

I walked Madisyn back to the club and told her gently, "It's been a long day for you. I'm surprised you're not starving. Let me take you back to your dorm. If you don't have anything going on, I'd like to pick you up sometime tomorrow morning – spend the day with you."

She stopped by my bike and looked up at me. I took my glasses off while she searched my face.

"I *am* tired, *and* I'm starving. I didn't even think about that until you said something about it just now. I would like to go home, and..." she hesitated, finally nodded and said a little more quietly, "I would like that about tomorrow, too."

"Okay." I nodded. "Sounds good. How about you text me whenever you get up and we'll play it fast and loose?" I asked.

"That sounds good, too," she said and her shoulders eased.

I smiled and said, "Alright. I'd take you out to grab a bite, but I've got something I've got to get to tonight."

"Yeah?" she asked.

"Club business," I said, putting my sunglasses back on. "Which won't always be something I can share."

"Why's that?" she asked, and I simply stared at her until she shifted uncomfortably and capitulated.

"Okay, alright," she said and averted her eyes from my face.

"Trust me when I say it isn't malicious," I said. I brought up a hand to brush my thumb along her cheek. She seemed to like when I did that. "It's for your own good," I told her.

"Well, I guess that's something to talk about the next time we see each other," she said. "Honestly, it sounds like a heavy topic and I'm tapped on energy and the emotional reserves to have that discussion right this minute."

"Let me take you home, then," I said.

"Well, back to my dorm," she corrected me, which I found curious. "Home doesn't really feel like home anymore – just the place where I grew up, you know? Even that feels... I don't know, like a lie now, I guess."

Ouch. I knew that feeling myself even though I hadn't felt it in many years. There was one point, though, when I was close to graduating from college, after my mother died, but before I was fully out from under my father's thumb...

"I underestimated how close you and your brother were," I said, and I know I didn't sound happy about it. I wasn't. It was really starting to sink in how hurt she was and I hadn't wanted to hurt her. I'd wanted her to be angry. Angry with her brother and done with his bullshit, but she wasn't like me and angry hadn't been her default. I'd fucked that up.

She sucked in a deep breath and heaved out the heaviest sigh I think I'd ever heard and said, "Yeah, well, that makes two of us. So don't feel too bad."

I scowled and let my hand drop to her shoulder as I towed her into my arms. That tickle of guilt that I'd felt earlier damn near crushed me under its sudden weight and I indeed felt bad and worse.

"Bike or cage?" I asked her.

"Bike is fine," she muttered, her voice muffled against my chest.

She surprised me with that answer with as much as she hated the helmet on her head, but I admit, I was pleased, the shot and chaser of the two emotions a heady thing.

"Okay, let's get you back to your dorm, then," I said.

We mounted up and took off. I'd told the boys we'd get started when I got back even before she and I had headed to Bonaventure. I was sure I'd get some shit from some of 'em when I did get back, over making a big deal about her, but that shit would be premature. My thoughts on her spending the day with me tomorrow included us hanging around the clubhouse. Maybe going to Bonaventure so she could work on her painting if the weather held. It was supposed to thunderstorm throughout the day.

She looked tired and a little forlorn as she took off her helmet just

133

as soon as she got off the bike out front of her dorm. She made to hand it back to me. I shook my head and called out, "It's yours. I bought it for you."

She looked surprised. I took off my own helmet and all but demanded, "Give me a kiss for the road."

She smiled at that, and she really was easy to please. The key to her just wasn't money or anything flashy. For having been raised a rich kid, she'd somehow won the genetic lottery on not being greedy or entitled. She'd been missed with both of those genes.

She took a step forward and leaned down. I captured the back of her head with my hand, pulling her into the kiss I leaned up into, but conscientious enough to not pull her off balance with the hot pipes so close. I didn't need her stumbling into them. That would be bad. I liked her fair skin soft and smooth. Unblemished by burns from a hot exhaust was the way I preferred her legs, especially for the next time I could get them wrapped around my hips.

"Mm." She stepped back and I let her go.

"Text me when you get up tomorrow and you're ready for company," I said.

"I will." She nodded, and I thrust a chin at her building's door.

She went to it, casting a glance behind her in my direction. I waited until she was behind the locked door before I put my helmet on and rode back to the club.

Tonight, the planning phase began on Castañeda's little familial drama. I thought to myself, *how ironic it was I was so steeped in family dramas for a man who had no family of his own... at least not blood family.*

My brothers in the club filled the cracks and gaps on that one.

Chapter Seventeen

Madisyn...

I got into the building and took the stairs up to my floor. I'd texted Valory off and on with updates here and there and a few pictures of the painting I was working on in Bonaventure, so she wouldn't worry. I'd told her when we left Bonaventure and texted as I went up the stairs.

Okay, Mom. I'm home.

She was waiting in our open dorm room doorway by the time I got out of the stairwell onto our floor.

"Really?" she demanded, but she was grinning. "Mom? Did you just *Mom* me?"

I laughed and nodded. "I did!"

"Get in here and tell me everything," she demanded, taking my pack from me after I slid it off my shoulders.

"Can I get a shower first? I've been outside and sweating my ass off like all day."

"No," she said. "Levi was fit to be tied when we talked. Said that dude bro was being a total fucking asshole and that you were just putting up with it."

"For a little while," I said, dropping onto the edge of my bed with a gusty sigh. "Not for long, though."

"Did you slap him? Please tell me you slapped him."

I laughed a little and told the truth. "Kind of? I mean, I really lost my temper and I hit him, but like in the chest. I didn't even try to go for his face. That would just be wrong."

"Wait, you actually *did* hit him, though?" She stared at me open-mouthed and I felt myself color deeply.

"Yeah," I said. "I'm not proud of it, like at all. Violence isn't the answer to anything, you know?"

"I beg to differ," she said, putting my backpack where it belonged and going over to her own bed to flounce down on it, facing me. "Violence was absolutely the answer when it came to the Nazi's."

I rolled my eyes. "Okay, but Synister isn't a Nazi."

"He's an asshole," she said with a shrug. "Nazis were assholes."

I snorted and said, "Yeah, not the same thing – like at all."

She rolled her eyes at me. I groaned and got up, moving around to gather up my shower stuff and robe.

"So, you hit him, and what'd he do?"

"Held me off like I was an annoying gnat and looked amused right up until I started crying."

"He made you cry?" she demanded, sitting up straighter, looking murderous.

"Sort of," I said. "Zeke is the real reason I was crying."

"You mean Zeke was there and he let him be an asshole to you and didn't say anything?"

"Okay, hold on. Let me go take a shower. Seriously, order us some food, and I'll be back before you know it. I *promise,* I will spill *all* the tea."

"You had me at 'order us some food,'" she said and held out her hand. I put my phone into it and she opened it up with my PIN. We always ordered from my app. I had the upgrade or whatever to prioritize delivery, and I had no trouble paying. Valory didn't have much extra even with her part-time job.

I took a while in the shower and when I got back to the room, Valory looked up from her phone and said, "Yeah, I told you!" She tapped her screen and held the phone up more pronounced and said, "Proof of life, you Gomer! See, she's fine."

"Hey, Syn! I told you I would check on you."

"Hey, Levi," I said. I made a face at Valory for showing me with my hair a nest of snakes and in just my robe to Levi.

"Whoa, what's that face for?" his voice called out from the phone.

"For Valory, not you!" I called back.

"Oh, okay, then."

"Tea," Valory said. "Spill it."

I flopped down on my bed after putting my shower caddy of all my stuff away, and I sighed.

"Okay, buckle up, it's a lot," I said.

"We're all ears," I heard from her phone and she turned it so I could see Levi who was lying in his bed somewhere with headphones in, raising the mic to his lips to speak into it quietly.

"What the?" I asked.

"My moms is sleeping. She's got the night shift this week."

"Oh," I said and then I launched into the whole sordid tale.

We were interrupted by our food arriving, and the rest of my saga was told between bites. By the end, Levi was complaining we were making him hungry, and had a couple of good laughs at some of my thoughts and how I would have liked to deal with some things versus how I did.

Still, Valory looked worried and Levi wasn't all that thrilled either when I told them I would be giving Synister another chance.

"We're supposed to hang out tomorrow. Have sort of a lazy Sunday. I'm sort of hoping we can go back to Bonaventure and I can paint some more, but that really depends on the weather, I guess."

"Oh, cool. You got to go to Bonaventure, too?" Levi asked.

"Yeah, sorry, I was sort of focused on telling you all about how things went with Synister that I forgot to mention that part," I said. "Did you finish your drawing from Colonial Park?"

Levi held up his sketch pad. He hadn't gotten to coloring, but he was almost done inking the pencil lines with a fine-tip black pen. It was looking sharp.

"I can't wait to see it colored," I said.

"Yeah, I should hopefully finish it tomorrow," he said with a yawn. One that Valory echoed.

"Don't do that!" she admonished him.

"Sorry." He grinned. "Peace out ladies. I need my beauty rest."

"G'night," Val and I chorused.

The screen dipped and went back to the app Valory had used to FaceTime him.

"Thank you, guys, for looking out for me," I said and she nodded.

"We love you, girl," she said with a sigh. "I just don't think this guy is right for you."

"Probably not," I agreed. "But I think he's interesting. Sort of this bizarre crush of Mr. Darcy from *Pride and Prejudice* and Heathcliff from *Wuthering Heights*.

"Yeah, no, that really didn't help your case," she said. "Now I've just gone from 'I don't think I like him' to 'I know I really don't like him' with the whole Heathcliff comparison."

I snorted and shook my head.

"Whether you like or don't like him..." I said. "As he likes to remind me, '*our business isn't concluded*' and so he's going to be around for a little while longer if for nothing else than for that." Valory giggled when I'd tried to sound all, well, *sinister* and affect Synister's voice for the whole business not being concluded thing.

"Seriously," Val said. "Why are men?"

"I have no idea," I said with a sigh. "If I find out, I'll let you know."

"I just hope tomorrow goes better than today for you," she said with a sigh. "You talk to Zeke yet?"

"No," I said. "I will when I'm ready. Honestly, I'm so disappointed in him, I'm really not ready yet, you know?"

"You maybe smacked the shit out of the wrong person," she said as she thought about things.

"I know, right?" I said.

"Well, he's your brother, so I'm sure there will be plenty of opportunities to in the future."

I sighed, thinking back to that house that Synister and I had pulled Zeke out of earlier today. "Only if he gets his act together," I said.

"Yeah, well, he will. He has to," she said and I forced a smile. I knew she meant it to be comforting, but she lacked the ability to put any real conviction behind her words. I did too, and it broke my heart for a different reason.

God, where had it all gone so wrong? I wondered. I honestly didn't have an answer for that. If I did, I might have had some kind of a hope in fixing it. I think the only person capable of fixing *anything* about the entire situation surrounding my brother and his gambling habits was Jesus and he hadn't been around in a long, long, time.

Or maybe Savannah's very own devil... I thought, but no, Zeke already owed Synister quite the large debt that I was paying off for him. Not that it wasn't fun in some ways because *woof.* No, I couldn't and wouldn't ask Synister to fix it because then *I* would owe him. It was bad enough Zeke owing him. I didn't want to know what it would be like to be indebted to Synister firsthand. Vicariously was more than enough.

The next morning, I woke from a fitful sleep. I'd kept tossing and turning, waking up for no reason, and I didn't feel rested at all... but still. I was curious, and Synister *had* said something about playing it fast and loose. I was curious on if slow and lazy would be a speed he'd be willing to take for the day.

Only one way to find out.

Hey, I just woke up but I kind of slept like crap. I know you said you wanted to play things fast and loose today, but the only way I'm going to be able to do anything is if it's at the pace of slow and lazy. Ok?

I sighed at the ceiling and looked over to Valory's twin bed. She wasn't in it. I remembered that she had that thing she was going and doing this morning. Some church thing with her grandmother who was staunchly religious but sweet as could be and not pushy about it.

My phone went off on my chest and it was Synister.

Be by in 20. Lazy Sunday sounds good. Dress comfortably. We'll start with brunch.

I snorted and closed my eyes. Food sounded good. Brunch was one of my weaknesses. Still, I didn't know that he understood the literal definition of *lazy* when he said something like "we'll start with brunch."

I mean, *did the man ever slow down?*

Probably not.

I leveraged myself up out of bed and I made it quickly, fluffing the pillows and trying to decide if whatever my idea of casual was, if it was going to fly with Synister. I sincerely hoped so, because I seriously didn't want to deal with another trip to some random boutique with a bitchy French women, no matter how lovely her assistant had been.

I went down to the bathroom, used it, washed my face, and did my morning skincare routine. Fuck, if I was putting on any makeup. He could deal with the dark circles under my eyes and me looking like a feral raccoon. To be quite honest, I was feeling kind of feral after how poorly I'd slept the night before. Today was not the day for any bullshit, and I was certainly not the one.

Once back in my room, I found myself, hands on my hips, looking at my meager collection of clothes and wondering just what to do about the whole dress casually thing. Like wondering if my version of casual varied widely from his idea of it because yeah – our *dress for dinner* – was legit two *very* different things.

I finally resorted to texting him.

What's your version of casual? I don't want another "dress for dinner" incident.

I was mildly annoyed when he simply texted back, **driving.**

Not helpful, I sent back, then thought about it a second and went all in, telling him, **I literally had my roommate who is in fashion design pick my last outfit out of my clothes and look how that turned out.**

He didn't answer. I blew out a breath and decided on settling for what was genuinely comfortable for *me*. I was just about too damn tired for any of these games today.

My phone rang almost as soon as I was dressed. I picked it up without looking and asked, "So what'll it be?"

"Syn? What're you talking about?" Zeke asked.

"I don't want to talk to you," I said, and he let out a gusty sigh. "I'm dead serious, Zeke. I don't even know who you are anymore!"

I went to end the call and heard him say in a panicked voice, "Wait, wait, wait, wait, wait!" But I *was* dead serious. I ended the call and then rejected the next three that he tried to make in rapid succession.

A knock fell on my dorm room door and I jumped.

When I opened it, Synister was on the other side.

"Oh, hey!" I swallowed hard and peeked out into the hallway, looking this way and that. It was empty.

"How did you get in?"

"Walked right in behind somebody," he said and he was scowling. "Some people have no sense of danger or consideration that other people may or may not be in some kind of it. They'll just let anyone piggy back right on in to a secured building like it's nothing."

He held out the bag from the boutique and I took it.

"You alright?" he asked.

"Yeah, why?" I asked, taking the bag and setting it on my bed.

"Heard you talking to your brother through the door," he said.

"Oh." I hugged myself.

"You look good," he said. I looked down at myself and the pair of leggings and fitted spaghetti strap tank top I had on. I was in unrelieved black, but that was because I had an off-the-shoulder top that was supposed to go over it.

"Thank you," I said, and I noticed he hadn't crossed the threshold. I asked, "Um, so what was your plan for the day?"

"Brunch and then spend some time at the clubhouse."

"Do you think we could go back to Bonaventure?" I asked.

"Bring your stuff. It's iffy because of the weather, but if it holds, I don't see why not," he said.

"Okay." I passed him my artist's pack and he took it, shouldering it easily. It looked small on him but ginormous on me.

"Um, two seconds and I'll be right out," I murmured. He didn't argue, simply nodded, and swung the door shut. I slipped my oversized shirt over my head, made sure it covered my butt, and took up my purse. My phone went off again and I sighed as I rejected Zeke's call, *yet again*, and stepped out into the hall with Synister.

"Either turn it off or leave it here," he said.

I looked up at him after rejecting the call. He stepped closer and took the phone from my hand gently.

"I can't," I blurted out. "My roommate Valory would freak if she couldn't get a hold of me."

"Text her my number. She can get a hold of you that way."

I nodded and did just that, telling her what was up and that everything was okay, just Zeke wouldn't knock it off and I needed a break from him and all of his bullshit.

I don't like it, she said and I sighed, but then another text came through that made me feel better. ***Don't turn off your phone, just silence it completely and ignore it. Then I can still see where you are.***

I told Synister what she said and he smirked.

"Whatever makes you feel better, but you're no place safer in this city than with me."

Until I'm not, I thought to myself, but I wisely kept my mouth shut. I silenced my phone completely as Zeke tried yet again, and I ignored it just as completely, stashing my phone in the pocket of my artist's pack that also held my wallet.

"Oh, do I need the helmet?" I asked.

"I'm no fair-weather rider, but I don't expect you to ride in just any weather, so no. I have the Land Rover today."

"Okay," I said. He reached out and steered me back down the hall and it occurred to me. "How did you know which room was mine?"

He snorted and said, "There's a directory in the lobby, Madisyn."

"Oh – right." I felt myself color with embarrassment as he went for the stairs and held the door open for me.

I led the way, and sure enough, parked at the curb outside the dorm's lobby doors was the sleek unrelieved black Land Rover I'd seen parked at the clubhouse the day before.

Synister got my door for me and I climbed up inside. He shut me in and opened the door to the back seat behind me and slipped my pack onto the floorboards.

"Where are we going?" I asked when he settled in behind the wheel.

"Best brunch in Savannah," he declared.

"And where's that?" I asked, tilting my head, and taking in his profile. The first time I'd seen him, I'd thought him intimidating and not particularly handsome. The second time I'd seen him in that tailored suit and corset vest thing, I'd found him extremely attractive. Now, in another simple black tee, leather jacket, and butter-soft broken-in jeans that were just beginning to fray? Ruggedly handsome came to mind.

I think I was starting to like Synister's chameleon ways. I mean, he really did have that kind of quiet confidence, that I certainly felt like I lacked in all ways, that helped him blend seamlessly into any and every situation.

He turned to me and raised an eyebrow, saying nothing with

words but clearly "you'll see" by his expression alone as he started the expensive vehicle with the push of a button.

I settled back into my seat and put on my seatbelt.

I guess I was getting some kind of comfortable with him, because I was certainly starting to trust and believe that while I was in his presence, at least physically, I would be fine.

Chapter Eighteen

S **ynister...**
Even despite her careful but light makeup, she looked tired. Her eyes, now hidden behind a pair of brand name sunglasses, had held dark circles. I did believe a nap was in my kitten's future.

We brunched at one of the most popular spots in Savannah. Today, we waited. I didn't feel like flexing my power. Some days were meant for flying under the radar and blending into the crowd. There were balances and counterweights to being one of the elites. There was something to be said for being just another man on the street. I happened to enjoy both worlds and lazy Sundays, so today we blended and I kept things lowkey. I think I did it mostly for Madisyn, though. She was sweetly naïve for having been raised rich, or simply didn't go for the power dynamics and sport of it all. She didn't seem to go for the expensive trappings and power plays. The simplicity of it was unique to her, and her natural humbleness when she'd been raised from anything other than humble beginnings impressed me.

We were seated and silent as we ate. It was a comfortable silence with just a smattering of small talk. Talk of favorite breakfast things and what the week might hold for either of us, mostly her.

My "day job," as it were, was boring. Certainly, in counterpart to her art and her vibrancy and enthusiastic observation of life. How she loved to capture new things as though they were old, with her oils and brushes on her squares and rectangles of canvas.

I'd been suitably impressed with her art in the cemetery the day before, and I knew my mother would have loved her instantly.

She certainly moved me with her ways, and I loved that it was simply naturally just *her* and no wiles at play.

We left the restaurant and strolled in the summertime heat and humidity at a leisurely pace back to my SUV. I opened her door for her and she raised her sunglasses to hold back her hair as she got up into her seat. She had a bit of a faraway look in her eyes as soon as she settled in, before I could close the door. It caught my attention. She looked like she wanted to say something, but couldn't decide if she should or not. I paused and leaned a shoulder against the doorjamb, my curiosity ignited.

I patiently waited her out, but I'm afraid my patience fled in the face of my curiosity. I finally prompted her with a low, "What is it?"

I'm afraid I wasn't very practiced at soothing. Commanding was more my speed, but she'd proven to be a delicate flower. I found that with her, I was *wanting* to downshift my speed and take things a little slower, right up until she did something so unconsciously and naturally sexy, and I essentially turned into a bull in a China shop.

I kept glimpsing her in my mind's eye, arching beneath me, her arms twining around me, her lithe body sensual and warm against mine, and I wanted more of that. With an intensity that I was willing to change some of my behaviors to suit her, but only for her, which was wholly out of my character.

She looked up at me, and her blue eyes were soft and her lips curved in a gentle and yet almost somber smile.

"I don't know if it feels like the right thing to do," she said. "But I guess, I just feel the need to say 'thank you' right now. Today, so far, has been... nice. Things... things feel a little different today. Like you're trying to make me more comfortable and I appreciate the effort," she said.

I couldn't help myself. I smirked and lowered my mouth to hers and pressed my lips against her petal soft ones. I just barely sucked her bottom lip between my teeth, grazing it gently.

She sucked in a sharp breath and blushed immediately. I loved the reaction I got from it. My cock stirred in my jeans at the faint pink dusting her nose and across her cheeks, and I pulled back.

Her lids fluttered open and she looked up at me a bit dazed and asked softly, "What was that for?"

I simply smiled and shut her door for her, walking around the back of the Rover to get into the driver's side.

She said nothing and neither did I, as I drove us the scant few minutes out to the club.

I pulled around back and in through the main bay doors, parking efficiently and turning off the cage.

She was staring out the passenger side window, vacantly, her mind a million miles away from the here and now. The way her shoulders drooped and the story her posture told was that she was *tired*. Not just the tired that a lack of sleep or rest brought; although that may have been part of it too. No, this was a soul deep type of weary, and I could tell her brother and maybe even herself were at the heart of it.

"A lot of deep thoughts going on in there," I commented, and reached out to smooth a hand over the back of her silken hair. She huffed a slight laugh and nodded tiredly.

"Come on," I said, and didn't pry.

I got out of the Rover and she followed suit, climbing down and asking after the sharp report of my door closing, "Should I grab my art kit?"

"No, not right now," I said, coming around the car, and she nodded. I held out my hand to her and she shut her door much more softly than I'd shut mine, to the point I said, "Make sure it's shut."

She bumped her shapely ass against the door panel and I heard a click, but the whole thing was so childlike and innocent, I couldn't suppress my smile. She certainly had a way about her.

She took my hand and trailed after me as I took her upstairs to find some of the guys. There was no one up at the bar, near the pool tables, or the dart boards. The ceiling fans spun lazily over the open floor plan, the air conditioning working to cool the space efficiently and quietly, to the point Madisyn huddled in on herself and gave a little shiver.

I heard the slider open and one of the boys called out from the deck. I headed around the corner that way.

"Oh, hey, man." Requiem threw me some chin.

"Where y'all at?" I asked and he jerked his head behind him.

"Down below, setting up to watch a movie and do some grilling back at the house later. Why?" he asked, eyeing Madisyn who shyly looked away.

"Thought we might join you," I said, heavy on the sarcasm when I added, "That alright with you?"

Requiem snorted and bypassed the question, asking, "What're you drinking?"

I looked to Madisyn and she gave a little shrug. "Get her a mimosa. I'll take a Bloody Mary."

"You got it," he said with a nod. He passed us to go for the bar as I towed her to the open slider to take her down the steps and underneath the solid deck. No rain got through that bitch, making it so we had an outdoor space whenever we wanted down below. It was a narrow deck for smoking and the like up here, with some tables and chairs. Things were hollowed out and niched up under the jut of the building below it for a bigger outdoor party space when we wanted it – which was honestly most, if not all the time.

There was a whicker sectional down here in a charcoal gray that was large enough to sleep all thirteen of us if we wanted after a night of hard partying. Upon seeing me with Madi, Shade got his ass up off the big chaise end that was wide enough to fit the both of us. It ran along the bottom of the lowered projection screen, a little close for my taste, but it was also the most comfortable spot in the clubhouse for cuddling and watching whatever.

Shade dusted off the top of his close-cut sandy-blond head and fluffed out his beard that was a shade or two darker than what he had on top. He liked to look good and pour on the charm around women. Didn't matter who she belonged to. He was a giant flirt – but I had to hand it to him, as flirtatious as he could and would be, he knew where the line was and he only crossed it if a dude pissed him off. He knew how to stay in his lane and we had enough respect that he would firmly stay inside the lines where Madi was concerned. Especially noting when I put my arm around her when I went to make the introductions.

"Madisyn," I said. "That fucker over there is Shade. He flirts with anything with a skirt but he'll stay in his lane if you tell him to." Shade grinned, put a middle finger to his forehead, and saluted me.

"You saw Requiem upstairs," I threw in. I jerked my chin over to Hangman who was fucking with the laptop on its pedestal, cuing up whatever we were fixing to watch on the projector that'd been set up in its bracket near the ceiling.

"That's Hangman," I said, and Hangman nodded without looking at Madi, which was fine by me.

"Those two creepy fuckers are Grim and Reaper, and you won't see them apart very often." I thrust my chin in the direction of the two aforementioned brothers sitting on the sectional, Grim's arm along the back of it, and behind Reaper's shoulders, his feet up on the blocky ottoman. Reaper sat up, his forearms on his thighs, hands flexing absently like he wished he had someone's neck between 'em to wring.

That was Reaper, though. If he wasn't fighting, fucking, or riding, he was antsy and on edge, and seemed to need Grim to keep him in check.

Grim raised his open beer in a silent toast in Madi's direction while Reaper stared a hole in her soul from behind his round hippy glasses that were tinted blue.

Madi raised her hand and curled her fingers in a weak wave and unconsciously tucked herself a little closer into my side.

"Anyone else here that I missed?" I asked.

"Nah," Grim said and took a pull off his beer.

"Where the fuck is everybody?" I asked, leading Madi over to the chaise end of the couch and sitting down. I worked off my boots while she stood near me, looking warmer but still hugging herself like she was cold. My guys had that effect on people. They didn't tend to warm up unless they had a reason to.

A round of shrugs was answer to my question as I lay back on the chaise in the corner and waved Madi down to join me. She sat, and Shade darted forward with a welcoming grin and said, "Allow me, my lady." He slipped her shoes off one at a time. I nodded when Madi looked to me and I loved that she did.

She murmured, "Thank you," and let the flirty bastard take her shoes and line them up neatly next to mine.

Her shoes off, she turned and tucked close to me, her back to the rest of the guys. She cuddled against my chest as I pressed her head to my shoulder.

Absently, I kissed her forehead as the screen next to us switched and she relaxed into me.

The damn chaise on this end was almost as wide as a queen-sized bed, and we liked it like that. It was good for fucking when we partied, and I felt my cock stir at the thought of doing Madi on it one night while the boys looked on with jealousy. Hell, just having her sweet body curled into mine was enough to get me going, but I simply held her and just *thought* about what I wanted to do to her in front of these guys.

For now, she was still new to her sexuality, so I would have to ease her into it, presupposing we got that far and she didn't make things overly difficult. I'd maybe start today if the opportunity presented itself.

Today, I was all about starting off by resting with her, giving her the space that she needed to get it together, but with the way she felt against my chest and in my arms? It may be a short reprieve for her because *god damn.*

"What the fuck are we watching?" I asked when Requiem and Shade got back with the drinks.

"Zombie shit," Hangman answered and I chuckled.

We liked our horror and zombie shit.

"My lady, my liege." Shade leaned down with our drinks on a tray and I took them, one at a time, and set them on the rail-like table built along the back of the couch.

I took a generous mouthful of mine and swallowed, coughing slightly, and asked, "Fucking strong enough? How many shots you put in there and what kind of vodka did you fucking use?"

"The good shit. Quit being a pussy." Requiem winked at Madisyn as he took a seat out here. She was trying to suppress her giggle by turning her face back into my chest from where she'd twisted to see Shade at her back.

I chuckled in good humor but I would get the fucker back later.

We settled in to start the show, which was apparently zombies on a train or some shit, and wasn't American made. All the while, I massaged Madisyn's back and neck with my one hand that had clean access to it, knowing it would put her out against me.

She snuggled close. After a while, it was Reaper, who got up to take a piss, but he came back with one of the blankets we kept around the clubhouse, laying the throw over her gently, his gaze unreadable, his expression non-descript.

"Thanks," I grunted and he gave a nod and fucked back off over to Grim.

Those two were fuckin' weird. Not quite gay, but not quite bi, either. I didn't know what the hell you called it when it came to them. They didn't really do any chicks unless they were sharing or swapping partners and they never seemed to fuck either each other or a bitch solo. If one was getting it? They both were getting it. But if anyone said anything derogatory about them being some kind of gay in their direction? Depending on the severity, they either lost some teeth or would have their jaw wired shut for weeks.

Those two were constantly scrapping with the law and the club spent thousands upon thousands on them in defense fees for assault. It was to the point the club had voted to put them on a sort of house arrest for a time, where the only places they were allowed to go was work, the clubhouse, and home – just to rein them in a little bit. Otherwise, they had to be around other brothers to keep their dangerous asses in check.

I didn't honestly care or put a lot of other thought into things with them other than whatever they did to get their freak on? It wasn't for me.

I liked what was mine to be *mine*; but oh damn, did I like to show off what I had and what no other motherfucker could touch. Madisyn was no exception.

Chapter Nineteen

Madisyn...

I didn't remember drifting off to sleep against Synister, but I must have. I also must have turned, because when I woke, my back was against him, his arm around me in such a way that he'd slipped his hand into the front of the waistband of my leggings. I sucked in a sharp breath as he teased my clit gently with his fingertips, and I looked up at him. He smirked down at me and gave me one of his hard looks that was almost a veritable *dare* to defy him on this.

I swallowed hard and looked around. Most of his men were focused on the screen and the projected images on it of zombies and mayhem. A few looked our way and he gripped my pussy hard for a second in warning. I very nearly sagged with relief that somehow at some point, a blanket had been draped over me. I tried to close my eyes before anyone noticed I'd come awake but...

"Welcome back," Requiem said and lifted his beer in salute.

I tried a smile, but froze as Synister began teasing my pussy lips and clit with his fingers again, gentler this time.

I managed a nervous smile in Requiem's direction and a polite nod while subtly trying to squeeze my thighs together. He spread his hand forcefully and my sort of knee-jerk reaction was to stop and part my legs just a little bit more so as not to draw attention.

I liked the feeling of his hand on my pussy, playing with me and teasing me, but everything about my proper Southern upbringing *screamed* at me that this was *so wrong* being in front of other people like this and to somehow get Synister to stop things before it went too far.

Synister gave a subtle grunt that could have passed for something on the screen but I knew it was for me. A subtle sound of approval for me parting my thighs just a little as he had his way with my pussy, in front of everyone without tipping anyone off to a thing.

That was the problem, though. I wasn't worried in the slightest about *him* tipping anyone off. I was worried about me and my face, which, Lord have mercy, always seemed to be in need of deliverance!

I felt color paint my cheeks and I *hated it*. Hated how every thought and every feeling played across my expression in real time and how I'd never really done anything to correct it up until meeting Synister. To be quite honest, I'd never *had* to. I'd always been a good girl, dammit! But Lord help me, being quote unquote *bad* was feeling so damn good.

He stroked that bundle of nerves and I held my breath, trying not to gasp or to squirm. Trying valiantly not to tip a single one of the other men who surrounded us that anything untoward was going on over here because *what would my mother think?* I knew it was a stupid thing to worry about but my anxiety didn't seem to care and chose that to be the perfect thing to hyper fixate on.

Nothing to see here, just keep watching the screen! I thought but my legs gave a subtle little trembling twitch, and it caught the eye of at least one of them. The one called Reaper, who turned his attention in our direction.

A slight smile tugged at the corner of his mouth and he elbowed Grim. I thought I would die right then and there, studiously averting my eyes in the direction of the screen as my cheeks flamed.

I could feel their eyes on me. I tried not to let on that anything at all was happening over here and eventually they turned their attention back to the horror on the projector. I sat against Synister, horrified by what he was doing to me in plain view of everyone without my brain honestly coming up with a single earthly reason *why*, other than it was *so out of character of me*.

I swallowed hard and sat rock-still and rigid against him, but that seemed to steel his resolve even more. He wasn't going to let me up until I came against his hand and *oh*, how he played me.

He played me like his favorite instrument, his fingers slicking through my folds and over my clit as that tingling vibration of pleasure flitted along every vein and nerve within my body.

"Oh!" the rest of the guys called out in unison, and I jumped at the sudden sound as the vibration of Synister's – well, *sinister* laughter thrummed against my spine.

He turned his head and kissed my temple. I closed my eyes and just tried to relax. It didn't take any time at all to reach the conclusion that he wasn't about to give up or stop until he'd wrung an orgasm out of me in front of all of his friends. The best I could hope for, locked in the steel bands of his arms, was that I could let the sensations flow through me and somehow get off without any of them being any wiser – but I knew better.

If I was being perfectly honest with myself, the thought of it did something to me – a rush of heat going to the apex of my thighs and I wanted it. I wanted it badly, to come, but my panic surged and I fought it down. And eventually?

I sighed and capitulated, closing my eyes and resting against him as though I were simply going back to sleep. I hoped against hope I played at least a semi-convincing part that I was just tired and drifting back off as he worked his hand subtly against the most intimate parts of my body.

I tried to keep my breathing slow and even, as what I can only describe as something akin to pressure built between my thighs, making my pelvic region feel heavy, like the atmosphere out here felt heavy with impending rain.

The way he stroked my clit, gentle and slow at first, seemed to build, even as the sky rumbled out somewhere beyond the covered area where we all sat comfortably and protected.

"There's that afternoon thundershower they said was going to be rolling through," someone commented, but without opening my eyes, I couldn't tell you who. Although, it'd come from the direction where Grim and Reaper sat close together. My anxiety spiked when they talked, as I could *almost* convince the panic center of my brain that we were alone out here. That it was just me, and just Syn, and no one else – as long as they didn't talk.

"Yeah," Synister said and he heaved a yawn, speeding up the slicking of his finger, up and down over that sensitive nub. I could have killed him for saying anything at all. It just destroyed the illusion I was trying so hard to build, to give him what he wanted, but still have my way and keep it just between us and spare myself the embarrassment.

I cuddled back into him and made a point to dig my elbow into his side in such a way that I hoped it was uncomfortable. He pinched my clit just enough to make me quickly back off. I rolled my head back and glared up at him as he impassively looked down at me, the only thing letting me know that he had anything to "say" about it, the slight wicked upturn of the corner of his mouth and those dark eyes that spoke to my soul, letting me know unequivocally that *he* was in charge.

"Just make her come already," Hangman said, and I dropped my head and stared at him, wide-eyed. He didn't even look at me, just took a drink from his beer and stared fixedly at the movie screen which rippled with a gust of wind.

Requiem and Shade snickered. Reaper was openly staring at me with a dead sort of look that I couldn't even begin to consider what he was thinking. Grim was much like Hangman, just watching the screen, which rippled again and strained against the four points of paracord or whatever they used to anchor it.

I looked up at Synister mortified. He pulled his hand from the front of my leggings and made a great show of sucking my essence off his fingers.

"When I feel like it," he said, and he stared coolly at me.

I felt my face grow hot with absolute mortification at the lot of them, as several of the guys started laughing. I firmly felt like the butt of some joke between them.

"You're un-fucking-believable," I said low, just for him. I practically vaulted out of my seat, pushing the blanket aside and sitting up, shoving my feet into first one of my shoes then the other, fishing at the heels with a finger to seat my foot quickly.

"Bathroom?" I asked. Reaper was the one to get up and open up a door down here, behind the couch on the other side, and gesture in the classic *"right this way."* I darted around the large sectional and inside just as thunder boomed hard enough overhead to rattle windows in panes and get a "Whoa!" out of a couple of the guys at the suddenness of it.

It was a mostly empty room except for a couple of couches and the like down here. Almost like a casual conference setting but with a big television against the far wall. There was only one other door straight across from me. I went right for it, right through it, and found myself in the garage. I felt some of the pent up just *argh* drain out of me at being somewhere at least a little familiar and went for the bathroom that I knew was down here, shutting and locking myself inside.

I stood at the sink and pressed my thighs together, staring at my too-wide blue eyes in the mirror above it as I clutched the cool edge of the hard porcelain. The coolness against my hands seemed to travel up my arms and cool my flaming cheeks as well, as I stared at my ghost-white face framed in the artful and intentional sneaking tendrils of my blonde hair escaping my messy bun.

I wanted to scream at the girl in the mirror. *Just what are you doing with him!? What is wrong with you!? Why do you like this?* but I didn't make a sound. I just stared at her long and longer and felt the tears well in my eyes because dammit, as uncomfortable as I had been, him doing that to me in front of them, the rational and non-hysterical part of mine whispered out of the back of my head, *You're alright. It's alright. They couldn't see anything and not a one of them made that big a deal about it. Honestly, Madisyn. You're the only one freaking out here and it felt good, didn't it?*

That was my problem, wasn't it?

It felt good.

Not just the way he touched and teased my pussy, but the way I felt snug against him with his arms around me like that.

I'd never been one to fall asleep in random places. I was kind of a control freak in that regard, although I didn't know what or if anything had ever specifically *happened* to make me that way.

Seriously, though. I couldn't sleep in public. Not on trains, buses, or planes. I couldn't drowse or nap on the beach or in a park. The only time I effectively slept was at home or in a bed where I was behind locked doors. I had just *always* been that way.

I turned on the tap and splashed cold water on my face, sniffing, worried, and wondering just *why* I kept coming back for more where Synister was concerned. The man was kind of more than an unmitigated *ass*.

Like, he was a *jerk*, and if I were Valory, or any other girl telling me what I'd been up to and how I'd been treated up to this point, I would have been the *first* one to tell the girl – *run.*

...but God had he felt so good. What hadn't, was their laughter at me, though. It took me back in my memories of how when we were small, my brother's friends would make fun of me until I cried. When I would go to my mom or dad, they would be busy and would tell me I had to stand up for myself or get a thicker skin.

When I'd gone back outside, it'd been my brother Zeke to defend me. He'd fought every last one of them and there'd been scrapes and bloody noses. He'd gotten in so much trouble for fighting but he'd tried. He really had. It'd lessened their cruelty, but like any kid of seven or eight, he'd caved to peer pressure. I'd always been excluded and still had been made fun of just never to the point they'd made me cry like that again. At least not often... and so, in the end, I had to admit once again that my feelings right now, on what'd transpired, were more than likely another case of me being too sensitive. They were, in fact, more than likely a "me" problem that I needed to breathe through and let go. But it didn't make me hate it any less.

"Madisyn..." Synister's voice came deep, but muffled through the bathroom door. "Open up."

"Just a minute!" I called back. I shut off the tap and grabbed a fistful of paper towels from the dispenser to mop the water off of my face.

"Madisyn..." he intoned again.

I called out harshly and exasperated, "Just a *minute!*"

I jerked open the door and he had his forearm pressed to the jamb on the other side just up over his head. He loomed over me and I stared up at him defiantly, angry for a couple of reasons. One, for what he'd done out there, and two, that I just couldn't seem to get enough.

"You have two choices," he said and the look in his eyes... we weren't playing.

"Oh?" I demanded.

"One, I fuck you here, in front of the guys, and they can be a bunch of jealous cunts, which you should know, *I live for that shit.* Or two, you get in the Rover right now, I take you back to my place, I fuck you there, and you stay the night with me."

"Door number two," I said immediately, because the way he was looking at me, there wasn't a third option, even if I wanted to make one. Which I did. I had class tomorrow and I was hoping that I could convince him to let me go back to my dorm after we were through, but damn was I turned on and damn did I need to do something about how my body seemed to *scream* for his deeper attentions.

Stupid hormones.

"Get in the Rover and text your friend."

"I have class tomorrow," I said, trying to open negotiations to split the difference with him.

"If we get up in time," he said and pushed off from the doorframe to let me pass.

"I hate you," I said impulsively, my wild anger and resentment from that mistreated little girl rising up and lashing out. I didn't hate him. What I meant was I hated how *difficult* he always had to be.

"Makes for a better ride between those thighs of yours," he said, completely deadpan.

"Jesus Christ!" I declared in disbelief. He always had a comeback and it always had to be so crude! It was like it was next to impossible to have a serious conversation with him!

"No," he said. "I won't settle for anything short of you screaming 'God' when I'm inside you."

Holy shit.

I swallowed hard and shook my head. I said, "We need to talk about how you treat me."

"Pillow talk. After I make you feel so good, you'd like to think you found God," he said.

"You're incorrigible!" I cried out in disbelief. He shrugged and stepped back.

"Your fault," he said. "You just smell and taste so damn good."

I stuttered to a stop mid-step and said, "Are you for real?"

He stared at me, impassive, and said, "For every second you delay getting in that cage, I'm going to spank that ass, Madisyn. One..."

I stared up at him and he arched a brow. "Two."

I stared a heartbeat more, just enough time for him to say, "Three," and I bolted in the direction of the SUV and got in.

He got to five before I made it into the passenger seat and I stared at him, saying, "You said for every second I *delayed*!"

"Good to know you don't think I'm joking, 'cause I'm not. You're right though. I'm not unfair. Three." He shut the door on me and rounded the front of the hood.

Again, the refrain, the voice inside my head, screamed out at me, *what is wrong with you? Why do you like this?* But it was undeniable the butterflies in my stomach and the heat blossoming between my thighs as I squeezed them together. My sopping wet panties was the silent answer and the only one I really needed. Synister had awakened something in me. A voracious appetite for sex, it would seem, but still, some fucking *boundaries* needed to be put in place because, and I reiterate, *Jesus Christ!*

He got into the luxury SUV and started it up. I sat with my hands tucked between my thighs and rigid in the passenger seat. I was irritated with him, but mad at myself and over it, all at the same time. I was swamped with frustration and confusion, and I didn't know what to do about any of it.

"Text your friend," he reminded me and handed me his unlocked phone. I sighed and did as I was told, with some sort of relief settling over my shoulders and along the back of my head, down my spine, in a tingling rush.

It suddenly clicked why it was... *nice,* in a perverted sense of the word, to be with Synister.

I didn't have to make the decisions.

I didn't have to be the adultiest adult in the room, which God knows I'd been since I was a teen. Especially when it came to my brother. Our parents were jet setting off before we were even out of high school, and most of the household responsibilities fell to me because, you know, *girls are more mature than boys,* and *Madisyn, you're so sensible.*

When I was around Synister, there was honestly none of that. Just a sense of "do as I say and everything will be fine." Good Lord was it oh so fine with how he'd moved over and inside me that first time. How fucking *good* it felt to just let someone else be in control and to make the decisions. But *oh* the mess it was making of me with how I felt no sense of control over anything anymore, and how I was grappling with that in so many ways.

I texted Valory that I was staying at Synister's, that I would be back at the dorm sometime tomorrow and not to wait up. She asked if my phone was still blowing up and I'd told her I hadn't honestly looked. I really just wanted to turn it off. She demanded Synister's address if I was going to do that. I texted the fact that it was on Whitaker Street and that it was a mansion that was impossible to miss. It was huge and yellow with big white Greek columns in a semi-circle and right across the street from Forsyth Park and the grand fountain in it.

She texted back after a few moments, an address and a screenshot from the search engine's street view and I confirmed yup, that was the one.

"You texting a novel?" he asked and I looked over at him.

"Telling her where you live so I can turn off my phone," I said.

He grunted but not like he was unhappy about it. He said to me, "I'm sitting right here. You could have just asked. It's 513 Whitaker."

"I guess I'm not talking to you," I said. "You're being pushy and a jerk."

He rolled to a stop on the side of the road and looked at me.

"Really now?" he asked.

"Yeah, really," I said. "What the fuck was that in front of your friends?"

"I wanted to play with your pussy. What's wrong with that?" he asked, giving me a savage grin.

"Ever hear of fucking *consent*?" I demanded.

"You didn't tell me to stop," he said with a shrug, and I felt my cheeks start to flame.

"What did you think my elbow in your ribs was all about?"

"Closed mouths don't get fed, Madi. You want something from me, you have to say it."

"Fine. I don't want you to touch me like that when we have an audience," I said.

"That was just warming you up," he said with a one-shouldered shrug. "Eventually, I'm going to fuck you in front of all of them. I want every motherfucker in there wanting and wishing they could have you like I do. It turns me on, knowing they want what they can't have and that you're mine."

I could have caught flies with how my mouth fell agape and stayed there.

Partially because, *no, sir!* But also... also... *goddamn, why did that turn me on just thinking about it?*

"Don't worry," he said, searching my face. "I'll try to ease you into it."

I shut my mouth, my teeth audibly clacking together, and turned away from him to stare out the windshield as I let all that information percolate.

"We good?" he asked.

"I don't fucking know!" I snapped and he chuckled.

"Close enough. I'm taking you home and I'm going to fuck you into a coma. Everything else can be sorted out after I rock your world."

"I think my world has been rocked enough by you," I muttered, crossing my arms over my stomach, and turning to stare resolutely out the passenger side window.

"Mm-mm," he said. "I'm just getting started with you."

There was a finality to his tone that made me look at him, but instead of this absolutely dead serious and terrifying look that I expected to match that voice, he was smiling and honestly looked as happy as I'd ever seen him.

"All of this is a lot and very confusing," I said softly. He reached over and put a hand on top of my thigh, massaging the muscle deep.

He didn't say anything else, but his touch was both sure and reassuring.

He navigated us through the pounding rain and lightning to Whitaker. Hitting a button on his dash display, the gate in front of the mansion swung inward. He rolled into the drive and up under the covered carriage port beside the front steps and shut off the car.

"Come on," he said. His voice, while still steel and iron, had gentled to where it'd wrapped itself in silk. He reached behind my

163

seat and dragged my artist pack to the front and got out, shouldering it.

I got out too, and came around the hood, the thrum of the rain loud on the roof overhead and the pavement of the drive to either side of the overhang. The rumble of thunder was a distant groan now, as the storm rolled through, moving slowly, and letting it all out all over the grand house.

He held out his hand and I closed my eyes, feeling my shoulders drop in something akin to defeat. I somehow felt weak of character when I reached out and took it. He towed me along, up the broad covered and sweeping steps to the heavy and ornate front door.

I hung back just slightly when he opened the door, and I heard music blaring from somewhere inside. He tugged me along and I took an intrepid breath. I felt like I plunged into his world further as soon as I slipped through the portal of his front door, and he reached back to shut it behind us.

There was a beautiful man standing there, going from the kitchen out somewhere into the rest of the house, with a big mug in his hand. He stopped and eyed Synister and then looked at me. The way he looked me over was just this side of uncomfortable. Not in a *he was sexualizing me with that look* way, but moreover, he was looking at me with such a curiosity, like I was an interesting specimen.

"Sup?" he asked, and I couldn't be sure if he was talking to me or Synister.

"Torment, this is Madisyn. Madi, this is Torment." Synister introduced us.

"Hi," I said a bit meekly.

"Cool," Torment said and he raised an eyebrow at Syn. "You guys fuckin'?"

"That's the plan," Synister said coolly. "Madi's staying with me tonight, so don't pull any shit."

Torment threw back his head, laughed and immediately wandered off back through another room and disappeared.

"What kind of shit would he pull?" I asked curiously, as Synister led me over to the stairs.

"With him, you never know. But whatever it is, it usually ends in tears. He'll behave," he said.

"How's that?" I asked, looking back down the stairs to see if I could catch a glimpse of him, but all that lingered was the pulse-pounding music from somewhere deeper into the large house.

"He doesn't, I'll beat his fucking ass," Synister declared nonchalantly. "Or have his ass beat. Depends on my mood at the time of infraction and what it is," he said.

"You're dead serious," I said, hanging back.

"As a heart attack," he said.

"Violence isn't the answer you know," I said, and he gave me a sinister look.

"Says the woman that did her best to beat my ass just yesterday."

I felt myself color.

"That was wrong of me," I said. "I'm sorry."

"Don't be," he said. "You're cute when you're mad. I like it when you're riled up."

I scoffed and he towed me the rest of the way up the stairs, laughing at me.

He let me precede him into his room. I swallowed hard as he shut the door behind us, ghosting past me, the sound of the strap of my bag slipping from his shoulder loud in the sudden quiet. Shutting the door had dulled the sound of the loud music in the house into practically nothing.

He set my bag onto one of the love seats in the room in front of the fireplace, and he turned to face me. I stood hugging myself and he said to me, "Turn off your phone."

"It's on silent," I protested, and he tilted his head.

"Turn it off."

"No," I said, and he raised an eyebrow.

"Why is it so important to you that I turn it off?" I demanded. "It's not bothering us."

He slipped my phone out of the pocket I'd put it in and frowned down at the screen.

"Fifty-seven missed calls," he said. "You're driving big brother a little crazy."

"Yeah, well, *you're* driving *me* a little crazy," I muttered.

"That a good thing or a bad thing?" he asked with a savage grin.

"A bad one," I answered without hesitation, and he dropped my phone to his side and advanced on me. I backpedaled as he crossed the room like the thunderhead crossed the sky outside. He captured my chin with his hand and the touch was firm, but careful, as he forced my chin up to meet his eyes.

"You do pretty admirably at putting up with me," he said, his lips almost barely touching my own, his breath warm on my face.

"At what cost?" I asked. "My sanity?"

"Stop resisting, go with the flow, and you'd be having a much better time."

I gave an exasperated scoffing cry and rolled my eyes, his fingers tightening along my jaw. My eyes immediately snapped to his in alarm.

"Don't do that," he said.

"Do what?" I asked breathy. "Find all this back-and-forth yo-yo bullshit exhausting?"

He grinned and said, "I like to play with my prey a little sometimes. One of the things I love about you," he searched my face with those liquid dark eyes of his, "is that you only put up with it so far."

"Y—!"

I didn't even get to say what I was going to say because his mouth was on mine, silencing me, and dammit if I didn't absolutely *swoon* into him.

Chapter Twenty

Synister...

She tasted citrus and sweet, like summer honey on a salty wind, and I couldn't get enough of her. I was starting to find I liked it when she got fed up. She turned into this beautiful blushing wild thing if you riled her up just right. I tossed her phone onto the bed behind her and pulled her against my body.

The other thing I loved about Madisyn was her body betrayed her every thought. Like now. Her hands cupped my face without her even thinking about it, and she all but plastered her body to the front of mine.

I slid my one hand into the back of her leggings and gripped her shapely ass, *hard,* fetching her up against me and trapping her practically on her toes, making her ride atop the thigh of my leg that I'd thrust between hers.

I had her firmly in hand, enough that I let my other hand that'd gripped her chin fall to join the first in her leggings. I gripped her other ass cheek, moving her against my leg and causing what I knew was a delicious friction between hers. She moaned into my mouth, and I felt my lips curl in pleasure.

"I'm going to fuck you so good and you're going to watch me do it," I growled into her ear. She gasped and wrapped her arms around my shoulders.

I picked her up and set her back on the bed and she let me go, lying back and kicking off her shoes as I pulled my tee off over my head.

The way her blue eyes lit up with the motion and the reveal of my chest and shoulders made me feel like a God, but I wouldn't stop or be satisfied until she was wailing it.

I kicked off my own shoes and hooked my fingers into her leggings and panties alike, peeling the material down her legs and off. She arched and pulled her shirt over her head. I reached forward, snapping my fingers with the clasp of her front-closing bra between them, unleashing her breasts from the constraining lacy material.

Her body was nude and perfect, on display for me, and I let my eyes drink their fill. She tried to cover herself with her arms at one point, unsure, still shy and clinging to hangups from her old life, and I captured her wrist with my hand and pulled it away from her breasts.

"Don't ever hide from me," I told her. "You're too beautiful to ever hide yourself from anyone." On impulse and without thinking, I lowered my mouth to the inside of her wrist and placed a single soft press of lips to the underside, below where my thumb and fingers met.

She sucked in a sharp breath, her eyes wide as she watched me, and I went to my knees beside the bed.

I wrapped my arms around her thighs and dragged her ass right on up to the edge. She gave a surprised yelp, and stiffened with the sudden motion, but quickly went languid as I put my mouth against her pussy.

God damn, she tasted good this way, too. Like a fine champagne with a hint of sugar. I plunged my tongue inside her, as far as I could, and lapped at her sweetness as she arched and gripped the covers to either side of her hips. I reached up and wrapped my hand around one of her balled-up fists. After a couple of insistent tugs, she let the comforter go.

I put her hand on my head and teased her clit with my tongue. She wrapped those fingers in my hair like I liked. I flicked that little kernel of pleasure with my tongue until her second hand joined the first, and she gripped my hair and wantonly pulled my face tight against her sweet snatch.

I worked her with my mouth until she writhed, her hips rising and falling unbidden, which is the point I thrust my middle finger up inside her. She cried out, her hips jerking and lifting suddenly. I made that come-hither motion with my finger, stroking the roof of her cunt and smiled as she went crazy for it.

Her moans were rhythmic sharp cries that echoed off the ceiling, and I swear coated the walls of my stark black-and-white bedroom with a prism of her passion. I lived for that shit. I loved how she reacted to every touch I made to her sexy body, as though my finger-prints branded her, searing her soul with a permanent mark of my presence – or even better, unlocked her like my touch was the only one that could fucking do it.

Fuck, that turned me on. I was hard to the point of pain in my jeans. My cock pressed tight and restricted against the prison of denim, the tip weeping precum at such a rate, there was a wet spot forming on the outside that I felt by touch when I went left-handed to uncoordinatedly free myself from belt, button, and zip.

Madisyn was none the wiser at what was coming. I had her riding that fine edge of orgasm. Just when I thought she might spill over, I stilled my fingers inside her, and backed off with my tongue.

She made a whining noise of protest, but I ignored it, giving her seconds to cool down before edging her again. I wanted to see if I could get her so worked up that when I shoved inside her for real, she would come around my cock instantly.

I fisted myself in my left hand and stroked myself. With the flavor of her still tantalizing my tongue and the hot slickness around my hand, her sweet clean scent filling my nose, shit... this woman was a feast for the senses and she was *mine*.

I didn't care anymore. I was in a place I didn't want to let her go, and so, some kind of deal or accord had to be reached.

She shuddered, her legs trembling finely, and I took the cue that she was going to go. Swiftly and efficiently, I stood and guided my cock inside her, driving deep, no barriers between us and *holy fuck*, she felt heavenly. She gasped and writhed as I shoved as deep as I could go, while simultaneously pulling her down the bed to meet my thrust.

She cried out, and her body arched provocatively, her blonde hair wild around her angelic face, her eyes closed as she experienced everything that I did to her. Her face so exquisitely contorted in beautiful agony as she came around me, her pussy milking me and causing me to still and ride out her orgasm before I re-struck a rhythm. I needed to give myself a breather before I came, too. I wasn't ready to pull out of her yet. Not at all. I didn't want to come yet.

"Fuck yeah, baby. Just like that," I praised through gritted teeth. I kept my body pressed tight to hers, and rolled my hips up and down to rub the inside of her walls and keep the orgasm she was experiencing rolling.

"Oh, God!" she cried out, and I felt my grin go from feral to absolutely *savage* in its triumph.

"I told you, baby. Now, that's it, come for me. Ah, yeah! So good!"

Fuck she was the sweetest conquest I'd ever undertaken.

Chapter Twenty-One

Madisyn...

I couldn't tell if Synister was just a madman or a mad genius. Whatever he was, when he did these kinds of things to me, it felt thoroughly as though the madness was spreading.

I lost my mind when he made me come the first time, but I lost my heart a little when he delved arms beneath me and cradled me close against his chest, kissing me gently and sweetly, my own sex still perfuming his face. I didn't know if I liked that, but the way he planted a sweet kiss to my chin, along my jaw, and paid close attention to that spot in the side of my neck that sent shivers down my whole body?

Oof, *Lord*. All I could do was cling to him back, my arms around his shoulders and neck, my lips frantically placing butterfly kisses along the well-muscled and rounded cap of his shoulder, as he settled his full weight atop me and simply held me until I could breathe normally again.

"Mm." He made a satisfied sound. "Good girl, now turn over so I can spank that ass. I believe I owe you three."

I jerked my head back and stared up at him open-mouthed but he was *dead serious!*

"You're serious!" My mouth echoed the thought almost as quickly as it'd entered my brain.

"Madisyn..." he stared down at me impassive, and I swallowed hard.

"I don't know if I want to be hit, how about that?" I demanded, my voice trembling.

He looked away from me, rolled his eyes and muttered, "Jesus Christ, I keep forgetting how innocent you are." He looked down at me and rolled his hips and I gasped.

"Have I physically hurt you yet?" he demanded.

"No," I half-answered half-moaned.

"Then turn the fuck over and trust me."

He pulled out of me and I rolled onto my stomach. He put a hand on my hip and pulled me up half onto my knees and half onto my arms. He ripped a pillow from the top of the bed to put it under my hips. I sucked in a breath and settled into a natural feeling position where my ass was up. My pussy felt exposed, and honestly, I felt like I was offering myself up.

He rested a hand on my ass and smoothed his thumb over my pussy lips, rubbing them in circles, plunging the digit inside me to where I gasped and jerked forward out of an almost defensive subconscious habit.

Smack!

I jumped and yelped and pushed my ass back up, his thumb plunging deeper inside of me.

"That's one," he remarked, as the stinging slap to my ass settled into a deep warmth.

He disappeared and I looked back to him shucking off the rest of his clothes. He got back up on the bed behind me, and I faced forward, blushing profusely as he'd had his cock wrapped in his fist. He'd clambered up and the head was swollen and looked almost angry. He nudged my opening with the head of his dick and I closed my eyes, gripping the covers in front of me, unsure.

I expected him to be rough, but he wasn't at all. He slid into me slowly, making noises of appreciation, and I started to relent and relax. The feel of him gliding into me made me moan and then it happened again. His hand came crashing down on my other ass cheek with a sharp report, and the wave of stinging pain made me drop my stomach low to the bed, but *oh!* Combined with the feel of him inside me?

Oh, God...

I felt my pussy tighten and spasm around him in something akin to an orgasm, but not quite, as he made a cry or a groan of his own in ecstatic approval.

He thrust in and out of me quickly but no less gently. The strokes easy and smooth, and I felt that feeling low in my body start again. That golden blush of first light and that struggling climb to unearthly heights beginning to make its appearance.

"That was two, baby. Fuck yeah, mm!" he said from behind me, his voice strained. He put his hand on my back and his thumb made me jerk as he rested it on my asshole.

"Someday, I'm going to fuck this too," he declared as he teased it with the pad of his thumb. I made this feral squealing noise that I couldn't even begin to tell you if it was in desire or protest.

Smack!

I shrieked and writhed from the last one and decided I *didn't* like that one! That the smack having landed on my already sore and warm ass cheek was too much. I dropped and his hands went to both my hips. He *drove* into me with a fierceness I hadn't expected but that completely distracted me from the red glow of my ass cheek.

He fucked me with a punishing force that left me hanging on for dear life but that also... oh, man, oh fuck, oh, *yes!*

I closed my eyes and the golden wash of energy flooded with tsunami force throughout my body. The intensity of it became too much and I shot up onto my knees, at which point one of Synister's arms went around my waist, his other hand locking on my throat to hold me back against him. He shoved me down onto his cock, and held me tight, somehow keeping his hips rotating *just enough,* and I was overwhelmed. I felt like I was suddenly drowning in him. Try as I might to slow this ride down from its extreme and terrifying speed, he was having none of it...

...and then his breath came hot against my neck, stirring my hair, his voice lovely, dark, and soothing to my ear.

"You're okay, baby. I've got you. You just ride that high and enjoy it."

A strangled, "Mm!" was all I could manage. With his hand on me, his arms holding me so securely, and his voice soothing in my ear as he worked my pussy with his cock – well, I found my god in that shining moment of chaos and confusingly diametrically opposite sensations that clashed against one another within me... and *he called himself Synister*.

Chapter Twenty-Two

Synister...

"Ah!" she cried, and it wasn't a good sound.

"Hold still," I ordered her gently. She submitted to my demand so beautifully, easing back down against my chest where I held her.

I was working the tangled ponytail holder out of her long soft tresses from where it'd gotten snarled during the course of our passions.

"Ow!" she cried and her hand flew up to stop mine.

I chuckled and said, "It's alright, let go. I've got it now." She glared at me with mistrust and I raised an eyebrow. We stared at one another for a while, and she did what she usually did and backed down. I'd noticed it was taking longer and longer and that she had a core of steel in there.

I held her hair tight, closer to her scalp, and worked the tangled hair elastic free, doing my best to tease it out of the golden strands of her hair without breaking or tearing them to get the job done.

"Thank you," she said when I handed it to her.

"You're welcome," I said and combed my fingers through her hair, gently working at the knots and tangles while she sighed out and rested against me.

"I wish you could be like this all the time," she said.

I stilled and asked, "What's that supposed to mean?"

She pushed up and turned to look at me, her blue eyes wide in surprise as she looked at me like I couldn't be serious. I cocked my head and considered her. My mother's voice echoed out of the dark recesses of my mind, telling me that I already knew... and yeah... I guess I did.

"Sweet to me," she said finally, choosing her words carefully.

"I'm not used to being sweet, or kind, or gentle, Madisyn," I told her. She cocked her head and looked at me. There was something about her expression that was bittersweet.

"That makes my heart hurt for you," she said. I felt myself scowl, but she didn't back down. She just let those blue eyes of hers rove my face while her feelings played out over hers. She was so beautiful and expressive, and the expressions she wore now? They were sort of sad. Maybe even wistful, as though she looked at me and was thinking about what could be or what could have been if some things had been different for me... but that last?

Well, we would never know, now, would we? Because you couldn't change your past, and mine just was what it was.

"I don't want or need your pity, Madisyn," I told her, but I belied my harsh words and iron tone with a soft caress of her long, if tangled, tresses. She closed her eyes and turned into the touch, just barely, and settled back down, huddling against me, laying her ear over where my heart should be.

"I guess I just wish you could be like this with me more often," she said as I gave her a squeeze and kissed the top of her head. She sniffed and a patter of a warm tear hit my skin.

I knew what she meant. I became more affectionate in these times we were alone together. Heaped touches and cuddles on her, and I was sure, to an extent, that it made her feel some type of way that... well, I guess I could only guess but never really know, lest we talked about it. I wasn't very good at talking about feelings.

She was such a lovely and delicate creature. I honestly vacillated between being annoyed by that and besotted with her for it.

She was soft, loving, and loyal. All the things a man should want in a mate or partner, but I didn't know how to do the whole relationship thing. While I wanted to keep Madisyn longer, I wasn't sure how. I certainly knew that while it was the right move for me, would it be the right one for her?

No.

No, I knew that it wasn't, which is partially why I kept up my games – for her own good. But it was becoming a struggle. Even after only a few days together, she'd worked her way under my skin in such a way that no other woman had.

"Why are you crying?" I asked her, even as my hands, unbidden, made motions of comfort for her – one massaging the back of her neck, to ease the tension in her, the other stroking up and down her exposed arm where it rested around my ribs.

"I don't know," she said with a self-deprecating little laugh. "My brother is a gambling addict, I'm having sex with you to pay off his debt, and it hurts that he won't *stop*. That he's kind of expecting me to do it now. I'm so tired of trying to live my life and graduate and everything else. Yet it's like I'm always and forever expected to be the responsible one and clean up after him."

That last part piqued my interest. "By whom?" I asked. "Who expects you to do those things?"

"Mom and Dad started it, I guess," she said faintly, and she told me about some of how they'd grown up. About the parents all but abandoning ship on them once they hit fifteen and sixteen and how when they did, going off, jet setting and bouncing from conference to conference for their work overseas. That it was Madisyn, the youngest, who was expected to run the household and corral her older brother, even though by all rights as the parents had told *him*, he was the elder and in charge.

They'd handed him all the power and saddled Madisyn with all the responsibility. I felt the unfairness of it all in her despair at her perceived failures, which weren't hers to own.

I said as much. "It sounds to me as though you were set up for failure, kitten. You never had a chance."

"It's more than that," she said and sniffed again, wiping at her tears. "I'm just so overwhelmed by it all. By everything."

I held her a little tighter and felt a chink open up in the armor around my shriveled black heart as the thought echoed in my head... *how I hate that for you.*

"Sorry," she said and heaved a big breath, letting it out slowly, the warm current of air skipping over my abs in eddies and whorls like water over stone.

"Don't be," I said. "Do you feel better?"

"A little," she confessed. "But you're no therapist."

I barked a laugh at that and agreed, chuckling. "No, I am not. I'm fairly sure that if I were to see one, they'd quit the profession shortly thereafter."

She giggled and put her hand to her mouth. Although I couldn't see her face with the angle, she lay upon me, it was a nice sensation.

"Somehow, I could see that," she said.

A knock fell at my door and I called out, "Yeah?"

"Grilling up some food down here. Get your asses up and come eat!" Specter called through the door.

"Yeah!" I called back and Madisyn sighed and gave a little shudder.

"What?" I asked her softly.

"Was that Specter?" she asked.

"Yes," I said.

"I don't like him," she confessed. "He scares me."

I tried not to make a sound and cut the sinister laugh that tried to bubble up out of me to a "Hm," before I said, "They should all scare you, kitten. That's the type of men we are, but look at me."

She pushed herself off me, and looked at me, one hand on my

chest over my heart, which I felt that damn chink in the armor open up just that little bit more with the look of trust in her eyes, at least about this...

"As scary as they are, as long as you're with me and in my bed, they're on your side because you're on mine. Understand?"

"No," she said. "But I think that's less important than I believe you that it's true."

I smiled and reached up, stroking a thumb along her cheek, and tucking some of her wild mane behind her ear.

"Then you're learning, and fast," I said. "I can appreciate that about you."

"We should get dressed," she said softly.

"Come on, get off me. Whatever they're doing down there will keep long enough to get cleaned up and you more comfortable. I want you in one of my shirts or robes."

She looked hesitant. "Can't I just get dressed in what I was wearing?"

I shook my head. "I promise to keep you safe, and I promise no one will touch you but me. You're beautiful, and sexy, and I want to show that off."

"Why is that so important to you?" she asked.

"It's a power play," I said with a shrug. "And I like power."

She swallowed hard, took back her hand, and sat at my side, thinking about things.

"Plus, I like to dress you up," I said. "It's a guilty pleasure of mine."

She cocked her head and asked, "Did you just give me one of your secrets?"

"I did," I said, sitting up. "Does it make you feel better?"

She contemplated that a second and said, "It does. Does it really make you happy to dress me like some kind of a Barbie doll?"

I smirked. "One, Barbie doesn't have anything on you, and two, yes it does. Let me ask you something, though? Does knowing one of my guilty pleasures make you feel more powerful than a moment ago?" I asked, and she looked surprised.

"I don't know about *powerful*, but maybe a little more in control?"

"Same difference, sweetheart," I said. "Same difference."

She looked a mix of troubled and thoughtful, but didn't say anything after that.

Chapter Twenty-Three

Madisyn...

We showered, but I did my best with keeping my hair up and not getting it wet. I just didn't feel like it. Synister was good to have around to that end, as he held it up for me as I turned to rinse the lightly scented designer soap or whatever he had in here off my body. It smelled nice, somewhere between masculine with notes of tobacco, and feminine with hints of vanilla.

Not at all what I would have picked coming from him. He said he liked it because his spicy cologne layered nicely over it.

"You have an eye for detail," I murmured, and he'd smiled genuinely at the compliment.

"Coming from an artist like you, I'll take that as high praise indeed," he said, and he kissed me. One of those sweetly long and lingering kisses that'd left me swooning into his hard body as he'd held me close. The kind in all the movies where the heroine's foot came off the ground and somehow you could believe that all was right with the world... except nothing could be further from the truth in Synister's world.

I didn't fully understand it. I just knew it was fraught with danger and that when you flirted with illegal dealings and the word on the street created such a palpable fear surrounding these men and their club... well, it was only going to be a matter of time before some kind of disaster struck.

I had such mixed feelings about that, you know? On the one hand, as much and as often as Synister frustrated and infuriated me, I didn't want to see anything bad happen to him. Not when he touched me with such careful consideration when we were alone like this. Not when he seemed to *really listen* to me when I became so over-whelmed and couldn't seem to contain it all myself anymore... like just the moments before, in bed and my confessions about my family.

I hadn't told a single other soul how I'd really felt about that, or how it'd been for me growing up in my teenage years. He'd listened to me, patiently, and what's more, he hadn't tried to gaslight me or tell me my feelings weren't valid. He'd just silently absorbed it and had let his hands do all the talking and his hands... *God*... he knew how to silently comfort. The way he touched me was all I had ever dreamed of.

Like seriously, once upon a time, I had thought to myself how I would *bleed* to have someone touch me and hold me the right way. In that way that made me feel like nothing out there could hurt me. Not physically, not mentally, and not emotionally. If I was being honest with myself, I had to admit that as much as Synister poked, prodded, and outright *smashed* some of my boundaries, it was because I had locked myself into this seemingly safe space in order to garner parental and societal approval.

But to what end?

What did that approval get me? I didn't know that it was neces-sarily *comfort* per se. It certainly wasn't any type of security – lest why would I be here? Not just naked in the shower with one of the most powerful men of Savannah, but the *president* of the *Iron Wraiths*...

I guess I'd expected judgment, and to be laughed at and made fun of by Synister and his men. To feel worse about myself. But just when I would start to feel those things, it was like he sensed just how far was too far and would stop them just at, or just over the line of my comfort zone.

I guess that's to say, the last thing I had expected from him was understanding. But when he'd spoken that bit of validation into the air, about me being set up for failure, I had very nearly sagged with relief. That was *so true* and I would give anything, anything at all for my parents to recognize that, and to say they were sorry, or that they understood it was unfair, but alas, I knew that would never happen.

Still, Synister understood, and something in his touch, and in his softly spoken wisdom on the subject had started the healing process within me. My inner teenager very nearly lost it with relief that finally *somebody* had not only listened but had *heard* me.

That was a powerful thing.

It left me in a difficult place, because while it *certainly* didn't make up for any of Synister's rough treatment of me outside the walls of his bedroom, it made me want to forgive him anyway, which I knew wasn't necessarily healthy or good. I know, I know! If Valory had been standing in front of me, she would have been hard pressed not to slap some sense into me, and that's what made this so hard! I think that I was just so desperate to be seen and heard that even a drop made me want to chase that sensation of acceptance into the ether – and that was problematic.

Maybe I did need therapy because *Lord have mercy!*

"You look far away. Want to come back to me?" I jerked my head up and looked at Synister, his dark eyes searching mine and contemplative.

"I was just thinking how nice this is but how toxic the whole situation is for me at the same time. How my best friend would slap some sense into me if she could hear my thoughts right now."

Synister didn't look precisely happy about any of that, and he reached behind me and turned off the tap.

The shower quit, and I reflexively crossed my arms over my breasts and stood a bit awkwardly in the hush of his bathroom.

"Let me get a towel," he said gently. "Don't move."

He looked... unhappy. Thoughtful, but guarded, and I instantly felt bad for being just a little too honest.

"Listen," I said when he came back to me with a large bath sheet, a towel wrapped low around his hips and water still running in gentle drops and rivulets down his chest. He focused on wrapping me up and rubbing me briskly but nicely through the absorbent cloth. "I'm sorry. That may have come out harsh and—"

"Don't ever apologize for being honest," he said, and his voice was back to velvet-wrapped iron with an undercurrent of heat that could have been anger. His dark eyes flashed as he captured mine with them, and he said, "Never, kitten. I don't care if you're worried about hurting my feelings. I want to hear it. Hurt them if you have to. That's my problem to deal with. You're right. I suppose my normal is a normal person's toxic or out of hand. Just because I thrive in such an environment doesn't mean I can expect you to."

I stared up at him open-mouthed and said, "Apology accepted."

He gave me a crooked smile. Good Lord, when he did that, all open and all pretenses dropped, he was so damned handsome. Achingly so.

"I didn't apologize," he said. "I don't ever apologize."

"I beg to differ," I said quietly, and something came over his face. Something akin to appreciation but much deeper than that. He looked me over, a so-serious look on his face, and then he brought his mouth down over mine.

The kiss was something new, something... I don't know. It was wonderful, soulful, and deep, and I found myself melting into him, my arms going around his neck as he crushed me to him and our lips moved against one another's and our tongues clashed.

God, I loved the way he kissed. All in, and like he would devour me if he could.

"I'm glad you get me," he whispered from a scant centimeter from my lips. I didn't open my eyes, simply nodding as he pressed his forehead to mine.

"Let's get you dried off and join the rest of the boys," he said, and I swallowed hard, my lips red and swollen from his kiss.

I croaked out, "Alright."

Of course, being around the intimidating lot of them was pretty much the *last* thing I wanted to do but there wasn't any escaping it.

I dried off the rest of the way while he disappeared around into his walk-in closet and searched through it. I wrapped the towel around me, just below my arm pits and secured it. I availed myself of the comb he kept on the vanity, working slowly at the ends of my hair and teasing out the knots, getting the last couple inches free of them and working my way up.

He came back wearing satin pajama bottoms slung low on his hips and shirtless. I forgot to breathe for a second as I drank his physique in, and my hands stuttered to a stop at his reflection behind me in the glass over the sink.

"Here, let me," he said, slipping up behind me and opening a drawer to the vanity. He withdrew a brush and gathered my hair into a tail, holding it fast and starting at the ends, as I had done, brushing through it briskly and efficiently. He was careful when he snagged in a particularly tough tangle. When he was sure there were no more knots, he let my hair go, and dragged the brush from scalp to tip gently, in slow, long, strokes that had my eyes slipping shut.

If I could, I would have purred like the kitten he'd called me.

"Here," he said, setting the brush aside. He took down the robe from the back of the door. It wasn't lost on me that it matched his pants.

On him, it might have fallen just below his knee or to mid-calf. On me? It swept along the ground, which I guess wasn't too bothersome as we were in the house.

"Turn," he ordered, and he tugged the towel and took it from me, settling the two halves of the robe over my breasts but leaving a long line of skin visible from throat to nearly navel as he tied it off at my waist.

"Really?" I asked, more amused than anything, arching a brow and trying to suppress my smile.

"Like I said, I like showing off what's mine. I live for making some of those fuckers jealous," he said. With hands on my ass, warm through the satin, he trapped me between his hard body and the vanity.

"Oh, is that what I am now?" I asked mildly, but my chest tightened up on me with the possessive notion from him.

He looked away, as though he realized he'd gotten too comfortable and let something slip that he shouldn't. He looked back at me and played it off cool when he said, "Until our business is concluded." But the mask had slipped and I'd seen it.

He wanted me, and I didn't honestly know how to feel about that. I mean...

"To be continued?" I asked softly. I was hungry, my stomach gnawing at my backbone and demanding sustenance. After all, brunch had been hours and hours ago.

He cocked his head, searched my face and asked, "Why don't you sound opposed to the idea?"

"At the moment," I said honestly, raising my chin a bit defiantly. "I'm very opposed, and frightened by the idea. You would have to be a lot nicer to me around other people in order for me to consider it. I mean, as nice as you are right now."

He thought about it and spoke in the language that he seemed to know best – the art of making a deal or negotiating.

"Make you a deal, kitten," he said. "A sweet one."

"I'm listening," I said softly.

"All the bullshit with your brother that got you in my bed in the first place?"

"Yes?" I asked.

"Done. Right here, right now. You won't hear another word about it. Our business on that front *is* concluded."

"But?" I asked, hearing it without hearing it linger in the air.

"But the business between you and me? It's just beginning."

"Okaaaay...." I drew the word out, reluctantly, waiting for the other shoe to drop, or the rest.

"We go downstairs, we have dinner with the rest of the guys that're here. We take things a little slower and figure it out. You come back here with me, we spend the night together, and I'll get you to your class first thing in the morning, even if I have to put my business on hold to drive you myself."

"Then what?" I asked, and he smiled, knowing he was towing me in.

"The rest is a series of negotiations. We take it one day at a time, one event after another, and we see..."

I stared at him and tilted my head, caution ruling the day as I asked, "Can I think about it?"

"For as long as you like," he said gravely. "In the meantime, we go downstairs and have some dinner, and then we can come back up here and get you some more rest."

"Rest?" I asked, arching a brow and he chuckled darkly.

Snake bite quick, his head darted forward and he kissed the tip of my nose with a quick peck and a very verbal "Muah!"

I giggled and put a hand to my nose as he tickled me, which made me struggle. I *almost* slipped a nip from the robe. I went to clutch the panels together and he said "Ah!" I stopped and my eyes widened.

"If I'm willing to make some concessions, you've got to meet me half way on some things. When we're in my house, or at the club, I get to play a little. Out in *public,* I'll behave more."

I gave him a flat, considering look, and said reluctantly, "Okay."

"Good girl," he declared, and he kissed me in that way that took my breath away all over again.

We went downstairs. The music had been turned down to something tolerable and a bunch of masculine laughter and voices filtered up the stairway to us.

We found a bunch of the guys standing in the kitchen and I reluctantly hung back.

"Hey," one of the guys called to Synister, and Synister jerked his chin in the air in a nod.

"Yo, Syn, what do you want to drink?" Specter asked from where he was at the fridge.

"Oh, um, water?" I asked, and everyone stopped and stared at me. I blushed and stammered out a "Sorry," as Specter turned and looked at me confused.

"Okay," he said, catching some kind of look from Synister over my head as Synister's hands fell onto my shoulders, kneading them through the satin cloth over my back and causing the slick fabric to gape precariously to the point my mouth went dry. "Let me try that again. Water for Little Syn. Original Syn, what do you want?"

"Gimme a beer," Synister said.

"How long have you gone by Syn?" Everyone kind of froze at the voice and turned slowly to Reaper, who had been the one to speak, his voice a lovely tenor and soft.

"Um, ever since my brother was a toddler and wouldn't say Mad or Madi but would say Syn whenever my parents tried to teach him my name. So, it kind of became Syn or Synnie and sometimes Synnie Syn Syn," I rushed out in a babble that I hoped would be coherent.

Way to over share, Madisyn! I thought to myself, blushing at some of the looks the guys exchanged and the tittering of laughter that felt like it was at my expense. Like, *get a load of her,* or *is she for real?*

I burned with humiliation and felt stupid, but then Synister's thumbs dug gently between my shoulders, silently urging me to loosen up.

"What was it when you were in trouble?" someone asked, and I swallowed hard.

"Madisyn Jayne," I said. "It was always Madisyn Jayne, or Madisyn Jayne Reynolds if I really fucked up."

"Ooo, first and middle," Torment said and sucked in a breath through his gritted teeth, picking up a platter of raw steaks and backing out through the kitchen door into the backyard. I could smell a grill wafting in before it shushed shut behind him.

"I'll have to remember that for when I'm serious," Synister said, taking a can of beer from Specter.

"Ew, please don't," I said, and he chuckled. I knew that one was already a lost cause just by the pitch of the rumbling from his chest.

"Thanks," Specter said as another man handed him a glass and he filled it with ice and then water from the front of the fridge.

"Thank you," I said, taking the glass from him. He turned back to the fridge, turned around to me and dropped a strawberry into the top of the glass.

He winked at me. I just kind of looked startled and thought it was a good thing I wasn't allergic to them... but at the same time, *why was he so weirdly suddenly sweet?*

"Where we doing this?" Synister asked.

Requiem tsked and said, "Inside. Tor's out there working the grill, but the storms are just sort of rolling through continuously. In here is the best option for dining."

"Could always build a covered walkway out to the pavilion." Grim looked thoughtful as he stared out the back windows off the kitchen.

"Or get a bucket of umbrellas to go back and forth," a man who seemed young mentioned.

"Jesus Christ, Pooky. Where do you come up with this shit?" someone asked. The youngest man shrugged. I didn't say anything, but *Pooky?*

I looked to Synister curiously and all he did was look back and smirk, taking a sip of his beer.

We wound up in the dining room and when I say dining room, I mean it was a long banquet table in here. And when I say banquet table, I mean the thing had to seat at least... *twenty-four?*

Synister took up the place at the head of the table, gently leading me in that direction with his fingers intertwined with mine. I sipped my water, the liquid cool and refreshing as it flooded my parched mouth from all the panting I'd done upstairs.

He pulled me down into his lap before I could take a seat to either side of him. I didn't know exactly how that would work for me, you know, actually *eating* or how this was supposed to go.

I was a lost babe in the woods with these men, and being the only woman in a room full of them was decidedly uncomfortable.

Did I trust that Synister had them all in hand and would protect me? I mean, while he was here and present, yes, but he couldn't always be around. I think that was the crux of why his insistence on "showing me off" as he called it, and making the rest of them intentionally jealous, rubbed me the wrong way so hard.

Because he couldn't *always* be around. As a woman, we were practically trained since birth to be modest, be careful, to make ourselves small and to always be careful because it didn't matter what men did. It would always be our fault somehow or some way.

I didn't know if it was something I should even bring up to Synister when we were alone for fear of having my feelings and concerns dismissed. All I knew was that as I sat on his lap, his hand on top of my thigh, the other at my hip steadying me, I was deathly afraid of his robe slipping and exposing more than I was comfortable baring.

Something obviously showed on my face, because in a gesture wholly unlike him, he made sure to arrange the material over my legs to conceal more, not less. I flicked my gaze to his and he cocked his head and raised an eyebrow, giving me the barest of solemn nods.

I tried to relax, marginally, but I still felt as though I sat like stone on his lap.

The light began to fail, coming through the banks of windows overlooking the backyard of the mansion. With the storms rolling through, it was as though it hastened sunset on with the thick, low hanging, cloud cover, but the men didn't seem all that fazed.

"Oh, hey." Requiem stopped by the table and the seat to Synister's left. He looked down the line of the table and called out, "Move it down so the lady can have a seat so she can properly eat."

Wordlessly, the men down the left side of the table got up and moved down one seat to open up the one by Synister's left hand.

"Oh, thank you," I said. He let me go but his hands lingered in places on me as he helped me up subtly so that I could take the seat that'd been offered.

"No need," Requiem said with a sniff.

"We all here?" Synister asked, looking down the table.

"Looks like it," a man I'd had yet to meet said, taking the seat at Synister's right hand.

"I'll make introductions when everyone's seated," Synister said to me, his voice low and considerate. I nodded silently and let my eyes rove the table and the men seated across from me.

I mean, it wasn't exactly rocket science, considering most wore their vest things and their pseudonym or whatever was emblazoned on a patch right there on their chest.

Across from me sat Corvus, who according to his patches was the vice president. He had a beard and a longer sweep of hair that was swept back and gelled into place. Not quite long enough to do anything with by way of a hair elastic or anything. His eyes were brown with a warm golden cast to them like a really fine-aged whiskey or bourbon with the light coming through the glass.

Requiem, who was next to me, put a hand on my arm. I jumped slightly and turned to him. He had short brown hair and a short well-trimmed beard as compared to Corvus, but that wasn't fair. While Corvus's beard was something I would call medium length, it was well maintained. As in he probably took a heated brush or something to it every morning.

"You want some more water?" Requiem asked me, his muddy brown eyes kind but guarded, as though he couldn't decide what to make of me yet.

"Oh, thank you, that would be lovely," I said as my glass was only half full by now and I would surely run out before the meal was through.

"Cool, be right back. You like pineapple?"

"Yes, why?" I asked.

He smiled. "I'll throw an extra strawberry and some pineapple in there for some flavor."

I smiled genuinely and said, "Thank you."

He walked back the way of the kitchen. I glanced toward Synister who nodded at me while he sat stoic and listened to the different conversations that overlapped and rushed down the table like a babbling brook.

I sort of resumed making my own silent introductions and looked back to Corvus. The chair beside his was empty, and the next, too. Then there was Grim and Reaper who I'd met earlier that day at the club.

Reaper was staring openly at me, and I felt myself blush and look quickly away under the uncomfortable scrutiny. But not before I caught Grim elbowing him lightly in the ribs which seemed to break his spell and had him turn to the man. Grim was ruggedly handsome with black hair, shiny with those blue-and-purple highlights like a crow's wing under the lights. That natural way most women would kill for. He had a dark shadow of equally black stubble along his jaw, chin, and upper lip, and sparkling blue eyes now that he had his aviators off.

Reaper was... awkward in the social arena, and I had to wonder if he might be on the spectrum. I mean, it didn't really excuse the creepy staring if he was or wasn't, but it certainly might be the reason for it. He was taller than Grim by over a head, and had medium-brown hair styled in an almost flat top, but definitely more modern and nicer to look at than the old style. His eye color was inscrutable from behind those blue tinted hippy glasses, but if I had to guess, they weren't brown, nor blue... maybe hazel or green?

"Ho!" A man came bustling into the dining room, hands laden with a tray each, one piled with steaming grilled corn on the cob, the other with what looked like grilled – something. I couldn't exactly tell what yet. Maybe chicken.

He set things down on the table to a bunch of the guys making some noise about it being about time while others just gave out an appreciative, "Alright!"

He disappeared back the way of the kitchen and the one they called Pooky started ferrying out dishes and platters to dress the table with and feed the hungry horde that waited.

When Torment, the beautiful man from earlier when we'd first come to the house, came in from outside, it was to a rowdy cheer as though they hailed some conquering hero.

"Give it up for the chef!" Shade shouted, and someone down the table on the left let out an earsplitting whistle. I had to laugh a little.

The man set a big plate of what looked like steaks down on the table in front of our end of it and took a sweeping bow to the loud cheering and applause before seating himself two seats down from Corvus at Synister's right hand.

"Alright, you fucking heathens!" Synister called out. The guys around table settled down as the last of the plates and serving bowls made their way to the table and everyone that it seemed was here took their seats.

"Not hard to notice we have a lady in our presence." He shifted in his seat and intoned my name. "Madisyn," he said and I looked to him. "That's Corvus," he said, pointing to the man on his right whose identity I'd already surmised. "You've met Specter." I nodded politely to him and he gave me a look that I couldn't honestly define, but there was certainly something off-putting about it.

"Then there's Torment." The chef, who I'd already met, who winked one of his hazel-green eyes at me and gave me an uncomfortably lascivious look as he shook some of his brown hair somewhere between light and medium back off his forehead.

"Grim and Reaper." Synister re-introduced the two men together as though they were one, which I found interesting. "And finally for that side of the table is Fear."

Fear lifted his hand in a wave and he was, well, pretty much model-perfect and a jock from what I could tell. His chestnut hair perfectly styled and his brown eyes that liquid dark and deep but lighter than Synister's. I forced a bright smile for politeness' sake and gave him a nod.

"Now to the left, down at the end there is Spooky, our prospect," Synister said.

Specter called out, "Yeah! Pooky!" at which a bunch of the guys laughed and Spooky looked slightly embarrassed. He seemed like a, I don't know... good kid? Maybe my age or so, definitely younger than the rest of them. He kind of reminded me of that actor from the American Pie movies – Stiffler was his character. Except darker, his hair and eyes with an almost Latin American cast to them.

He'd been the one to suggest something about umbrellas to go back and forth somewhere outside during the rain. I thought it'd been a sweet and whimsical idea.

"Then Revenant," Synister said, and a man half stood up and gave a nod so I could see him. All I caught was dishwater blond hair in a regular men's cut and a flash of blue eyes along with a *striking* resemblance to that British actor who last played James Bond. The one with two first names. He seriously looked like him from several Bond flicks ago when he was younger and had first started them. To the point, I was pretty sure, the theme song was going to get stuck in my head just from thinking it.

Ah, yep. There it was on a loop.

Great.

"That one's Death." He could have been Fear's modeling buddy because they were cut from the same cloth in the looks department – except Death's face was less chiseled in the jaw, and his hair was a darker brown. Just brown enough so as not to be black. His eyes were a haunting silvery gray and his smile? Wow. Panty dropping for almost any other girl, but I just wasn't interested. Probably because I *was* boning Synister – but for anyone else? Yeah, he was pretty hot. I could see it.

"Shade, you know." Shade winked at me and turned his smile up. I remembered Synister's warning that he would flirt with anything in a skirt.

"Hangman you've met," he said. Hangman didn't even bother to look up from where his eyes were fixed on his sweating bottle of beer and the play of his fingers stroking up and down the moisture beading on the outside of the dark brown glass.

"That's Haint," he said, who was a rough, almost Middle Eastern looking man with a medium long straight ironed beard threaded with salt, and deep dark eyes almost a match for Syn's.

"And you've met Requiem," he said finally. I said hi to the man next to me who had been at the club and had made us drinks.

"Hi," I said with a faint laugh.

"We meet again," he said with a smile.

"Everyone, this is Madisyn. She's mine and off-limits," Synister declared.

I heard a couple of snorts, a shit, and an "awww," or two. I didn't look to see who had said any of it. Instead, I'd simply blushed and fixed my eyes on my waiting and empty plate. I didn't understand why, but even though Synister had spoken perfect English, it might as well have been a foreign language to me. As in the way the men around us reacted to the proclamation of *"she's mine and off-limits,"* it was as if the words held more meaning behind them. I couldn't put more thought into it than that scant observation, however, because Specter's voice cut through the thought with, "Cool, now that's out of the way, let's fuckin' eat!"

I glanced his way and wished I hadn't as his eyes were boring a hole into me. Fixed on me in a decidedly unfriendly look that chilled me.

I glanced to Synister to see if he noticed. Other than the usual grim set line to his sensual mouth, there was nothing to say he'd been the wiser. I kept things to myself, as I really didn't want to rock the boat or upset anyone, but I was uncomfortable. Not just from Specter's look, but from how exposed I felt in just Synister's robe in a room full of men.

I tried not to let it visibly faze me as Requiem asked if I wanted some of the greens he was dishing up on his plate. I smiled, nodded, and politely said, "Please and thank you." He told me to say when and did it for me as though I was a child, which was more sweet than annoying to be honest.

"We've got it all, baby," Synister declared. "Chicken, Pork, Steak, you name it."

"Chicken sounds wonderful," I said, and Synister stabbed a breast or thigh off the platter of chicken and shook it off his fork onto my plate. I smiled ruefully, as it looked as though the men were intent on serving me, which I just didn't understand. I mean, I was an adult and perfectly capable.

I mean, these were hard men. I didn't think hard men doted on women like this.

"You like seafood?" Corvus asked me from across the table.

"Yes," I said.

"Not allergic to any of it like shellfish?" Torment asked around a mouthful of something.

"No, why?" I asked.

"Oh, you *gotta* try his ceviche," Shade called and passed a dish this way.

"Okay," I said, as I plucked a corn on the cob from a platter of it that was offered to me before someone else could do it or put it on my plate for me.

Shade passed the serving dish up the line and Requiem dished a small amount onto my plate.

"Try it and make sure you like it, baby. That shit is as good as gold around here," Synister told me.

I tried the traditional Southern American dish and my eyes lit up. It was perfectly balanced, spiced, and prepared. No flavor from the citrus to the cilantro, to the tomatoes to the fish overwhelming the others.

"That's amazing!" I declared.

"Ha! Yeah. Got the recipe off of Castañeda's boy, Renaldo, the last time we had to stand around waiting for forever and a fuckin' day." A sharp clack against Synister's plate made us all freeze. I looked up slowly and caught him, elbow on the arm of his chair, rubbing his forehead, like he had a headache. He fixed Torment with a withering look and Torment's eyes went from Synister to me and back to Synister.

"What?" Torment demanded. "That's all I'm saying." He lifted a shoulder in a shrug and Synister made a noise of consternation in his throat.

I took another bite of the grilled chicken breast which had been perfectly marinated in white wine, garlic, herbs, and spices, keeping my gaze anywhere but at the men around me.

I didn't know who *Castañeda* was, but I was sure I didn't *want* to know. If it *was* one thing that I'd learned growing up rich, is when you heard something that you weren't supposed to hear, was how to *keep it to yourself.*

A lesson that if it were Zeke sitting here? That would have been lost on him. He probably would have asked. I didn't. I asked what was in the marinade that was on the chicken instead. When I looked back to Synister after Torment had waxed eloquently about his cooking, there was an almost proud and appreciative smile curving his lips.

"I didn't expect us all to be here," Synister said later on, replying to something Corvus had said.

"Shit happens," Corvus replied and gave me a wink. Some of the men were decidedly more charming than others. Some just didn't seem to care. Others, Specter specifically, seemed to have a giant chip on their shoulders.

"Yeah, well, Spooky can clean up and we can still discuss. I'll just take Madi back upstairs first."

"Roger that," Corvus said casually.

Again, even if I didn't like being talked about while I was literally sitting *right here*... time and place, and this was neither the time, nor the place.

"Should I excuse myself now?" I asked softly.

"No," Synister said. "You don't want to miss dessert."

"Made my key lime pies last night," Torment declared.

"That actually sounds amazing," I said, laughing, and he nodded.

"Best shit you'll find outside Florida and The Keys themselves," Requiem boasted.

"Really now?" I asked.

"Fuck yeah," Specter said across from me, and I think it was the nicest thing I'd ever heard him say to this point.

Dinner was amazing, and I tried to rise to help Spooky clear plates and decimated platters away, but Synister caught my wrist and I lowered myself back into my seat.

"Spooky knows what he signed up for with this, don't you, Pook?" Corvus asked.

"Yes indeed," Spooky declared, picking up my plate and giving me a wink, as he placed it on the stack of dishes.

"Today, you're a guest, and guests don't clean," Synister declared.

"Fair enough," I murmured. "Thank you," I said to Spooky who flashed a smile at me.

"Listen to her, *thanking* the prospect," Specter said and he laughed to a smattering of chuckles and outright laughter around us. I couldn't help but feel made fun of, and I especially hated that feeling when it was for simply *being nice*.

"Never hurts to be polite," I said defensively.

"Specter." Synister's voice held a note of warning, and Specter fixed me with a hard look.

"Must have a pussy made out of gold, huh, little sister?" he asked, and Synister's hand smashed down on the table, making plates and flatware rattle and jump.

"One more fucking word in Madi's direction like that, and we're going to have a problem," Synister declared. Specter opened his mouth and Synister cut him off before he could say anything with, "Fucking *try me*."

Specter shut his mouth with an almost audible clack but glared murder in Synister's direction who simply stared back, posture rigid.

"Dude, let it go," Corvus said from beside Specter. "Read the fucking room, man. You're on your own with this one."

Specter looked up and down the table, and Shade said, "I, for one, would love watching you get your ass spanked by Daddy."

"Man, fuck you," Specter muttered but he backed down to a bunch of laughter and *still*, even though he was being totally bi-polar in my direction tonight, mostly erring on the side of being a douchebag, I couldn't help but feel for him.

Doesn't feel so good to be the butt of the joke, does it? I thought to myself.

Silence fell over the length of the giant banquet table until Torment piped up with, "So... pie?"

Some laughter tittered around the gleaming wood's surface, and he pushed back, taking some of the half empty platters with him and went for the kitchen.

I stared at the table top in front of me and didn't say a word. Synister reached out, chasing some of my hair hiding my face from him back behind my ear and I swallowed hard, cheeks flaming with a mix of discomfort and embarrassment, and refused to look right away.

When I did, his expression was neutral but held an edge of gentleness where his dark eyes roved over me.

"I'll handle it," he said softly.

"It's fine," I lied. "There's nothing to handle."

"That's not your decision to make, it's mine. And I say there is and it'll be handled. I'm sorry you're being treated rudely as a guest in my home."

I heard Requiem suck in a breath beside me and I looked his way sharply.

He pulled his lips back from his teeth in an "eek" expression and said very quietly and very succinctly, "Specter fucked around and he's going to find out on this one."

"What's that supposed to mean?" I asked before I could stop the question from escaping.

"That's club business," Synister said, and he took my hand in his atop the table. "Just if I say it'll be handled, trust that it'll be handled."

I nodded quietly, because the look on his face? It was as good as a guarantee.

Specter looked thoughtful across the table and looked at where Synister held my hand, his thumb stroking back and forth along the back of it. His expression was a curious one that I couldn't quite define.

Chapter Twenty-Four

Synister...

It was a pleasure watching Madisyn take her first bite of Torment's pie. The man was a professional high-end chef by trade and loved his fucking craft. Just about as much as he loved his knives... which is honestly why I think he got into it in the first place. His knife work was unparalleled by anything other than his cruelty. I'd watched him slice razor thin strips off a guy and make the fucker eat himself before.

To watch what his silken key lime pie did to Madi, though? Almost made me jealous. Her eyes fluttered shut and her eyes rolled back in her head in pure bliss the moment the cool and creamy confection touched her tongue. The way she rolled the bite as it dissolved in her mouth made me instantly rock fucking hard beneath the table.

Night had fallen outside the glass of the floor-to-ceiling banquet room windows and I discovered that her presence at my side, along with the club that I'd built from the ground up... Let's just say when it was me and all of my brothers, I held a sense of satisfaction, an almost completion. But with Madisyn here, it went beyond that. It felt... *cozy*. Dare I say, I even felt *contented*.

That was a foreign concept to me.

I never had enough, or felt like anything was enough, but with Madisyn, I felt some kind of whole. Complete. Content.

Of all the things that were different where she was concerned, *that one thing* was the thing that made her more precious than all the riches in the world. I needed to sit with that for a while.

I think the rest of my men had sensed it... all except for Specter, that is.

Of course, I would address his disrespect later. First, I intended to enjoy my dessert. Well, the one that Torment had crafted at any rate. I couldn't tell you how much it fucking turned me on, picturing setting Madisyn's ass on the table in front of me, licking her sweet pussy as my men watched and she moaned.

Fuck.

I needed to figure out how to have my cake and eat it too in that department, and all I could come up with was simply getting her used to being around them. Showing her that there wouldn't be any judgment and that she would be perfectly safe.

That last one seemed to be the crux of her hangup. I watched her face the whole evening, and what most would consider a lack of confidence, I saw something else, and a glance or two down the table confirmed it for me.

Fear.

Torment and Reaper were the ones to know. Reaper stared at her in that way that told me everything I needed to know. The way I would catch Torment looking with that joker's grin of his simply confirmed it.

They could smell her fear like a shark scented blood in the water.

"Oh, my God. That was better than sex," Madisyn complimented Tor. The rest of the guys all looked at me, a moment of silence, and they all burst out laughing.

I had to laugh too.

"Better than sex, you say? Guess I'll just have to try harder."

She blanched and covered her mouth with both her hands and once again impressed me with her ability to turn such a bright shade of crimson, while simultaneously having all the blood drain from her face. Such a gorgeous paradox, she was.

"It's just an expression!" she cried, as some of the men around the table howled with laughter, some even going so far as to fall completely out of their chairs.

Even Reaper laughed, and he rarely *laughed* at anything.

"I'm glad you enjoyed it," I said, grinning. "I'm still going to make you pay for that, though."

"Oh, God!" she cried, and I decided I would indeed have my dessert.

"Come here, Madisyn," I ordered and slid my plate away.

She got up and came over to me as I pushed my chair back from the table. The guys were starting to settle down. She was so embarrassed and had no one but herself to blame.

She stepped in front of me and I lifted her, setting her ass on my place setting. She squeaked, gripping the edge of the table with her knuckles mottled white. I looked up at her and asked her softly, "Do you trust me to keep you safe?"

"When you're around, yes. It's what could happen when you're not around that scares me."

Honest answer, and one I could appreciate.

"Whether I'm around or not, this club has rules and rules you don't break... ever."

"I don't understand," she said.

"Laws are meant to be broken," Corvus said from my right hand. "The rules of this club go beyond that, sweetheart."

"Requiem," I called to my sergeant-at-arms. "What would happen if any of you touched what was mine or your brothers without permission?"

"It'd be brought to this table and punishment would be decided and meted out by me or Torment. Unless it was one or the both of us then you, Corvus, or a volunteer would handle it."

"Specter," I called out. "If someone was found guilty of mishandling another brother's property, what would the punishment be?"

"If you're lucky, you'd just get your ass beat. Not so lucky, you'd lose your life. Real unlucky, you'd live but your ass would be kicked out this club."

"So, if I told you, every last one of you motherfuckers present, that Madisyn Reynolds here is *mine,* what would that mean?" I demanded.

"Respect your brother. Respect his property. Protect your brother. Protect his property. Lay down your life for your brother. Lay down your life for his property." They all recited it from heart, from memory, as they were the core tenants of this club.

Madisyn shivered in front of me as the chant died and the sound rung from the rafters and dripped from the chandelier above us.

"Open your legs," I demanded, staring her square in the eyes. Her blue eyes were haunted but there was something else behind them. A sort of understanding to them. She parted her knees hesitantly and I swept the satin material of my robe off the tops of her thighs.

I kept my eyes fixed to hers as I lowered my mouth to the apex of her thighs, only diverting them to my prize when her heaving breasts got in the way of continued eye contact.

She gasped and made a strangled noise, as my tongue parted her folds and I gave that first lick to her pussy. My hands found her ass as I scooted my chair forward and pulled her closer to the edge of the table, closer to my mouth.

She panted and her body arched in that sinuous sexy way that was simply natural to her, and I heard one of the guys groan a few seats away.

"Oh, shit, that's nice," one of them said. I smiled to myself as I plunged my tongue into her sweetness. *Fuck, yeah, it is.*

"Oh!"

Madisyn's cry was the cry of a woman losing her senses and all semblance of control. The sound music to my ears, and so sweet to me.

I hummed in appreciation and stroked her from opening to clit with long, languorous strokes of my tongue, spending some time at that hard kernel of joy at the top of her sex, letting it get acquainted with the tip of my tongue.

I took one of my hands from her hip and introduced my middle finger into her pussy. She was soaking wet and ready for me, and I liked that. Loved that she was ready for me when just a bit ago, it seemed as though the thought of letting me do this to her in front of my men would make her dry up faster than the Sahara in a hundred-year drought.

She moved her hands from the edge of the table and put them flat against the gleaming surface. I'm pretty sure I heard one or two belt buckles let go.

I was good with that. Didn't mind one bit if they jerked off to what they saw. What was mine was theirs in one context and one context only – as a visual aide. This was the closest they would ever get to this woman's pussy. Let them get as much enjoyment out of it as they could.

I rolled my eyes up Madi's body, but her head was thrown back. So caught up in what I was doing to her, she'd lost herself completely in the sensations, my robe front gaping. Her perfect tits pushed out from the slick satin material and were on full display.

I worked her both from inside and out, taking her higher and higher into the clouds until she became one with the lightning, letting it flit and flicker along her veins, her pussy contracting around my fingers as I rubbed the roof of her slick cunt with them. I took my other hand, suckled at her clit, and pressed down *just so* from the outside, just over her pubic bone, bringing the branching nerves from the other side of her clit down against my pressing and rubbing fingers inside of her, and she cried out.

Her hands gave out and she collapsed onto her back. She came, arching so beautifully, her hair fanning out around her head in a golden halo around her beautifully and exquisitely tortured face, and I carried on with that torture. I didn't let up, even when she became so over sensitive, she was sure she would probably die. She likely thought she pissed herself with how much fluid was gushing from her cunt.

So, she *was* a squirter. I liked that!

I finally stopped, stood, and wiped my mouth with the back of my hand. I stared down at her lovely spent figure as she stared up at me, ashen, her blue eyes heavy lidded, and her stare almost blank.

I took my straining cock out from over the waistband of my pajama bottoms and wrapped my arms around her thighs, dragging her back down the table until her ass was barely on it. And when I drove into her? It was the most satisfying thing.

I grunted, and worked myself in and out of her, her tits bouncing, her hands grasping the edge of the table as she panted and pulled herself down to meet the forward thrust of my cock. *Oh God!* She was more than a princess. She was proving to be my *queen* as she let go and let me do with her what I willed in front of God and everyone, and that got me so fucking hard. The way she got so fucking wet for me!

"Come on, baby," I urged. "One more. You've got one for me, I know it. Give it to me!" I placed my thumb against her clit and worked it in circles, determined to drag another orgasm from her.

My hips and ass *burned* from the effort of my continued strokes but I was determined. I fucked that perfect pink pussy of hers without hesitation, without mercy. When I felt it start to tighten up around my dick, I knew she was almost there.

She panted, and all but begged me with her sultry bedroom eyes to give it to her, to make it good, and I was determined to do just that for her.

I bent over her, slid an arm beneath her lower back, getting her to arch, driving up into her hard and harder. Her pants turned into cries that punctuated every thrust until with a high, thin wail, she came, screaming around me. I had to rip myself from her so I wouldn't come inside her. I shot on her stomach, some of the jets reaching as high as her tits, and one or two as high as her lovely throat. She collapsed back onto the table, panting, covering her mouth with both of her hands.

I bent over her and wrapped my arms around her, cradling her head with my hand and urging her to put her arms around me. She did, and I stepped around one of her knees and effortlessly slipped an arm beneath one and lifted her.

"Back for that meeting as soon as I get my woman settled," I growled.

All I heard was a faint, dazed, "Good deal," as I swept out of the banquet room and through the parlor, hitting the stars and powering up them to the upstairs.

I took Madisyn to my room, kicking the door shut behind us, and went straight to the bathroom, setting her onto the edge of the sink and vanity. She was hyperventilating, and I stepped back just enough for her to lose her shit on me.

She smacked me, tears streaming down her face as her emotions rode her into the ground. She screeched, "I don't know whether to love you or hate you for that!"

I tried not to chuckle or laugh but it was hard. I caught her wrists and pulled her against me and held her, shushing her.

"I told you I didn't want to do that!" she wailed and sobbed against my chest.

I shushed her, soothed her, and tilted her head back. I smoothed her hair back off of her tear-stained face.

"Then why did you part your legs?" I asked her, trying to get her to *think* beyond the war of emotions playing out on her face.

"I don't know!" she cried. "I-I-I-"

"Shh, shh, it's okay. I've got you," I soothed and she calmed down eventually. At least from trying to hit me anyhow. She still sat there, her breathing ragged, her panting slowing.

"Hear me out," I said. "I think you parted those lovely thighs of yours for me for a couple of reasons. One, and most importantly, because you *do* trust me to keep you safe." She sniffed and nodded, but kept her head down. "And two, because you crave it," I said.

"Crave *what?*" she demanded.

"The feeling of having someone be proud of you," I said, gripping her face between my hands and forcing her head up to look at me. "And I *am*. I am *so very proud of you*. I promise you – no, look at me!" She'd tried to jerk her head back, to look away, but I wouldn't let her.

"*Look at me!*" I commanded and she stilled and did. "I'm not bull-shitting you, kitten. I'm proud of you. I'm grateful for the gift you gave me and my brothers down there, sharing yourself so selflessly like that. I *promise you*, what happens in this house and what happens in that clubhouse, *stays* in this house and in that clubhouse. You'll never hear any of us speak on it outside these walls or the club walls – ever. Do you understand me?"

"You're the Vegas of Savannah, I got you," she said and she sniffed, overwhelmed tears slipping down the shattered walls of her comfort zone, and yeah – some of her boundaries, too.

"Fuck yeah we are," I said with a slight laugh, and I praised her. I had to. "You were so fucking hot down there."

I pulled her back into me and kissed her forehead. She put her arms around me and shivered but not from cold. Her skin was too heated for that.

"You're good, baby. I promise you. You're safe. You're good." I tucked her head against my chest and kissed her forehead, her temple, and the top of her head, even as I still buzzed from the thrill of it.

She didn't say anything. I think she was too shocked at her own want, desire, and passion, overwhelming what she thought was her common sense.

"Let me get you cleaned up," I whispered, and she sniffed and nodded.

I let her go just long enough to start the shower again and to help her down from the vanity and out of the tangle of my robe. I let it, and my pants, fall to the floor and said, "Hold your hair up for me. That's my girl."

She did as she was told and it was glorious. I washed her and myself clean, got us out and dried off, and picked her up once again to take her to my bed. I tucked her in and got into my bedside drawer and shook a muscle relaxer out of my prescription bottle.

"I want you to take this. It'll help you sleep," I said.

She took it, tossed it back, and drank from the glass of water I had nearby without even asking what it was.

I tucked her in and she settled beneath the covers.

"I have some business with the boys. I'll be up soon," I told her.

"It's whatever. Just go," she said, and I could tell she was miserable. I couldn't help her with that. Some things you had to sort out for yourself. That being said, I could also tell by how her hand lingered in mine, gripping it once before she let go that her anger wasn't so much anger but a panicked confusion at the tumultuous feelings that she was having at having just been freshly fucked in front of a group of strangers.

I kissed her sweetly and she kissed me back and sniffed.

"I won't be long," I promised her.

"Okay," she said again with that edge of misery to her tone.

I went into my closet and pulled on a fresh pair of pewter pajama bottoms, tying the drawstring securely.

She lay huddled on her side, beneath the blankets, facing the windows, her back to the rest of the room.

"Back soon," I told her, but she didn't respond.

I shut the door behind me and sighed, heading back down to the banquet hall.

I entered to a standing ovation. I chuckled but deep down, I was worried I may have broken something in her.

The table had been cleared and I returned to its head, retaking my seat.

"Pook, did you get everyone's phones in the bag?"

"I did indeed," Spooky answered.

"Good. Go upstairs and stand guard outside my door. Do *not* let Madisyn know you're out there. She's resting."

"You got it," he said, and he jogged out of the room. I glimpsed him taking the stairs two at a time through the parlor.

I sighed. "To order," I declared and rapped my knuckles on the table.

"The Castañeda thing," Haint, our secretary, called.

"Right," I said. "Torment, Grim, and Reaper. You're on it?"

"Like Sonic," Torment declared, tipping his chair back on two legs.

"Reconnaissance on that?" I asked.

"Got the kid's routine on lock," Grim affirmed.

"When you pulling the trigger, so to speak?" Corvus asked and it was a valid question.

"Friday night," Grim declared.

"Good deal," I said. "When you have the package secured, call me in," I said.

"You're the boss." Grim sent me a little salute.

"Next shipment," Haint declared, when I looked back his way.

"Hangman, Death, Specter, and Requiem, you're up," I said.

"Yup," Requiem said from my left. He was back in his official seat at my left hand. The other three nodded.

"Next?" I asked.

"The Avery fight," Haint rattled off.

"Right. There was trouble with the venue, yeah?"

"Handled," Corvus declared. "Got an old warehouse out near the river. It's outside Savannah PD's jurisdiction and thus outside the city prosecutors. The county sheriff's been paid off and were all too happy to take your corporation's *generous* donation to their educational program for kids to keep them off the Moll-E and other nasty little drugs." He smirked.

"Anything else?" I asked.

Haint shook his head.

"Last order of business." I fixed Specter with a hard look. "I'm going to let that little debacle earlier with my property slide because I genuinely believe your dumbass couldn't read the fucking room. But you disrespect her again, I'm not going to stop punching until you've swallowed teeth. Do I make myself clear?"

Specter nodded gravely.

"Make it fucking right," I said, and he kept nodding. He knew exactly my meaning.

"Get the word out, she's mine and everything that entails," I told my men.

"Never pictured you with a woman like her," Corvus said, tilting his head. "But it weirdly makes sense."

"Didn't ask anyone's opinion," I said.

He grinned and said, "Well, you got it anyway."

I braced my elbows on the arms of my chair and steepled my fingers.

"Anyone else have anything they want or need to bring to the table that isn't about my choice in who I'm keeping?"

There was a smattering of other business, nothing especially heavy. Just a few things – the next clubhouse rager after the next big fight, some shit about online stuff on the dark web promoting the next fight. Shit like that.

We managed to wrap things up inside an hour.

"Any of you fuckers need to, you're welcome to stay," I said, getting up. "Meeting adjourned."

I stood as each came to me and clasped hands and bumped shoulders. We always closed church out with respect. When Specter got to me, we hugged it out.

"I'll make it right," he said with a nod.

"We're good," I said, just to be clear that he needed to make it right with Madisyn. I did so by stating obviously, "An opportunity will present itself. It always does."

He nodded, and I excused myself and went upstairs. Spooky was leaning against the wall opposite my door.

"Good dog," I said with a wink, and he grinned and shook his head. "Wait here. I'm going to grab some things so you can put them in the wash for me if you don't mind."

"Don't mind at all," he said.

Right answer.

I gathered Madi's things and the pajama pieces we'd ruined downstairs and took them to Spooky, thrusting them into his arms.

"If you get them in the dryer, great. If not, get them there in the morning as soon as you wake up and it should be fine," I said.

"You got it," he answered back, and he went down the stairs.

I let myself back into my room and threw the lock like I always did.

I got into bed and eased up behind her. She startled and turned to face me. I lay back as she cuddled into me and laid her head on my shoulder.

I held her close and smiled.

"Decided you weren't mad at me?" I asked.

"No," she said petulantly.

"So, you *are* mad at me?" I demanded.

"You're such an asshole," she said with a huffed-out breath.

"Yeah?"

"Yeah."

"Why?"

She muttered something under her breath and didn't answer. I jostled her gently.

"I said you needed to be nicer to me, and you do, well, for all of five minutes and then *that*," she complained. I grinned. "What happened to 'easing me into it?'"

"I thought giving you two orgasms was being *very nice*," I said slyly, and she pinched my nipple.

"Ow! Did you just pinch my goddamned nipple?" I demanded, laughing.

"Yes, but somehow I think you liked it," she said.

I chuckled darkly. "Touché, kitten. Touché."

She wasn't precisely wrong. I did like it in the right applications, but it was still unpleasant.

"You're learning, baby," I said and I kissed her forehead. She sighed out. The way she was draped across me and so limp, I knew the muscle relaxer had taken full effect.

"I wasn't lying. I would never lie to you about things like that. I am *very* proud of you."

"Shut up and let me sleep," she grumbled. I chuckled and gave her a light squeeze.

She clung to me and I liked that too. I reached out and switched out the bedside lamp and we were plunged into darkness.

"I feel like I should say I'm sorry for reacting like I did," she said quietly. "I just... I don't know why I did that. Why I... I guess once you started, it felt good but... I don't know. I—"

"Shhhh." I held her close. "I don't make apologies," I told her. "But I will concede that yes, you're right. I took that too fast – but god damn, baby. If you could only see you the way I do."

She sniffed and snuggled closer, and I gave her what she was looking for. I held her tight and rubbed my hands over her smooth and sensual body wherever they could reach.

"Please don't make it my fault," she whispered.

I said, "No. That was on me being the impatient bastard I am." I kissed her forehead.

She was silent and I closed my eyes.

I slept entirely too well with her tucked into my side.

Chapter Twenty-Five

Madisyn...

I still can't believe I'd let him do that to me. That I'd allowed myself to fall under the spell that he'd cast with his voice and those eyes, through his power and control. He'd held out the forbidden fruit and I couldn't help but trust him, because whether he was being sweet and kind or a total fucking asshole, a liar Synister was not. To have that entire room of thirteen men affirm what he was saying, and to take that leap, had been a siren's call and I was weak. I wanted to believe him, and at the same time, I hadn't. Well, the joke was on me.

Synister was a man of his word and part of me was glad that he had, because *fuck,* had it felt good and *fuck,* had I felt powerful. But also, *goddammit,* had I been such a fucking weak ass! Ugh!

It was as though I was one with an addictive personality as well, only my addiction had turned out to be Synister's kiss and that look of praise in his dark eyes. The worship I felt he bestowed upon me, and all I had to do was bend to his will – and bend I did.

It was a hard and confusing time to be me. It was also mentally and emotionally *exhausting*.

I woke before Synister did and I felt so relaxed, but also sore from his attentions the day before – both on the dining room table and in his bed before that. I stared at him as he slept beside me, and I watched him sleep for a while.

Something about sleep smoothed out his hard and sharp edges and it was... nice.

My thoughts trailed back to last night, at how the men had watched us with naked want on their faces. How they'd looked at Synister as though they'd give anything to be him, and at me like they only wished they could have a taste. *Jesus*, Synister had been right. It had been a powerful thing.

I didn't think I had ever simultaneously felt so in control and *out of it* at the same time in my *life*... and that was, I think, what had me so upset.

I had always prided myself on being the good girl, had strived forever and a day for praise and adoration from people who couldn't be bothered to reach out a hand when I was drowning and who always expected more or better out of me no matter what. Yes, I was talking about my parents, who no matter how hard I tried just couldn't be bothered. Not when Zeke was their golden child. Even when Zeke kept getting in trouble, it was always "not now Madisyn, your brother needs us, or needs you to do X thing more."

I felt like the invisible girl. Last night, I felt as though I'd been *seen* and all it'd taken was one step off the moral high ground to plummet to being sucked on like I was dessert and fucked on some-one's dining room table. In some ways, I felt like it wasn't *fair*.

I was angry and resentful at doing literally everything right for no return, and all it took was catching the eye of the devil of Savannah himself, and throwing caution to the wind and suddenly...

Shit.

I breathed in through my nose and out through my mouth and slipped from Synister's bed.

That more than anything is what I had been angry with him for this time. For shattering my illusion that I was in any kind of control.

Though I hunted for them, I couldn't find my clothes from the day before. I stared at Synister, asleep in his bed, and honestly? I didn't have the heart to wake him. Plus, I didn't really feel like going to my morning classes. That last part should have scared me or at least tipped me off that I maybe was falling into some kind of depression or was having some kind of a – a – a collapse or something.

Something about that last night had shattered some things for me. Had rocked my foundation, and I didn't know *how* to feel or come back from it.

I sighed and went in and found his shirts in the closet. I pulled down a white button-down. I pulled it on and as I buttoned it, I wandered over to the window and looked across at the fountain at Forsyth Park, peeking through the trees and the swaying Spanish moss. I glanced over my shoulder at my artist's pack.

Fuck it, I thought to myself. *Might as well do what always heals my soul.*

I opened the French door onto the patio and stepped out. It was warm but not hot or oppressive yet, being so early. I set to work, setting up and carefully setting my works in progress from Bonaventure and Colonial Park aside in favor of starting yet another new one. Only this one I was determined to stay here all day and finish, and fuck what anyone had to say about it. Even the king of the castle himself.

Right?

Right.

I did stop to hunt for my phone, which I found on the carpeted floor and half under the bed. I texted Valory that I was alright, and to send pictures of the view I was looking at. I told her I was going to take a mental health day today and paint the scene. She said she thought that was a good idea, but was I sure that I was doing okay?

I lied so as not to worry her and said yeah. Other than the rotten chaos going on inside my head, I guess I kind of had to admit to myself at least, that *yeah*, I was alright. I just needed to stop and take some time for myself and to, apparently, have it out with Synister

216

again. Either to get him to back off and slow down for real or tell him he needed to fuck off completely and leave me alone.

I was a fair bit of the way into the painting when I heard Synister stir behind me, but I paid him no mind. I kept carefully layering paint, knowing that I would never get this angle or this view of the fountain or park again if I stopped now.

"Morning, kitten," he said but I didn't turn around.

"Still mad at me?" he asked, and his arms slid around me. He buried his nose in the hair behind my ear.

"Not as mad as you're going to be when you see the front of your shirt," I said and he chuckled.

"It's just a fucking shirt," he said. "I'll buy another one."

I sniffed and sighed. He turned me around and made me look at him.

"What's this?" he demanded, curling his finger and tipping under my chin with his knuckle to make me look at him.

"I don't like feeling like this," I said.

"Like what, baby?" he asked.

"Confused, and used up, and just so tired." My voice broke on the last.

He sighed and said, "Hey, no. Come here."

"I swear you're like a little boy ripping the wings off a fly!" I warbled. "You get your gratification and damn the consequence for anyone else!"

He sighed then and held me tight. I sniffed again, holding my palate out and away from us, and said, "I don't know what I hate more, honestly. The fact I let you do these things to me, or the fact that I stick around for more when it hurts my soul!"

"Oh, baby," he murmured and he held me tight, and I just... *fuck*.

"I wish you could see you the way I do," he whispered into my hair. Hadn't he said as much last night? I couldn't remember everything after I'd taken that pill and it'd turned me to Jell-O.

"What, a toy or a-a-a piece of meat?" I demanded, trying to get my foggy memory after the fact to jumpstart.

"Brave, loyal, smart, beautiful, kind, caring, patient – certainly with my bullshit." I froze and leaned back slowly.

"You can't be serious," I said.

"Can't I?" he asked, and I detected no lie on his face.

"Why are you this way?" I demanded, and he looked vulnerable then.

He swallowed hard and lifted one shoulder into a shrug and looked out toward the fountain before saying something along the lines of, "I'm just like my father, I guess."

"What?" I asked.

He sighed, looked at me and told me, "I don't want you to go. I know I suck at showing it, but I *like you* and I really *do* want you to be mine. But I'm not a hearts-and-flowers kind of guy. I'm more a raze-and-ruin kind of motherfucker."

"Well, you're doing the latter just peachy," I said sardonically.

Half his mouth quirked up into a smile.

"Another thing I love about you... you're not afraid to call me on my bullshit when it's warranted."

He let me go and took a step back.

"Speaking of bullshit, where are my clothes?" I asked.

"In the wash. I had the prospect throw them in last night for me so they'd be fresh for you this morning."

"Mm." I made the noncommittal noise.

"I know it doesn't make up for pushing your comfort zone last night, but let me make you breakfast."

I sighed and looked at my painting and across the street.

"Leave it. Let me make you breakfast. Then you can come back up here an spend as long as you like finishing it."

I was hungry, so I agreed.

"Thank you," he said and took my hand. I set my palate down and took it. "Judging by the time, I take it you're skipping class today?"

"I need the mental health day," I said tiredly, despite how well rested my body felt. "Especially after last night. I mean, I... was that really me?"

"Fair," he said, and grinned. "And yeah. That was really my girl," he said, swinging our hands between us by our linked fingers.

He held out his other hand and I took it. He lured me carefully toward the door out into the hallway.

We found Torment in the kitchen, humming to himself and dancing around as he took things from the fridge and piled them on the counter.

"Ah!" He swept around the kitchen island and kneeled at my feet in a grandiose gesture of I don't know what, taking up my hand and kissing the back gallantly.

"A most splendid display last night, my lady!" he said and I felt myself blush. I looked to Synister who raised an eyebrow.

"Um," I said awkwardly. "Thanks."

Torment stood and said, "This momentous occasion calls for my crepes. Sweet, or savory?" he asked and then said, "Never mind. Sweet, for a sweet lady." He zipped around the kitchen island and started preparing things in a whirlwind of activity.

"Sit, sit!" he cried and gestured at the island before him.

Synister pulled out a stool for me and kissed my temple before actually asking me, "Will you be alright if I go check the laundry?"

I hesitated but for a moment before nodding my head. He promised me, "I'll be right back."

"Okay," I murmured.

Torment eyed me from across the counter as he sliced strawberries with a deftness that were I to try it, I would lose a finger. What was more impressive was that he stared at me while he did it.

"Stop overthinking it," he said after a moment, all pretenses at being happy-go-lucky simply gone in a snap. The change in him so abrupt, all I could do was sit there and blink at him, staring, waiting for some indication that I'd heard him right and that what he'd just said was real and not a figment of my imagination.

"What?" I asked.

"Last night," he said. "Seriously. Happens all the time around here. We're a bunch of freaks and perverts. Honestly, that was *so hot* and we appreciated the view. You're lovely and it was lovely of you to share yourself like that."

I felt myself blush a fierce crimson.

"I'm... um, I... that's just not me," I stammered. "I mean, that's not how I am."

"Correction," he said. "That *wasn't you* before last night, but now? Now that's most definitely you and way to go for being so daring."

I frowned like he was crazy and he grinned and winked at me, plucking the thought right out of my head by saying, "I'm certifiable. Yeah, for you, what you did might be making you feel like you're crazy, but all the best people in my estimation are a little nuts. At least from time to time. It's what makes life interesting."

I scrubbed my face with my hands and peeked from between my fingers, speechless.

"Ooo, breakfast," I heard behind me, and I turned as Grim and Reaper came around the corner. Grim made an exaggerated exultated bow with both arms held high in the air in my direction and said, "Good morning, my queen."

Behind him, Reaper cocked his head with a questioning look on his face, his eyes sweeping over me from my head to where I disappeared behind the counter as though to make sure I was alright. I nodded and he smiled faintly.

"Crepes or blintzes?" Grim asked, taking an orange out of a dish on the counter and tossing it in the air before catching it.

"Oooo, blintzes!" Tor answered, suddenly reconsidering what he was doing.

"Either or," Grim said with a shrug. "They're kissing cousins anyway. The real question I should be asking is savory or sweet?"

"Sweet for our sweet thing over there," Torment replied.

Reaper slid up on one of the stools, one apart from mine.

"I guess I'll juice some oranges," Grim said.

I looked around at all of them. They really were acting like what'd gone on last night was some kind of a regular occurrence and it somehow really *did* make me feel somehow better about things.

Synister returned a moment later with a neat pile of clothes and set them on the counter, sliding up on the stool between me and Reaper.

"An encore performance, perhaps?" Torment asked, looking between us, hopeful.

"I don't think so," I blurted and Grim laughed.

"I don't think I could handle another," Reaper said, and the rest of the kitchen froze and turned.

"He speaks," Tor said.

"Not that it wasn't hot and wonderful," Grim said, glancing from Reaper to me. "What my heteroflexible life mate is trying to say is it was maybe too much of a good thing."

I caught Reaper nodding on the other side of Synister who was laughing silently.

"Heteroflexible life mate?" Synister asked. "You know what? I don't want to know. Never mind."

"What brought you down first thing?" Grim asked. "Usually, you don't bother before like noon and when you do, it's just briefly for coffee."

"I told Madisyn I would make her breakfast but since Torment's in the kitchen, I'll let the master work."

"Damn right," Tor said and blew on his nails and rubbed them against his chest as though polishing them. It was pretty much then and only then I realized that they were *all* shirtless. I suddenly tried to look anywhere but at them.

"Is that paint?" Grim asked a second later after he'd juiced three or four oranges but realized suddenly, I was covered in colored flecks and streaks.

"Oh! Yeah," I said, looking down at myself. "I like to paint."

Reaper leaned back to look at me around Synister's back.

"Reaper loves art and artists. What do you paint?" Grim asked.

"All kinds of things," I said.

"She's painting Forsyth's fountain right now, from my balcony."

"Shit, really? Can we come check that out?" Grim asked.

"Oh, it isn't finished yet," I said.

"So?"

I colored faintly and murmured, "Sure, I guess."

Breakfast was a rather amazing affair of strawberry cheesecake blintzes which were a wee bit of a change up from crepes when a conversation came up about the differences between the two.

Torment was *beyond* a marvel with knives. The more I watched him, the more I realized that I'd never seen someone wield them with such a deftness before. He sliced the strawberries so impressively thin, they were transparent, and the filling and the blintzes themselves were absolutely decadent. I didn't know what was beyond *master* level for a chef, but Torment was certainly it, and I complimented his ability as so.

He looked well-pleased but it was well earned praise.

After breakfast, Synister put a hand to my back to guide me back upstairs.

"So, we good to see that painting?" Grim asked, wiping his mouth and tossing down his napkin by his plate.

"You fuckers better get your asses back here to help clean up," Torment said even as he took Grim's plate.

"We will, we will. Keep your fuckin' panties on."

"I could help," I offered. Synister's hand pressed slightly to my lower back enough that I looked up at him. He shook his head.

"You're a guest," he said.

I tipped my head and countered with, "Either I'm your guest or your girlfriend. You can't have it both ways." I raised my eyebrows and he smirked.

"Watch me," he shot back.

I rolled my eyes.

"Incorrigible," I muttered.

"He's right." Tor automatically sided with Synister.

I raised an eyebrow on him and said, "You *would* take his side."

"You're outnumbered and outgunned, princess. Might as well just go with the flow," Grim said, and I rolled my eyes even harder.

"Only my *dad* calls me princess," I said.

"I didn't know you had a daddy kink," Tor joked coolly at Synister.

"I don't. Come on, kitten. Let's show Grim and Reaper your talents."

"There it is!" Grim crowed and laughed.

"What?" I asked, clueless as to what they were on about but knowing it had something to do with pet names.

"Nothing," Torment said. "Nothing at all about you. We're just giving Syn a bad time."

"Like I said, come on, kitten. Torment's just living up to his name." Synister was smiling in that way that told me Torment was going to get it back, although it didn't have the wattage to the smile to make me afraid for the man. Rather, it was a playful if mischievous thing, and it had some of the tension easing out of me.

"Okay," I agreed.

Breakfast was as delicious as dinner the night before, although I wouldn't be making the same mistake as the whole "better than sex" comment as I had the night before. It was still really damn close!

The men joked, laughing, and talking about random small things. Torment talked about life as a private chef which led me to ask what Grim and Reaper did, which yielded some surprising results.

Grim was a contractor in high demand, doing high-end projects from historical restorations to modern builds and everything in between.

Reaper, however, was a mortician. I don't know why that didn't surprise me, but I think the fact that it *didn't* surprise me, surprised me more than his actual field of expertise – if that makes sense. There was a slightly uncomfortable silence before we just kind of moved on, so I didn't get to ask, or really want to know all that badly, for that matter, whether he worked in a hospital, mortuary, or for the state or what have you.

I mean, there was more than one way to work with the dead in that sort of capacity, wasn't there?

Synister took me back upstairs after the conversation flowed along for a bit, with Grim and Reaper in tow, and I stepped back out onto the balcony with my paintings. It wasn't very big out here, certainly not for all four of us, but that was okay. It seemed like Reaper was the only one really fascinated with what I was doing.

Grim hung back in the room, along with Syn, and Reaper looked over all three of my projects. From the Fountain peeking from the foliage on my easel to the two cemetery paintings leaning against the railing down low, waiting to go back in the back of the box here for transport.

Reaper pointed to the two cemetery ones and looked over his shoulder at Grim, his expression a little livelier than usual.

"He likes those two," Grim said, grinning. "How much when they're done?"

"Oh! Um, I don't know. I've never sold any of my artwork before, just sort of given them away as gifts or thrown them away when they were done and nobody wanted them."

Reaper looked stricken at the admission, putting both hands to his chest as though he were having a heart attack, which made me laugh.

"Finish those two," Grim declared, "and you have a buyer. I know that look from him."

I nodded and smiled. "I have to get back to Bonaventure for that one," I said, pointing. "That one I might be able to get back to Colonial Park between classes."

"Should go to Laurel Grove North. There are a couple of really cool spots and monuments in that one. Make it a three-painting series..." Grim, Synister, and I chatted some more about it while Reaper stared at the two that I'd yet to finish, rapt.

It was a nice talk, and left me... I don't know... feeling more normal about things, certainly more secure than I had felt in a while, and I was grateful for that.

Synister caught my eye and gave me a knowing smile. I felt a little silly, but still, I managed to smile back because I had to admit, on this? *He was right.*

Chapter Twenty-Six

Synister...

I let Madi finish her painting while I did some work up here at the small desk in my bedroom. She made the day go by much easier, with the view of her sexy silhouette through my now ruined shirt. The sun shining on all that gorgeous blonde hair made her seem like something made of pure light and sweetness.

She finished her painting after a few more hours and the day had sort of gotten away from us both.

She sighed, and turned to me after packing up her art, looking much more refreshed and happier for having indulged in it. Certainly, she was more relaxed.

"I need to take a shower, get dressed, head back to the dorms," she said to me. I looked up from over my laptop's screen and raised my eyebrows, nodding. I spoke into my earpiece and she frowned for a second, realized I was talking to someone on the line and colored furiously.

I smiled and winked at her. She took herself into the bathroom and the one and only regret I had was that I couldn't join her in there.

She came out dressed, hair hanging lank against her skull. I could appreciate having a woman who liked to be as clean as I did.

She smiled at me and briskly rubbed her hair between her towel-covered hands, and I leaned back and took her in.

"I hate letting you go," I said truthfully.

She nodded and said, "I know, but I have to go to class tomorrow. I have so much to do with finals coming up."

"Then let's get you back," I said with a sigh.

"I really would like to finish the Colonial Park and Bonaventure paintings," she said. "Maybe you could take me out to Bonaventure this weekend?"

I smiled and nodded.

"Saturday," I said. "I have a thing on Friday night for the club."

"That's perfectly alright," she said. "Friday, I can hang with Valory."

I nodded.

"Let me rinse off and get dressed," I said.

"Alright." She smiled brightly at me and I rose, my business concluded for today at least, and I took myself in to shower.

When I came out, she was talking on her phone softly, but her voice was strained as she sat on the love seat next to her packed-up artist's pack. She looked up at me sharply and said, "Yes, fine. Six Pence on Wednesday." She paused again. "I don't care, Zeke."

I frowned at that.

"Yes, fine," she said and she ended the call. "I had to get him to stop blowing up my phone somehow," she said with a shrug.

It'd only been her brother. I sighed and nodded. She relaxed her stiff posture marginally.

I held out my ruined shirt and said, "Keep it. Wear it over your clothes when you paint. I like the idea of it."

She beamed at that and took the cloth from me.

"Alright."

I took her back to her dorm, hooking a hand behind her head, and kissing her deeply before letting her go back to her life for the time being.

"Mm." She leaned back and I loved how her flawless skin was dusted a light pink over her nose and cheeks.

"Saturday," she said softly as though to confirm.

"Saturday," I agreed.

"Okay, bye." She slipped out of the Rover and shut the door, but I wouldn't budge from the loading zone in front of her place until she was securely behind the locked lobby doors.

I picked up my phone and called Corvus.

"Yo?" he answered on the first ring.

"The Island Boys called. They want to move game night from Thursday to tonight."

"Shit," he muttered.

"I was surprised, too," I said.

"Okay, let me text around and make some calls," he said.

"I can handle it personally if I need to," I said.

"I don't like it," he said automatically.

"Some shit has to happen to get it done," I replied.

"Fuck. Let me get off of here and I'll call you as soon as I can."

"Copy that," I said and the line went dead.

We talked in code about these things, but that had been the gist of the call I'd been on when Madisyn had finished her shower.

I drove myself home. By the time I was pulling in the driveway, Corvus was back on the line.

"It's you, me, and Fear," he said. "Everyone else had a thing and couldn't drop it to make it. Hangman'll have the game room open at his place. Be at the docks at nine to meet with the boys and it'll be game on."

"Roger, roger," I said.

"Cool. See you tonight," he said, and I ended the call.

I went about the rest of my fuckin' day. I headed for the club, parked the Rover, and got on the bike. Fear joined me, and we headed for the docks and my boat. Corvus was waiting for us at the river marina when we got there, his bike leaned and his butt on the seat, legs stretched out and crossed at the ankle as he fucked around with some game on his phone.

He looked up and threw chin at the sound of our approach, and we pulled into the same stall and parked ourselves.

"Any more details?" I asked.

"No," he said as he powered down his phone.

"Fuck," I grunted.

I keyed us through the gate and we went down the dock to our covered slip, boarding the speed boat and casting lines. I started the engine and backed us out and into open waters.

The ride out to the rendezvous point was only something like fifteen to twenty minutes for the exchange. The boys still in uniform, eyes a little wide, but they were tough as shit. Fuckin' Marines always were. Still, their tails were definitely singed and there'd been a close call.

I asked the big question, my arms crossed over my chest and my hands tucked into my pits, as Fear and Corvus loaded the crates along with two of the Marines from their boat to ours.

"Is this going to slow us down?" I asked.

"It'd be prudent, at least for a little while," the man said.

I sniffed. "We're lucky I'm a smart bastard and that I have a stockpile," I said. I worked out a rough timeline with him and he nodded along, listening.

"Should be doable," he said with a stiff nod, and I nodded back.

"Better be. These Columbians don't fuck around. I'm not sure if it's good karma or what, but something else is in the works that will buy us some good street cred with my buyer."

"Well," he spit. "I'll try my damnedest to keep the pipeline flowing, but the discrepancy was definitely noticed and some questions got asked. I don't know how much longer things'll be viable like this."

I nodded. "As long as you think you got it in hand and that what I've got in reserve will get us through…" I trailed off and he nodded.

"I'm pretty sure it will," he said, and we shook hands.

"With the favor I'm about to pull for our South American buddies, we stand to make a lot of fuckin' money," I told him, and he raised an eyebrow.

"How much money?" he asked.

I named the figure and he nodded slowly. "I'll see what I can do."

"I thought that might shore up your resolve some," I said with a savage grin.

"Ain't nothing on God's green earth wrong with any Marine's resolve," he said, and I held up my hands in surrender.

"Poor choice of a turn of phrase, friend."

He nodded and Corvus gave a low whistle.

"Guess that's it then," our contact said, looking on.

"Guess so," I declared.

"Don't call me, I'll call you," he said.

"As always," I agreed.

We fucked off in our respective directions, and Fear drove the boat back and away, in the direction of our next stop.

We pulled up quietly along the river at the back of Bonaventure Cemetery, the moon riding high in the sky, the light from her just enough. We had to do this shit under cover of darkness and quiet as possible. It was our luck and a little bit of planning ahead that helped us with our clandestine movements.

Hangman met us at the landing point and we rode up onto shore. Corvus jumped down, and we spent the next several minutes passing the crates from me and Fear down to Corvus and Hangman before we disembarked our vessel to join Hang and Cor on the riverbank.

"How we looking?" I asked Hangman, and he sniffed.

"Got it open already. Might need to turn on the sound system we take too long."

"Let's not take too fuckin' long, then."

"Roger that," he said. He and Cor hefted a crate between them while Fear and I took one up between us. It was hard work getting them up the bank and onto the palate on the forks of the forklift.

Hangman was one of the nighttime caretakers of Bonaventure,

and it made this shit easier, but not easy. As soon as we'd stacked the eight or nine crates of guns onto the palate, Hangman jumped up on the small propane powered forklift. I sat on the crates, Corvus joining me, as Fear leaped up onto the step and held onto the side of the heavy moving equipment.

Hangman drove us down the way, under the arching old oaks and swaying Spanish moss, into the first third of the cemetery inside the front gate.

There we stopped by the DeRenne vault. The bust of Wymberley Jones DeRenne watched in silent countenance as we took the crates one by one down into his family crypt. There was room for something like twenty-four bodies down here, the walls racked with open vaults waiting for more of the DeRenne descendants and dead, but only a few were sealed off with remains inside. The individual crypts were deep enough that they could fit four crates of guns a piece with only about six inches or so of overhang. The vault itself still remained vast enough that we had a few things down here – a six-foot folding table in front of old Wymberley's sealed off crypt with all manner of pliers, forceps, blades, and other things lined on it and a few chairs down here as well.

We stored more than just guns down here and there were occasions we brought a man or two down here too for information.

Once the forklifts dropped the vault lid down, it was as sound-proof as it would get. There was enough oxygen down here after we sealed it to last a few days if they didn't panic.

We went up top, and Corvus jumped onto the second forklift to help Hangman get the fuckin' lid back on things.

"Who'd you have out here to help you get this off?" I demanded, as it damn sure took *two* forklifts to get the job done.

"Requiem came out from the club long enough to do it before he had to fuck back off to whatever," Hangman said and sniffed. We were all sweating by now.

"I'll help you get these put back into the equipment shed," Corvus said. "Meet y'all back at the river."

"Yeah," I said, and Fear and I fucked back off that way.

It was a long walk, and it was hot and humid as balls out here. We made it back to the boat and were sitting on it waiting for Corvus when Fear perked up.

"Sounds like Hangman turned on the sound system," he said, and I frowned, straining to hear.

"Shouldn't have needed to," I said. "It's quiet as a damn graveyard out here."

Fear snorted. "It's a cemetery. Graveyards need a church on the grounds in order to be a graveyard."

I glared at him. "I know that, asshole. It's just an expression." He laughed at me, biting down on his bottom lip to keep from making too much noise. I raised eyebrows.

"That's not the recording," I said, as we heard laughter and a snatch of music carried on the faint breeze from the heart of Bonaventure.

"Then what the fuck is it?" he demanded, and I grinned.

"Come on, let's get the fuck out of here!" Corvus hissed and leaped, pulling himself up onto the boat.

"You look like you've seen a ghost," Fear said.

"You ain't hear that?" Corvus demanded.

"Yeah, it's the dinner party recording," Fear said.

"I just fuckin' told you," I said. "That ain't the recording."

"It isn't?" he asked.

"Nope," Corvus affirmed.

"Shit, is that the real ghost party then?" he demanded.

"Yep," I affirmed. "Time to fucking go."

We started the boat and I put it in reverse. For a moment, it felt like one of us would have to get off and shove off, but we busted loose and made it out of there, back to the marina and the bikes.

As I shut off the boat once we were back in my covered slip, Corvus said, "Smooth operation."

I nodded.

"Hell of a story to tell for the rest of the guys," Fear said.

"That it fucking is," I agreed.

I'd never heard the phantom dinner party of Bonaventure Cemetery for myself before. That was a new one. Usually, we just played a recording of a dinner party if we needed to, to cover any suspicious noises we might make when it sounded like we might need to.

Tonight was one for the books.

Chapter Twenty-Seven

Madisyn...
Synister texted with me throughout the week, even called a few times to make sure I was good and to see how things were going with my brother.

I'd told him the truth, that I wasn't really talking to Zeke, still. That Zeke was being better about not blowing me up and understood why I was pissed and that I wanted and needed space.

Valory was pretty much over every last one of the men in my life and had even at one point said, "If ever there was proof that you don't get to pick your sexuality, cis het white men are it. I mean, do you honestly think anyone in their right mind would put up with this amount of bullshit from them if they could just go lesbian and be done with it?"

It'd made me laugh. I mean, she wasn't wrong. Good Lord.

Classes and my finals that I'd had to take for this term had gone well in my estimation and when Friday rolled around, I was ready for that girls' night.

I was walking back from the grocery store with snacks to be ready for it when two men walking in my direction called out, "Reynolds? Madisyn Reynolds?"

I slowed and asked, "Yes?"

Faster than I could blink, one of them buried their fist in my gut. I gagged and dropped my groceries, falling to the ground just paces from my dorm's lobby door.

I couldn't breathe, though I tried to suck in air. I tried to push myself up off the sidewalk with both hands and one of them kicked me savagely. They were talking, saying something about money, and I couldn't get my panicked brain to think beyond the pain and my lack of air. How I needed air!

A heel came crashing down onto my hand, once then twice, and I felt some things snap on the first blow, and grind and pulverize on the second. I screamed, suddenly finding breath to do so, as the heel came crashing down *again*. I turned onto my back, grabbing my wrist, and crying, screaming, at my mangled hand.

One of them straddled me and grabbed me by the head. I stared up wide-eyed and terrified as he said, "You make sure Zeke gets me my *fucking* money!" Then he *slammed* my head back against the sidewalk. *It didn't even hurt*, and I was swallowed by the dark...

Chapter Twenty-Eight

S ynister...
My phone was buzzing incessantly in my fucking pocket
as I stared at the wide-eyed and gagged ginger kid in front of
me. Ross Bayley was a rich kid and descendant of one of the original
Hilton Head Island settlers, which means he would be missed. But
he certainly wouldn't be missed by the little boy he forever altered
when he was a teen.

I sat across from him and wiped some of the blood off the scalpel
in my hand with a scrap of his tee shirt. He wouldn't be running. I'd
nicked his Achilles so even if he did get loose, there wouldn't be any
running.

I sniffed.

"Tor, Reaper, I'm going to hand this over to you," I said. "Grim,
you let 'em do their worst. Hangman's waiting out there with a fresh
plot to plant him."

"You got it, Syn."

"Don't forget proof for Castañeda," I said.

"We got it from here, man." Torment grinned savagely and I
nodded. I got up from my seat and went up the steps up out of the

vault. Once out of the stagnant press of ancient moldering air down in the vault, I sucked in a lungful of clean if heavy air from off the river. Things smelled wet and green up here. I was all for it after the rank and fetid crypt and the reek of copper from the kid's blood.

I reached into the front of the coveralls I had on to burn later along with any traces of the kid's DNA on me, expecting to break it off in Corvus's ass for interrupting but it wasn't his name on the screen. *Valory.*

Who the fuck was Valory? And how had she gotten this number? I didn't ever remember fucking a Valory, let alone, I didn't remember giving any bitch named Valory my—

I answered, realizing that it was Madi's friend, and she'd been blowing me up for the last ten godddamn minutes.

"Madisyn?" I asked.

"No, Valory," a cold and angry voice met my ear. "We're at Memorial. They're taking her in to surgery now and she was asking for you. I didn't want to call you but—"

"What happened?" I demanded, my adrenaline surging.

"She was attacked outside our dorm," she said.

"I'm on my fucking way. Text me where in the hospital you are."

"Okay," she said. She sounded worried.

I stripped off the coveralls and threw them down into the vault as I made strides for the front of Bonaventure and the caretaker's cottage.

Hangman unlocked the gate and let me slip out onto the street. My bike was at the club and I *ran* up the street.

I didn't panic. Not yet. I needed to know how bad it was. I needed to know what was done. All I had was that she was hurt, *bad* by the sound of things, and that she was going into *surgery.* But layered under all of that was *some motherfucker was going to pay.*

I was half worried it was something I had done, or that this was about me – but no one in this city was that fucking stupid. Touching what was mine was tantamount to fucking suicide and yet... it hadn't been that long. The word hadn't had time to get out there.

No, the likelier scenario was it wasn't about me at all, but her fucking loser brother.

I rolled up at Memorial in a time that shouldn't have been humanly possible, and that by all rights should have landed me in their ER and possibly the surgical suite right next to Madisyn's.

I went to the desk on the surgical floor and asked the nurse or admin or what-the-fuck-ever she was what the status on Madisyn was.

"I need to know how Madisyn Reynolds is," I said, and I was a little surprised at how anxious my voice was when it escaped me.

"Can you spell that please?" she asked.

"M-a-d-i-s-o-n—"

"It's s-y-n," I heard to my right and I turned.

"I'm sorry?" I asked.

"Madisyn. It's spelled with a 'y' not an 'o'. Her parents trying to make her stand out or something, they put a 'y' in her middle name, too. Hi, I'm Valory. You must be Synister." She held out her hand and her look from behind her cat's eye glasses wasn't friendly.

"I am," I said, ignoring her hand. "How is she?"

"I'll see if her surgical team can provide an update," the woman behind the desk murmured at Valory's nod.

"What happened?" I demanded of Valory.

"You might as well come sit," she said, wrapping her cardigan around her round frame.

"What *happened?*" I demanded again.

"That shit might work on Syn," she said. "But I'm not that bitch." She stared at me for several heartbeats, waiting for me to nut up, but she was underestimating me. "For once, you can sit your ass down and be fucking cordial or I'll make some shit up and have hospital security kick your ass out."

Impressive.

"Just tell me how she is and what happened so I can take care of it," I said.

She cocked her head, her bangs catching on her lashes and twitching against her forehead when she blinked.

"She was attacked outside our dorm's lobby. I didn't see it. Broken ribs from where they kicked her. They're doing surgery to repair her hand. I don't know how, but they broke it real damn bad, and she has a skull fracture from where they bounced her head off the sidewalk. There's some swelling on her brain, a real bad concussion, but we don't know how bad, yet."

I moved woodenly, numbly, to a chair and dropped into it.

"Where's her brother?"

"Don't know that either. He's not answering his phone."

"Her parents?"

"Flying back from overseas."

"Why are they telling you anything?" I asked.

"I'm her emergency contact," she said.

"Valory Walsh for Madisyn Reynolds?" the woman from the desk called.

"Go. Fill me in after. I'm going to make some calls," I said.

"Okay." She went over to the woman, and I brought out my phone and called Requiem.

"Yo, what's up?" he asked.

"Got a problem," I said and I filled him in. "Find out who and why. Get Spooky down here. Fill in the rest of the guys. I want blood."

"Copy that, man," he said, and he hung up the phone.

I shoved my phone back into my cut as Valory tearfully made her way back over.

"They're working on her hand," she said. "I guess she's going to wake up with some kind of stabilizing device or whatever, holding the bones in place. It's her left hand, the one she draws and paints with."

Fuck.

I hung my head and raked a hand back through my wind-blown hair. I hadn't even fucked with a helmet for the ride over here.

Valory sank down into the seat beside me and looked at me.

"She's my best friend," she said.

"She'll be fine," I told her, not used to being conciliatory but knowing that would be what Madisyn would want me to do. "She's tough."

"Yeah but—"

"No 'buts,'" I said sternly. "She's going to be fine."

I settled back into the seat, adjusting my jacket and cut along my ribs, pulling them forward.

"She'd better be," she said and sniffed.

Whether she is or not, some motherfuckers gonna die, I thought to myself.

"What took you so long to answer your phone?" Valory demanded and I snorted.

"Business meeting," I said tersely.

"Dressed like that?" she asked, and I glared at her. She snorted and said, "I don't know what she sees in you."

"I don't know either," I said, and she seemed surprised by the admission and shut her mouth.

We waited. For hours and hours, we waited. None of the guys called or texted. They fucking knew better. Shit had to be handled and they were out there handling it. The only call I wanted was when they had the fucksticks that'd hurt Madisyn in hand.

Eventually a doctor came out and twitched his finger at us to follow him. Well, he twitched it at Valory. We got up and he didn't look happy to see me at all, but simply gritted his teeth and led us to a private consultation room that was a little too homey for my tastes. It was a room meant to sooth and deliver bad news in.

"Madisyn is resting comfortably in ICU. She came out of surgery just fine for her hand, but we're concerned enough about the swelling on her brain and the fracture to her occipital bone," he tapped the base of his skull in the back, "that we've deeply medicated her and we're keeping her on a ventilator just as a precaution for now. We won't be able to assess more until the swelling has gone down and we can bring her out of the medically induced sleep we have her in."

"I want to see her," I said.

"Are you family?" he demanded.

"No," Valory said. "Neither one of us are, though. Her parents are on a flight back from London. Please? Can we? Just for a little bit?" she begged.

"One at a time," the doctor said. "And only for a few minutes."

"Thank you." Valory looked relieved, but he was giving me a hard look.

"Don't look at me that way," I told him. "It's not my doing that got her here."

"I never said that it was," he said.

Valory sniffed. "One of the witnesses said they said something about her getting them money. This is probably Zeke's fault and he wouldn't answer his phone at all," Valory said.

"Whose Zeke?" the doctor asked.

"Her fucking worthless-ass gambling-addicted brother," Valory admitted, and I silently seethed beside her.

She needed to keep her fucking mouth shut and to stop over sharing.

"It'll be handled," I said, and begrudgingly added, "I have every faith in Savannah's finest."

The doctor looked at me like I'd surprised him. He also looked like he smelled bullshit, which was fine as long as he kept his mouth shut, which he did. He rose and said, "As soon as she's out of recovery and moved into ICU, I'll have someone come get you. You'll want to relocate to the ICU wing and their waiting room."

"Of course," Valory said, and then she asked the tough question. "Will her hand be okay? Like, will she ever be able to draw or paint normally?"

The surgeon looked at her with empathy and said, "The surgery went really well, but it's too early to tell. Part of it is up to Madisyn's body and how it heals. The other part is up to Madisyn herself and how she does with physical therapy etcetera. Only time will tell at this point, but I'm optimistic."

241

I kept my mouth shut because I knew, just because a mother was optimistic didn't mean a goddamn thing in the face of reality. But I *also* knew that sometimes optimism could pull a person through. I tried not to think of *my* mother and her crushed spirit. Of how she had been such a light and such an optimistic person for me, her only son, her only child. By the time she'd gotten sick, how my father had driven every ounce of light out of her eyes for herself and how she'd just stopped fighting. How she'd looked so hollow and tired by the time she'd been given her diagnosis and how she'd turned to me, told me how very much she'd loved me, but how she'd given up anyway.

I wasn't about to let history repeat itself.

I wanted very much to empower Madisyn and to help her overcome this any way that I could. Trust me when I say, money would be no object. She'd have the finest professionals in every field at her disposal if I had to pay to fly them the fuck in from elsewhere to make that happen for her.

We parted ways with the doctor and found our way through the winding halls of Memorial to the ICU's waiting room. Valory and I both checked in at the desk and were given special visitor's stickers for our clothing. A few more hours of waiting ensued.

The sun was well up outside the glass of the hospital windows and yet neither of us slept. Valory looked as though she was going to fall over, but she had an intrepid personality and a determination that was admirable.

Finally, someone came out and said we could see her, but only one at a time.

I let Valory go first and called up Spooky.

"Yeah, what's up?" he asked, and it was good that his ass was wide awake. "I'm here and outside."

Shit, I'd forgotten all about telling Requiem to send him my way.

"Go back and grab the Rover and bring it here. I'm going to need you to take Madisyn's roommate back to their dorm."

"On it," he said. I heard him moving, his bike firing up.

"Come up to the ICU waiting room to get her," I said and ended the call.

I waited for what felt like forever and finally, Valory came out, tearful again and I stood.

"My prospect is coming with a car to take you home," I said. "Back to your dorm. You need to get some rest. When you want to come back, text me. I'll make sure you're taken care of."

She looked up at me, mouth agape, and asked, "Why would you do that for me?"

I stared down at her a little dispassionately and said, "I'm not. I'm doing it for *her*. Don't get it twisted."

She nodded and said, "Thank you."

I nodded and went over to the orderly or nurse, or whatever, and followed them back to the alcove they were keeping my woman in.

She looked fucking *tragic*. All the tubes and IVs and bullshit marring her pale, perfect skin. The bruising shadowing her face and the pins and swelling in her hand was so bad anguish lanced my heart just looking at it, to the point I felt a very real physical pain in my chest.

I snapped pictures and sent them all to the group text with all the guys and then took a seat by her side. I slipped my hand under her whole one that rested by her hip, up under the railing of her hospital bed, and I lowered my head to brush the back of her fingers with my lips. The plastic tube of her IV touching the corner of my mouth made me want to start throwing things. Made me want to destroy the fucking room around us and scream my unending rage until the Heavens shook with fear and Hell opened under our feet.

"I've got you now, baby," I whispered, and I felt the hot press of emotion at the backs of my eyes. "I'm right here."

The only answer was the hiss and whir of the machines they had her on.

I don't know how long I sat with her, but when they came to try and shoo me out, one look and the nurse's shoulders dropped and she capitulated with, "Well, I suppose I can let you stay until her family arrives."

I nodded.

Her parents... I didn't hold a very high opinion of them. We'd have to see if that opinion changed upon meeting them.

I sat vigilant and sentinel at my woman's side like that for as long as I could, pushing the envelope until her parents arrived late that night.

"Oh, my baby!" her mother cried when they led her back.

I looked up, and her father's eyes fixed on me.

I recognized him.

"Micah Devlin?" he asked confused.

"Yeah," I said and looked back down to Madi's hand in mine, relinquishing it to the crisp white blanket at her hip.

"Why are you here?" he demanded.

"She's mine," I said simply.

"Beg your pardon?"

"She's my girlfriend," I said, and I stood and stretched. "I was out for a ride when I got the call from her roommate. I came as soon as I could. Haven't left since."

Her mother took my seat and gathered her daughter's hand between hers.

"Well, we have it now. Thank you for staying with her," her father said, and I tried not to snort at the dismissal.

"I'm going to let y'all have some time and I'll be back tonight," I said. He looked indignant, but then looked back to Madi in her hospital bed before finally nodding.

I left to the track of her mother's weeping. Once out of the ward where I could turn my phone back on – I'd been admonished for having it on near the equipment at one point – I called Requiem.

"What's the status on this shitshow?" I asked.

"Come on in to the club," he said. "Church and we can go over everything."

"Good deal," I said tiredly. "I'm on my way."

I got pulled over for not wearing a helmet on the way to the club. The cop was an asshole at first, but after I got done explaining that I was on my way to where it was at and the why of forgetting it some-time pushing the night before or two nights before, he let me off with a fucking warning like I didn't practically own his entire department.

I played it cool. They got some new brass up top – newly appointed and looking to make some kind of a name for themselves. I'd deal with it later. Right now, it was only a couple of minor incon-veniences but three strikes? Miss thang at the head of the department would be out so fast, she wouldn't know if she were coming or going.

When I got to the club, it was night, which was good. The sun needed to flee for fear of what she may be about to see with all of what we had going on. The moon was colder, calculating, and preda-tory. She and I had an accord.

I dragged ass up to the chapel where the boys were already assembled. Requiem set a glass of straight whiskey at my elbow without being asked, and Haint came around with the mylar bag for the phones before going out and dumping the lot on the bar.

Once he was seated, I called our shit to order.

I looked to Haint for the order of things, giving him a nod. I was too fucking tired to think straight and admittedly had a bias on what should be handled first, so I trusted my man to back me.

"The shipment," he said.

"Handled," I said. "But we have some upcoming bumps in the road. There's heat on Paris Island and our boys on that end need to lie low for a minute. We're going to have to dip into our backstock to keep things smooth with Castañeda and his boys. But that brings us right up against and into the next point which should be the Castañeda thing." I looked to Grim. "How'd the rest of that go?" I asked.

"Disappeared the pedo just fine," Grim said with a satisfied smirk. "Proof was delivered to Castañeda's errand boy, and I passed along the crew's compliments on his ceviche recipe," Torment said casually with a wicked smile that matched the undercurrent of his words. "Got a new one try on you boys. Arepas this time. We'll see how that goes."

There were some chuckles around the table and Reaper spoke, which was out of character for him.

"How's Madisyn?" he asked.

Everyone shifted or turned to look his way then back to me.

"Her parents are back in town. They're with her at Memorial now, which is good. I need some fuckin' sleep," I said. "Doctors are optimistic. They said surgery went well, but they've got her in a medically induced coma—" I was interrupted by mutterings and I waited for the chatter to die down. "She's got a skull fracture and swelling on her brain. They don't know about her hand and if she'll be able to paint or do her art thing yet. Way too soon to tell."

It got real quiet and I looked to Haint who nodded.

"Where are we at with that?" I demanded.

Requiem spoke up. "Cops don't know anything," he said. "My contacts at the department say that there were plenty of eyewitnesses, seeing as they attacked her on the fuckin' sidewalk in front of God and everyone. But if anyone took pictures or video, they bounced before the cops got there or they're planning on using it to clout chase on the internet."

I looked to Death who looked grim. "I've been up and down social media. Covered all the major platforms left to right and nothing has shown up yet," he said, and I swore.

"You'd think with all the fuckin' tourists in this town, someone would have videoed something like that."

"Until Madi wakes up, we're at a bit of an impasse," Corvus agreed.

"We got our ear to the ground, waiting for some dumb shit to start bragging, but nothing yet," Fear kicked in.

"Shit." I braced an elbow on the edge of the table and ran a hand over my face, grimacing at the scruff it went over. It was longer than I liked to tolerate.

"Why don't you try and get some sleep, Syn?" Cor asked. "We've got you, brother."

I nodded and said, "Find her fuckin' brother. Find out who he's run debts up with and start shaking down every other crew with any kind of gambling operation in the city and outside it – big or small. I don't fucking care. I think it's our best angle."

"Done," Requiem said.

"Let's call this shit so we can get to work," Grim declared.

I looked down either side of the table for an objection or a holdup, and when there was none, banged the gavel. They all got up.

"Heading home or crashing here?" Requiem asked.

"Here," I told him. "Cops are on thin ice. Dumb cunt pulled me over for not wearing a fucking helmet on the way here. Figure out what's got a bee in the brass's bonnet about us and either throw more money at it or bring it to the table, whichever you think is fastest or more prudent."

"Copy that."

He got up and I knocked back the rest of what was in my glass.

I wandered out to the nearest couch and collapsed on it, face-first, and was out before I finished falling.

Felt like O wasn't out for five goddamn minutes before Corvus was shaking my ass awake and shoving a cup of coffee blacker 'n my soul at me.

I pushed myself up and winced at how stiff I felt, and grated out, "What time is it?"

"Time for you to get up and head back up to Memorial. Had the prospect go back and keep an eye on your woman from the waiting room. Her parents left a while ago. Figured you didn't want to be away too fuckin' long."

I looked out the window, wincing as I sucked down some of the bitter brew. It was dark out.

"How long I been out?" I asked.

"All fuckin' day, dude."

"Shit," I muttered.

"It's not that late, just past sunset, really. Still a couple hours left for visiting hours."

"Fuck their visiting hours," I said.

He snorted and smirked.

"Figured you'd say some shit like that," he said.

"Any progress?" I asked.

"Worlds on notice that you're on a terror," he said. "Other than that? No. Nothing yet."

"Fuck," I muttered.

"Give it time. These assholes always fuck up somehow."

I nodded.

I got up after only half of the cup and took myself straight to the hospital. Fuck showering or any of that shit. It could wait.

Madisyn was just as I left her, except for one major change that let some of the tightness ease out of my chest. She was off the ventilator.

"She going to wake up soon, then?" I asked.

"Hard to say," the nurse said kindly as I took up my woman's hand. "The doctors are talking about weaning her off the drugs in the next few hours to days. Everything is looking better where her head is concerned. She's supposed to have another CT in the morning and if that comes back good, they'll start the process."

"How long does it usually take when they come off the drugs?" I asked.

"Depends on the person. Again, hours to days, sometimes depending on how bad the swelling or injury, although for most it's within the week. She seems like she's doing *really* well on that front. As soon as she's off the medication, it'll honestly be up to her."

I nodded and said, "Thanks for being honest."

"Normally, I'm not so frank, but you look like you could both use it and take it," he said. I nodded but didn't look in his direction. He left, and I sighed and pressed my lips to her skin.

I sat with her all night, and thankfully, no one said fuck all about it. Might have been something to do with my cut. Also, could have had something to do with me just generally being quiet and respectful.

Who fucking knows? I didn't care. All I cared about was that I was still here and Madi was breathing on her own and looked peaceful as she slept.

I couldn't ask for much else in the moment except knowing where her fucking piece of shit brother was and who he'd pissed off enough to make 'em come for my girl.

Chapter Twenty-Nine

Madisyn...

I'd never slept so deeply in my life, and it was a strange sort of sleep. One, where, at times, I was vaguely aware of things going on around me but it was as though it was all layered under thick, wet, wads of black cotton. Heavily buried beneath a weight of things unseen, words unheard, and feelings felt but not understood... as though something was missing in the translation.

It was as though I was deep, deep, underwater, only thicker than water, my consciousness submerged in the deep and the black. So far down but warm instead of cold... I'd always heard the depths of the ocean was a cold place. So cold... but I wasn't. No, I was warm. Warm and lying someplace where it felt as though I floated, as though suspended somewhere between. Between what, I didn't know.

It was hard fighting my way to the surface, as though I was swimming against a tough current, and I couldn't move my left hand, my dominant one, and my left was...

"Come on, baby... come back to me."

Synister's rich, warm, velvet voice beckoned me from somewhere in the darkness.

I sucked in a shuddering breath and pressed on. Finally, *finally*, after way too much effort, I was able to drag my eyelids open to see him.

"Hey," he whispered, and his hand smoothed along the top of my hair, brushing it back off of my forehead.

I instantly felt safe, the choking panic of a moment before gone. If Synister was here, then the only thing I had to worry about was any bullshit from *him*, right?

"Hey," I croaked out and my voice trembled and rasped. I coughed and, *oh God, that hurt!*

He lightly pressed a thumb to my forehead and whispered to me, "Easy! Easy, baby. That's it, deep breaths. Just breathe."

He was being so nice, no, *too* nice and that was enough to make panic seize me.

"What happened?" I croaked. He pressed his lips to my forehead as he leaned over me and I closed my eyes.

"Just rest, for me," he murmured against my skin. I tried to raise my hands to shove him off but a shooting pain went through my right and I cried out.

"Hey, no, don't do that," another voice called out from beside me, and Synister leaned back to reveal the hospital room I was in. I gasped, panic surging in my chest.

"Synister," I whined, and he gave my right hand a gentle squeeze.

He said, "Shhh, it's okay. You're going to be okay."

"What happened? Where's Zeke? Is he okay?"

"Was he there?" Synister asked, his tone plummeting and his already dark eyes somehow growing darker as he looked at me.

"No, it was men, two men, first one white – um, baggy sweatpants, and white tee shirts, a thick gold chain and the new Jordans," I said. "They wanted money. They told me I'd better tell Zeke and then—" I stopped, staring at my mutilated hand and the metal pieces around it and puncturing the skin. A strangled keening, a whining and high-pitched noise of panic filled the room. Synister leaned over me again and pressed my face to his shoulder.

The sounds muffled, and I belatedly realized through the drugs and the haze that the sounds were coming from *me*.

"Okay, that's enough," I heard from someone, a woman, on my right. "I'm going to have to ask you to leave."

I threw my good arm up and around Synister's back, pulling him down over me and clinging to him.

"Baby, breathe," he begged. "You've got to calm down for me."

Calm? I wondered. *How on earth was I expected to be* calm *at a time like this?*

"Hold still. I'm going to give her something in her IV," a voice said, and then, the world grew fuzzy around its edges and I couldn't hold on to him anymore. I couldn't hold on to *anything*. I was drifting, floating, a ghost again...

THE NEXT TIME I WOKE, Synister was gone, and Zeke lunged forward in the seat beside my bed.

"Syn?" he asked. He looked frightening as much as he looked frightened. His eyes were bloodshot from crying, and his hair and clothes were disheveled. I started to cry. He looked so worried. Worried about *me*. We were suddenly kids again, my big brother at my side, my protector from all the world's ills, standing up for me against his rotten friends and telling Mr. Torrance to go fuck himself when he was being creepy toward me when I was thirteen.

"Zeke?" I asked, needing to make sure this was real and not some figment of my imagination.

"Hey! Hey! It's good to see you!" he said and I sniffed.

"Zeke, you better run, or-or-or pay them, or *do something*!" I said and he shushed me.

"Shh, shh, shh, don't worry about any of that right now," he urged and I sniffed again. "It's gonna be okay," he promised. He hugged me, pressing my head into his shoulder as Synister had earlier, but *where was he?*

"I'm scared," I said.

He leaned back to look at me and said, "I know, and I'm gonna fix it. I promise."

I nodded, and he sighed. "I've been a really shit big brother. I was supposed to take care of you and look at you."

He shook his head and started to cry, and I sniffed.

"Don't cry," I said.

He sniffed too and said, "I'm so sorry, Syn, but I'm going to fix it. I'm going to make it right and then I *swear* I'm gonna get help. I'm never going to gamble again. So help me."

"Okay," I said, at a loss for what else to say.

We cried together. When the nurse came in to ask for him to step out so that she could empty my catheter bag and to check on some other things, he went. When the curtain was whisked back, my mom and dad were waiting, but Zeke? Zeke was gone. They said they hadn't seen him, and I worried and wondered, because something felt really final all of a sudden about seeing him, but I couldn't tell you why...

Chapter Thirty

S ynister...

    I'd gone home, gotten myself fresh with a hot shower that I let beat my tight shoulders and back into submission, and then was forced by Torment to sit my ass down and fuckin' *eat* something when all I wanted to do was get back to Memorial and to Madisyn's bedside.

The rest of the guys were out handling the club's various businesses, and when they weren't doing that? They were prowling the streets, asking around and looking for Madisyn's brother. Spooky rang me and I picked up on the first ring.

"Yeah, what is it?" I demanded around a mouthful of frittata.

"The eagle has landed," he said, and I was too riled to fuckin' play games.

"Speak fuckin' plainly, prospect. I'm not in the mood."

"Zeke Reynolds just went in to the ICU here at Memorial," he said.

"Fuck!" I got up, dropping my fork to the counter with a clatter. "Stay on him. I'm on my way."

"You got it," he said, and he ended the call before I could. I shoved my phone into the back pocket of my jeans while Torment looked on from across the counter at me with his eyebrows raised.

"Madi's brother is at Memorial with her," I said.

"Pooky on him?"

"Like white on rice," I said.

"I'll ride with you," Torment said. I didn't say anything, just shrugged into my jacket and cut like it was my armor and I was headed into battle like some dark knight.

"Wait up!" Tor called.

I called back, "Fuckin' catch up!"

I heard him say something and the heavy boot fall of one of the other brothers dogging my steps.

I mounted my bike in the driveway and looked over as Reaper mounted his, which was surprising, only in that it was just Reaper, no Grim. Still, Reaper was solid and reliable – and I would take him.

We rode like hell was on our heels and got to the hospital in record time, piling out the elevator to find Pook in the waiting room.

"Where is he?" I demanded.

"Hasn't come out yet," he said. "Mom and Dad just went in a few minutes ago."

I nodded and jerked my head at Reaper and we went past the desk.

"Hey, wait, you can't go in there! Where are your visitor badges?" someone called. When Reap and I reached Madisyn's room, it was just her mom and her dad with her. *No fucking brother.*

"No more than two." The charge nurse stopped us, and Madi's parents looked up and over at us.

"Sorry," I said. "I just really needed to see her, and that she was doing okay," I said and her troubled blue eyes bored into mine past her mom.

I put up my hands and said, "I've seen her, she's good – we're good. We'll wait our turn," I said gruffly. I turned to go but Reaper was rooted to the spot. He reached up slowly and took off his tinted glasses, and stared fixedly at Madisyn's hand, the swollen and purple one that looked as though it was ready to burst its skin, at the metal spider-legged framework plunged into her flesh, and the crust of blood around them...

I grabbed his arm and he looked me in the eye, his own vivid green ones staring at me flatly, blankly, something stirring behind them that sent the hair raising on the back of my neck.

"We're going for now, brother," I said, and he just stared at me, long and longer.

"Do we have a problem?" the charge nurse demanded.

"First time he's seen it, her hand. Give him a minute to process. My friend here is on the spectrum," I said. To Reaper, I said, "Easy, buddy. She's alive. She'll heal. She's going to be okay."

He just stared. I knew that this required delicacy, and that at any moment, when Reaper looked like that, he could be prone to *wild* and unforgettable amounts of violence.

"Come on," I said, and I gripped the sleeve of his jacket and pulled gently. He didn't so much as twitch, and then it was as though a switch flipped and he moved, turning with me, and walking for the big double doors leading out, the charge nurse walking with us.

"She'll be moving out of intensive care and onto a floor unit tomorrow or the next day," the nurse was saying, trying to be reassuring.

"How do I go about getting her a private room?" I asked.

"I don't know about all that. This isn't a private hospital. It's Memorial."

"What's the best private hospital there is?" I asked.

"Oh, I wouldn't even begin to know about that," she said with a little laugh and stopped as we reached the doors where security was walking up on the other side. The nurse waved them down and they paused. She said, "It's good you care so much about your lady friend, but please, no more stunts like this. Not just for her sake, but the staff and the other patients."

I nodded, and we went out. The desk person said "There they are..."

A little diplomacy and things were smoothed over, but we'd definitely lost her brother. He must have slipped out somehow. Maybe at the other end of the unit through a staff-only doorway or something. *Damnit.*

Reaper looked at me, and he looked dismayed.

"I'm really sorry, Syn. I swear, I was watching that door like a hawk, I didn't miss him coming out," Spooky said.

"It's alright, Pook. Go back to the mansion and get some sleep. Reaper and I will keep watch a while," I said. He nodded and he fucked right off. Didn't have to tell him twice. Reaper and I took a seat. He watched that door like he would burn a hole clean through it with his gaze.

It'd been five days since Madi was admitted. We'd been taking watch in shifts, but Spook was doing the majority of the watching and transporting her friend back and forth from the college. He'd been taking on the bulk of things like a champ and I'd remember it. I had to hand it to the kid, he was fuckin' loyal and that was good. Even now, he begrudgingly nodded and fucked off back to the mansion like I ordered.

I sighed and settled in for a long day of waiting around with my thumb up my ass, but I didn't have to wait too terribly long. Her parents came out about twenty minutes after they'd gone in.

They came over to where Reaper and I were sitting. Her father asked, "Do you want to tell me what that was all about?"

"No," I answered smoothly, and he looked bewildered. Madisyn's mother made a scoffing noise and I raised an eyebrow.

"I could tell them not to let you in, you know," she said and I snorted.

"Madisyn is an adult and can decide who is and isn't allowed in to see her. There's nothing wrong with her cognitive ability. She can override anything you have to say and she should at this point."

"What's that supposed to mean?" her father demanded, and I stood up smoothly in one easy motion.

"It means she's told me all I need to know about you," I said.

"About how you never listen to her, diminish her feelings, and how you handed your son all the power but Madi all the responsibility. It means that I hold you and your spoiled rich kid son responsible for her condition in there," I said. No mercy. No quarter.

"I beg your pardon!" her mother gasped.

"You have a lot of nerve." Her father's voice was low and held a thread of anger. It was impotent, though. No one in this city held more power than I did, and I knew it.

"More than you," I said blandly. "You can be as pissed as you want. I don't particularly give a damn. But you need to really sit with what I've said here and marinate in it. You need to know, Madisyn would have never even met me if it hadn't been for your son getting in over his head and her riding to the rescue to bail him out of trouble once again. Something that was *your* job as his parents, not hers."

On that note, I marched up to the desk and said, "Micah Devlin and Samuel Irwin for Madisyn Reynolds."

"Thank you." The desk clerk asked for ID and we provided it. Before long, we had our visitors' stickers and were marching back through the ICU's doors, back to my woman's side.

She was sitting up in bed, but her eyes were closed, the scrape up high on her cheekbone angry and scabbed over now, the bruising of her raccoon eye shiners deep shadows around her sockets. Reaper went around to her right side while I took the seat by her left and took up her hand in mine.

Her eyes popped open and she sucked in a sharp breath, turning her head in my direction.

"It's like Grand Central Station in here," she joked weakly.

"Yeah, well, pretty sure your parents are going to be urging you to see less of me in the very near future. Just thought I'd make mention in case your mom makes good on her threat to try and make it so I can't come back and see you anymore."

"Oh, no," she said faintly. "What did you do?" The dismay was stronger than her voice which sounded so weary.

"Told them the truth. That I hold them accountable for not

keeping your brother in check as parents are supposed to and leaving too much of a burden on you."

I kissed the backs of her fingers and she let out a bitter laugh.

"You aren't wrong, but there was likely a more diplomatic way to put things..." she sighed.

"Fuck diplomacy. I've been diplomatic enough today. Isn't that right, Reaper?"

Reaper grunted from where he was bent at the waist, peering at Madi's mangled hand like he was wanting the metal contraption piercing her flesh to give up its secrets.

She sighed again and her lashes fluttered into crescents against her under eye, and fluttered there.

I was quiet a time, just committing her lovely face, even as battered, and bruised as it was, to memory.

"You in a lot of pain?" I asked. She nodded and took a deep breath, letting it out slowly through her mouth.

"I'm sorry," she murmured. "I'm just so tired."

"Sleep is how we heal," I said, and she nodded faintly.

Reaper gave me a meaningful look and I nodded.

She opened her eyes as though she felt it through where my hand held hers, and she asked, "What?"

"I hate to ask, not because I don't need to know, but more because it might bring you pain... but the men who hurt you, what do you remember? What can you tell me about them? Is there anything else?"

I pressed another kiss to the backs of her fingers and she closed her eyes, her brow furrowing, but not from pain this time. No, she was thinking and thinking hard.

"One of them was clean shaven with blond hair and brown eyes. The other had long hair, slicked back, and in a curly ponytail. The blond one was dressed like a wannabe gangster type, the white tee, gray sweats, big chunky chain around his neck and the new Jordans."

"Okay, good. That's good," I encouraged. Yes, she'd already told me but I was hoping for more detail with the retelling. It was obvious to me she didn't remember the first round, but that was okay. She'd been coming out of medication... at least I hoped that was what it was.

"The other one, the one with his hair slicked back, he had one of those pencil-thin beard-mustache combo things going on with his face, and brown eyes, too, but also some gold teeth, only like white gold maybe – or silver. Not yellow gold and they were weird, like not a whole gold tooth, but like his canines were all metal. The eye teeth and the front teeth were just outlined in it? Is that crazy?"

"No, baby. That's good. Do you remember what he was wearing?"

"Black shoes. Like heavy, boots maybe, with khaki-colored cargo pants over them and a white tee with a bomber jacket over it. I remember thinking it was way too hot for a jacket."

It was likely he was concealing a gun with it, but I didn't tell her that. Reaper looked like a lightbulb went off with the description, and I didn't say anything. I was too intent on Madisyn getting things out.

"Anything else?" I asked.

"He's the one that stomped on my hand," she said and sniffed, looking at the swollen ruin of it in its surgically placed metal brace. "They don't know if I'll ever be able to hold a pencil or a paintbrush again."

"You will, kitten. You have to believe that," I said. "Don't cry, baby." I got up and hugged her close, leaning way over her bed to do it.

"You'll paint again," I said. "I'll do whatever it takes, hire the best doctors, the best physical therapists. Whatever you need."

"It means so much that you're even here," she said, her voice breaking on her sobs into the front of my cut.

"I take care of what's mine," I told her. She nodded against me, and I just kept holding her tight.

Her nurse came in and we broke apart.

"Well, Madisyn, your scan from this morning came back much

improved. You're doing well enough that we can move you out of ICU."

She smiled weakly and said, "Thank you." She held my hand with her good one as though it were her lifeline, and I held her hand back, determined she should feel every ounce of my intent to both help her heal and keep her safe.

～

I DIDN'T WANT to leave her, but she wanted to see her friends, Valory and Levi, who were waiting for her out in the waiting room. Reaper was getting antsy, and so I reluctantly left and nodded to Valory. I even begrudgingly nodded to Levi as they passed us to go in and see her. Valory had Madisyn's purse and a bag of her things with her, and I was glad for that. Hopefully, Madi's phone was with the rest of the items and when they had her moved, she would be able to text me.

I turned to Reaper once we were outside. "That description ring a bell?" I asked.

He waffled his hand back and forth, meaning yes, but no. I had to think that yes it rang a bell, but no, he couldn't place where he'd seen the motherfucker or what crew or whatever he was from.

"You gonna fuck him up as hard as I think you are, we get a hold of him?" He stared at me impassively, and I nodded.

"Thank you," I said and he nodded once.

We rode to the club. By the time we got there, Madi had texted, ***They're moving me today. I'll text you the room number when they do. Texting with my non-dominant hand is hard.***

I shot a placating text back and told her I would be there, but quickly turned my attention to the business at hand with who we had here.

"Big brother gave us the slip. Madi gave us a good description of her attackers, rang a bell for Reaper, but still no luck," I told

261

Requiem, just as my phone went off in my hand. I looked down at the screen and picked up.

"Yo, Specter, what's up?" I asked.

"You're not going to believe this shit," he said, and I heard him exhale.

"Spit it the fuck out," I grated.

"Bro just showed up looking for a place at the table," he said.

"What'd you tell him?" I asked.

"I gave it to him," he said. "I know you're looking, and I know you'd want me to keep him here. So get your ass down here before he wises up and bounces."

"On our way." I ended the call and filled the guys in that were here.

"Madisyn's brother just showed up to the River Street poker game. Specter gave him a seat at the table. Get the van. Reaper, you're with me."

Reaper fell into step beside me even as Requiem called after us, "Copy that!" about the van.

We rode out to River Street and pulled up the cobblestone path to where we could park our bikes, lucky that a space was even open. It was thick with tourists out here today and I realized belatedly that it had to be Friday or something already. I didn't know. I couldn't be sure. All the hours and days had blurred together since Madi's hospitalization.

My rage was building with every step that carried me to the side door to my own operation, and Specter looked practically luminous with his fucking excitement at the look on my face. He swept the door open, practically giddy, and dove in behind me and Reaper, shutting it tight behind us.

I didn't even break stride. I just marched up to the table and snatched Madisyn's brother by the front of his fuckin' shirt.

"Come here, you weasly little shit!" I barked. I couldn't contain myself anymore. I fucking lost it and started *waling* on him.

Players jumped up from the table, poker chips rattled and scattered, and over the sounds was the rhythmic pistoning of my arm coming back, my fist surging forward, and the grunts and wheezing of her brother as I smashed my fist *repeatedly* into his face. I punched until sweat popped out on my brow, my breath came in ragged gasps, and my gloved fist *ached* from the damage *it* was starting to take as I fucking wailed on him.

I dropped him limp and moaning to the unfinished concrete floor and barked my proclamation to all standing in shellshocked silence around us. "You didn't see shit, you didn't hear shit, you sure as fuck don't *say* shit or I'm gonna find you and fuckin' *kill you!* You understand me?"

I looked around at each and every motherfucker in attendance, and none of them looked like they were feeling froggy.

"Game over," I said between heaving breaths. "Get the fuck out. You'll be compensated for the ruined game."

My boys escorted the three other players to a different exit from the one we'd come through. I looked down at Zeke's mewling and whining pathetic self and told Reaper, "Get him up and secure him. I got questions."

This shit was just beginning for him, and it wasn't going to end well.

It took a while before he was conscious enough to be of any use to me, and all it served to do was piss me off more at how fuckin' *weak* he was. I sat across from him, the boys adjusting lights into his face to make this interrogation a real one and keep him disoriented.

"Wake the fuck up," I demanded, and kicked his foot. "I got questions."

He jerked his head up and squinted at the light. His nose was still leaking blood, his lips so puffy and swollen from my tender mercies, it was almost pitiful.

He mumbled a bunch of shit I couldn't make out, but his tone was begging. I was all out of fucks to give at this point about him. Not even for Madi, as by this point, he was a detriment to her. Clearly. I sniffed.

"Who you owe money to?" I demanded.

"You," he mumbled.

"Who *else* do you owe money to, you dumb piece of shit?"

"The Carpino's brothers," he mumbled, and I scowled. Then, the list just kept going like five different motherfuckers deep.

What the fuck?

"I got it," Specter muttered and he indeed had written them all down. I looked to Reaper, who gave a nod and went out – likely to text Grim on whatever job site he may or may not be on.

I trusted Reaper and Grim to find the motherfuckers specific to Madisyn's pain and have them trussed like a pair of Christmas turkeys, waiting for my specific attentions. For now, I had her brother in front of me and some tough decisions to make... which for me? Weren't tough at all.

"Req," I intoned and he looked to me. We got up and went out the side door. He leaned in to hear me as I pitched my voice low to fly under the radar of the babble of tourists walking by.

"Finish working him over until he hits his expiration date," I said. "Dump his ass in the river, no traces. We'll make these two mother-fuckers in particular he owes and pay the cops. They found him, took him out, disappeared – case closed," I said.

He nodded once and went back inside.

I could trust that it would be handled. It would be tricky with how active River Street was out here, but it *would* be handled.

I was sure his body would eventually be found in the river, and Madisyn and her family? They would feel pain, sure. They would mourn him, and miss him, and it would be another hard thing she would have to go through... but after? The pain would dull, and scar over. But looking at this whole fucking mess, I knew if we gave him the opportunity to live, it would just get messier. The heartbreak would be prolonged. She would always be a fuckin' target and that I couldn't fucking abide.

I decided in my own twisted fucking way, that I loved her too much to keep her on this fucking hell ride, but I knew she wouldn't see it this way, she wouldn't understand. So, we would handle this quietly. Permanently. So that she wouldn't have to. So that she could focus on healing, and on *her* life. I knew as long as big brother was around and fucking up, which just by coming here and trying this shit was a mark of what an irreversible fuckup he was, that she would always be the responsible one. She would always be there to clean up his mess, and she didn't have to. Not when I was here to spare her the anguish, and the hills and valleys of it all.

Did it make me a bastard? Yeah. Yeah, it did. I was alright with that, though. I would walk through hellfire coated in gasoline for her, and I was hell-bent on freeing her from the golden chains she'd been bound with, in favor of silk and velvet ribbons fair, to adorn her like the goddess she was.

I got back on my bike and sighed. Reaper's was already gone. As I sat there, the flow of humanity rushing up the street, people milling about and taking photos, crawling like ants up the hillside and steps, I felt like there was a light at the end of the tunnel on this particular saga... which felt mighty fine.

I took myself back to the hospital, to Madisyn, and to see the rest of this through.

Chapter Thirty-One

Madisyn...

My parents were doting to an extent, but I was also getting a lot of, I don't know... basically reprimands? For not telling them how bad things had gotten with Zeke, which wasn't *fair*. I had tried telling them, over and over again. But they hadn't wanted to hear it, brushing me and blowing me off, and basically saying that Zeke was an adult capable of being an adult and making adult decisions even if they were poor ones. But still. Somehow, some way, it was my fault for not speaking up sooner or whatever and their contradictory nature was *exhausting*.

Synister, by comparison, was so *nice* when he was around. Reminding me how I would have *bled* once upon a time just for someone to stand up for me, shelter me, and to hold me the right way.

He may not have said it out loud, but everything about his *actions* screamed that he cared. That he maybe even loved me, because he was always *there*. His visits long, as I healed in the hospital, work a seemingly secondary thing to his presence by my side. He and his men positively doted on me – Torment sending healthy and delicious meals, balanced for holistic healing of my injuries. Foods rich in vitamins, minerals, and calcium for the formation of strong bones, and also with anti-inflammatory properties, and so much better than anything I could have gotten on the hospital trays.

Synister insisted on only the best care, flying in specialists and doctors that were top in their field, to address my hand and give me the best possible chance at regaining full functionality in it.

But most importantly? He was there to hold me when they found Zeke's body in the river.

He'd been beaten so badly as to be unrecognizable, with multiple facial bone fractures and ribs that had been splintered and punctured the soft tissue, macerating his lungs and heart. The autopsy and investigation pointed to the fact that my brother had died horribly, and the leading suspects in the case were on the run somewhere. They believed, it was the same men who had attacked me, although they hadn't identified them yet.

Synister had been there when the police had come to talk to me and take my parents outside my hospital room. He had held me while I'd cried, had climbed into bed beside me, had sheltered me with his body, and had given me a place of solace to process all and everything that had cascaded and swamped me, burying me like an avalanche and suffocating me with misery all while I begged and pleaded for some unknown God to tell me, please, what had I done to deserve *any of this?*

Synister had been my rock through it all, holding me tightly, kissing my forehead, being my comfort and my shelter from my parents wailing and sudden overbearing and obnoxious overprotec- tiveness. Like they had suddenly realized they had a daughter and that I'd mattered too, when all they'd done was talk about Zeke and where was Zeke, and how they hoped nothing happened to Zeke. All while so much had happened to *me* and like I wasn't right here, lying in the hospital with my shattered and broken dreams falling from my mangled fingertips.

In that time, in that space, Synister had been my champion. When it'd come time for my release from the hospital? He'd been there as well, giving me someplace to go that would give me the best chance to *breathe,* out from the suffocating feeling my mother's demands and overbearing nature had wrought.

"Come home with me. Stay with me. I need you," he'd told me and I'd fallen into the idea, and gratefully so.

He'd been with me through my brother's funeral, had held me as we'd laid him to rest at Hillcrest Abbey East Cemetery. Watching his gleaming casket slide into the vault had been a special hell, and I'd crumbled, but Synister had been at my back and had lovingly held strong and been my strength throughout.

My parents, I felt, hated him for it. But all it did was build my resentment stronger, thrusting rebar into the wet cement of it as it hardened and I turned from them further.

Weeks went by, and my surgery to remove the apparatus from my hand came and went. Synister was there, as I went back and when I woke. If it wasn't him with me when the physical therapist came to the house, it was Reaper who was so silently sweet, rubbing scar-diminishing ointment into my hand at night with care, easing the stiffness from it. I was determined to get pencil and paintbrush alike back into my hand.

I had passed what finals I had taken before the attack, and had passed more belatedly when I'd healed enough to take them, my professors understanding and incredibly patient, which also had the tang of Synister to it. Although, I didn't know how.

All I knew was that in the mansion, I felt safe, and that when I left, it was with him by my side, or one of the other men... mostly Spooky, who drive me to see Valory and Levi on occasion.

Valory took some getting used to coming around the big house, but even she eventually grew comfortable enough to walk over on her own, just to see me. We could be found in the living room, the big television descended out of the ceiling where it was hidden, and our romantic and sappy girl shows and movies playing, to which the guys made fun of us, but only good naturedly, and none begrudged us the time in front of the screen.

They always laughingly said that when the estrogen levels reached critical mass within the home, they could always fuck off to the club to get right.

When it came to the club and their activities, it was very much don't ask and don't tell. Synister and I simply worked on that paradigm and it maintained the peace. It was worth a little blissful ignorance on my part for the way he moved inside and over me at night. At how safe, and how he carefully cultivated things to maintain my peace so that I could heal.

It was near Halloween and my upcoming birthday when he, Reaper, and Grim found me reading and fiddling with my highlighter with my hand. I tended to stretch and move this way and that to keep it from stiffening as much as to work on my dexterity as part of the recovery from the damage.

"Hey, kitten," he'd said softly from the doorway, and I'd looked up.

"Hey." At the serious looks on their faces, I felt mine fall. "What's wrong?"

He slipped onto the couch beside me and took my book from my lap, passing it to Grim who set it aside.

"We need to have a moment of pretenses stripped away," he said. I cocked my head to the side, as Grim sat on the coffee table in front of us and Reaper hovered, standing nearby.

I looked up to the silent man who I considered my friend and who had done so much to help in my healing so that I may one day continue with my deepest love and passion, my art. The look he gave me from behind his tinted glasses was... well, it was as serious as I had ever seen him.

"What's going on?" I asked softly.

"Truthfully, I need to know something," Synister said, reaching out and chasing some of my hair behind my ear, his fingertip raising tingles along my skin and setting butterflies off in my stomach as it ever did, even these many weeks stretching into months later.

"Go on," I murmured. "You're scaring me a little."

He shook his head. "No reason to ever be scared again, baby. I've got you, you know that... but..." he searched my face.

"Not helping," I said. "But what?"

"The men who attacked you, the ones who killed your brother," Grim said gently, and I looked to him, my eyes going wide.

"What about them?" I asked and my breath had fled, stolen by his words.

"They've resurfaced. We have it on good authority they're back around, and I need your feelings on some things," Synister said.

"What things?" I asked apprehensive.

He swallowed hard, and said, "On do you want the cops to handle it or do you want me to?"

I leaned back in my seat and stared at him, searching his face. I swallowed hard and thought about it, like I'd learned from him... about the implications of what he was asking. All the way through as far and as wide as I could consider, but under it all, I also had to *trust*. After living with him, sharing his bed, his gentle and tender touches and growing to understand his ways... trust him I did. I knew that he was smarter than me. I knew that he was far more ruthless, far more calculating, and that he had an entire hive mind of his men to aide him and to buy myself a little time on such a momentous decision on my part. I started talking, babbling, in the guise of talking it through like he'd shown me.

"If the police handle it, there could be a chance that there would be no justice," I murmured. "I know that. I know how things work."

He nodded once, his chin dipping to the black tee that covered his chest and raising back up, his dark eyes never leaving mine.

"It doesn't feel fair asking you to—" I stopped, knowing full well the weight of two lives rested in my hands and I looked down to the shiny, flat, pink scars that marred the hand that they'd so callously tried to destroy. My heart felt heavy in my chest and like it had failed to stop beating. Like it just filled and filled with blood, ballooning until it pressed painfully out against the cage of my ribs, bloated with my anguish and my grief.

"I would very much like for you to handle it," I said, the gravity of my words dropping like stones into a well, altering me forever. I couldn't say that I had any regrets about that.

I swallowed hard and the feeling as though I couldn't breathe didn't last nearly as long as I thought it should.

In a flash, Reaper had gone. I looked up at the blur of movement, at the back of him as he strode away.

"Vengeance is mine, sayeth my lady," Grim said with a wink, and he got up and went after Reaper.

Synister leaned forward and captured the back of my head with his hand, stroking tenderly down the side of my neck with his thumb as he brought my forehead to his lips.

"Thank you," he murmured against my skin reverently. I knew that as much as I trusted in him for this awful task, that he had put an awful lot of faith in *me*. I was reminded how this... *this* is what I had always wanted.

A partner. A lover and best friend who could confide in me and who that I could confide in. That we could trust in one another beyond measure. I just had never imagined it would be with things so incredibly *dark*. But fate had brought us here, and I was committed as he was committed to me.

I cupped the side of his face and drew back, raising my eyes to his and telling him gravely, "Just don't make any mistakes, and you come back to me."

"Always," he promised, and his mouth crushed down over mine.

I kissed him back and plunged my tongue past his lips to twine against his, and he groaned into my mouth. He tore his lips from mine with an impassioned breath and growled out, "To be continued," before he rose and strode from the room, leaving me once more to handle my business. I couldn't help but feel as though he was the sword of my vengeance but the wickedness of this? It was all mine.

I sighed, and the breath was a cleansing thing, as I reached over and pulled my schoolbook back into my lap and took up my high-lighter from the crack between its pages, resuming tapping the capped end against the edge of the book, stretching my injured hand as a certain peace settled over me once more. Only this peace? It was the mantle of death, and not one, but likely two and neither was I even a little bit sad about.

I suppose this was what it felt like to fully enter one's villain arc, or whatever, and I had to say... it was nothing short of *empowering*. I very much so liked the taste of this power.

Chapter Thirty-Two

S ynister...
   I was in love with my dark queen as never before when
   she'd bequeathed me her permission to deal with the two
fucks who'd so maimed her.

They had no idea what was coming. The Wraiths were out, the
hunt was on, and they wouldn't live the night. The suffering would
be grand, but we had to find them first. I wouldn't rest until they were
in our clutches.

I rode out with Grim and Reaper, and we made for the marina
and the slip with the speedboat. Requiem, Fear, Death, and Specter
were out there stalking our prey and would need us to be ready for
the handoff. Corvus and Hangman were standing by at the cemetery,
waiting near the forklifts to open the vault.

Haint, Revenant, Shade, and Spooky were all out there too, on
the lookout or ready to cause mayhem in other parts of the city as a
means to distract the cops who definitely drew the line on looking the
other way on murder. Especially when, to their mind, they had the
suspects to a high-profile murder of one of the city's elites in their
crosshairs.

Everyone had it out for these two motherfuckers. It was just a question of who got there first, and I guaranteed, it was going to be me.

There was a lot of trust, a lot of patience, and a lack of real communication going on between me and the rest of the boys, which is the way we preferred it. Coordinating something like premeditated murder required us to operate like a well-oiled machine to negate any trail back to us. It was something we were good at – making mother-fuckers disappear.

It was late and under the cover of darkness when the van pulled into the marina lot. Requiem's familiar whistle let us know the cargo had been secured. It'd been in part a trade in favors to Castañeda that this was even possible.

Felt like the Castañeda thing months back had been a gift from the gods for all of a pain in the ass it'd been, but it sure as hell was paying off now with how we had these douchebags in our tender loving care.

"Kill the cameras," I said, and Grim jogged up the dock to go up into the marina office, which I conveniently owned with one of my shell corps, to do just that.

When he reappeared, he passed the keys to Specter who jogged the way to the office to reengage them as soon as our wake had settled.

"Let's see what we've got," I said with a savage grin. Requiem opened up the sliding side door to the Sprinter van with a flourish, revealing both men trussed up with duct tape, their heads wrapped in it around the eyes and the mouth, arms behind their back wrapped from elbow to wrist, legs bound from knee to ankle.

I chuckled and said, "What'd you do? Use the whole roll?"

"Two," Requiem said. "One a piece."

Grim laughed as they struggled and tried to scream from around the tape.

"Let's get 'em in the boat."

Wordlessly, Reaper stepped forward and, already in his Tyvek suit over his clothes, he lifted the first wriggling man over his shoulder and resolutely marched him to the boat where he tossed him like a sack of potatoes onto the waiting plastic covering everything. He came back for the second bastard as Grim and I bid farewell to the rest of the boys who'd done their part.

"We'll hose and bleach the van and see you guys back at the house later," Requiem said. With a nod, I trailed Grim to the boat.

We set off up the river to the back side of Bonaventure where Hangman and Corvus met us.

"You boys have fun," Corvus said as he leaned against one of the forklifts, and we carried our quarry down into the crypt.

"This is going to be a motherfucking delight," Grim said with a grin.

Depended on what you were into, but he wasn't fucking wrong.

We were suited up and ready for the long haul tonight, both these boys tied to chairs and waiting for Reaper's attentions.

All that was missing was Torment to put the chef's kiss on this little get-together, but he was on some yacht off St. Simon's, making bank for an indeterminate amount of time. Such was life for a private chef.

We peeled the tape slow and left their faces for last, blaring lights only when the lid had been dropped on us up top. We wouldn't get got again until the next night, but we were ready for it. We'd had things prepared down here for a *while* now, for the eventuality that we would be hosting these two as our guests.

They were good and panicked by the time the tape came off their faces.

"So, which one of you smashed my woman's hand?" I asked casually.

"He did!" Blondie declared instantly, and I felt myself smile a nasty thing. I said, "There's one of your problems, boys. You could run, but you couldn't hide, and ain't none of it work when there's no loyalty."

"Oh, God!" the dark one said, and I felt my nasty smile turn up right into a nasty grin and I let my crazy show.

"Tell you what," I said. "You go ahead and scream for your god as long and as loud as you'd like, there, bud... and when he shows up? We'll stop."

His eyes went really wide after that, and I let my expression fall, leaning way back in my seat and crossing my arms over my chest.

"So, is what this happy bastard saying true? Did you do that to my woman's hand? Because what you say next is going to determine how much and how slow you die."

He stared at me in abject horror and boy did that just tickle me pink. I was in for a good night. A really good night, making both these boys scream.

"Yes," he finally said and I nodded.

"Good boy," I said. "Reaper..."

Reaper stepped forward and Grim wrestled dude's first hand flat onto the table between us.

"A joint at a time. Move slow," I said. He started screaming alright, and begging for his god... but wouldn't you know it? That motherfucker never showed up.

Chapter Thirty-Three

Madisyn...

It wasn't until much later that I woke to the sound of some of the men downstairs. I'd been rattling around in the large house all alone and had taken some solace in the fact that none of the others were here, which had meant that they were with Synister. That meant that they had Synister's back.

My worry for him had abated and I'd gone back to sleep in our large bed, the door standing open to the hallway, waiting for his return.

After more than two months, or maybe three, of living under his roof, I'd had to admit that he had been right. That I could trust him when he said that I was safe among the rest of the men of the Iron Wraiths. That I belonged to him and that *meant* something.

I drifted off again, and it wasn't until late morning that I woke. I woke to find Synister's side of the bed still cold. He hadn't returned to me. Not yet.

I got up, brushed my teeth and showered, then dressed for the day. I sighed and stared at the unfinished paintings of Colonial Park and Bonaventure, then looked down at my hand, holding it out and staring at the scars, breathing carefully as I willed the trembling in it to stop.

It was nothing to do with the injury that I trembled so badly, but rather the trauma. After some time of some steady breathing, the trembling started to still.

I wanted so badly to finish one or the both of them for Reaper, who so desperately and sweetly seemed to want me to return to my art, and *oh*, how I wanted to, too.

The last painting I'd finished of Forsyth fountain from the balcony's view was dried and sitting on my easel, which Synister had set up for me again in his room, at my insistence.

I wanted to wake up every day to my paints and my art waiting for me to take up my brush again. I wanted that reminder every day in front of me to strive for. I wanted my life back so *badly*, it wasn't even funny. But today, feeling the absence of Synister in his grand house, I realized I didn't want to go back.

I didn't want my life *back* the way it was. I just wanted my ability to do my art back. I wanted desperately my ability to close and latch the door on the painful parts of my recent past.

I took the Forsyth painting down and set it against the floor by the Colonial Park painting and took Colonial Park's back up, setting it in the frame and ignoring the painful stretching and tugging as I manipulated my hand in the simple task of securing the painting back in its place. Something I had done hundreds of times if not more and had always taken for granted before.

I texted Valory and Levi and asked them to meet me in Colonial Park, and they readily agreed. Then, taking up my pack and packing everything neatly and carefully away, I went into the closet Synister shared with me now, and pulled one of my most favorite articles of clothing out from where I had reverently stashed it.

The white, paint-stained shirt I'd pilfered from him and ruined. The one he'd told me to keep and to wear to protect my clothes.

I slipped it on over my jeans and the tank top I wore, and pulling my hair into a high ponytail in the bathroom, I looked at myself in the mirror and took a deep breath and let it out slowly.

"Are you really going to try this?" I asked my reflection, and my somber countenance reflected back at me. I forced an optimistic smile onto my face and said with a bravery I didn't feel, "Of course you are."

I took up my pack and slipped out into the hall and down the steps quietly, listening for any of the men from the club.

Content that all was quiet, I slipped out of the front of the mansion on my own and turned to face Whitaker.

The sun was shining, there were people walking by, and the sound of cascading water and lazy early autumn insects soothed my soul as I just stood, *alone*, and drank it all in.

Eventually, I forced my feet into motion, skipping down the front steps and out the front gate, turning and closing it behind me.

"Hey!" I looked up sharply to Specter standing in the doorway to the mansion. "You good?" he called down.

I waved and nodded and he nodded once.

"Got your phone?" he called, and I pulled it out of my back jeans' pocket and held it up. "Alright!" He waved me off and I struck out up the sidewalk in the direction of Monterey Square and the historic district beyond.

"Madisyn!" Valory called out in a singsong voice, and I waved to her and to Levi who were waiting outside the front gate to the park.

"Hey, girl! You're looking good!" Levi called as I got closer. Valory held out my favorite drink from the coffee shop just across the street and further up on the corner. I smiled and hugged first her and then Levi.

"Thank you!" I cried.

Valory said, "So, Synister let you off the ol' ball and chain, huh?"

I gave her a reproachful look and said, "It's not even like that, and you know it."

"I know. I just miss living with my best friend," she said with a dejected sigh.

I sniffed, sipping some of my drink and said, "I know, but, hey, I'm here now. I'm going to need some moral support for this. So let's go."

"Okay, what are we doing?" she asked.

"I'm going to try and finish my painting," I said.

She gasped and looked both floored and excited. "Shut the fuck up! Nuh-uh! You're ready?"

I swallowed hard and said, "I don't know, but we're about to find out. This could end in disaster so be prepared."

I made a funny face and Levi put his hand on my shoulder.

"We got you," he said, and we headed into the park and over to where we'd drawn and painted that day that felt so very long ago, last summer.

Levi and Valory helped me set up my easel. I didn't really need the help, but they insisted, arguing that it saved my hand for the real work of laying paint on canvas board.

I mean, they weren't wrong, but still.

I buttoned up Synister's shirt to protect my clothes and took an intrepid breath, putting some splotches of my oils out of the tube onto my palate, and that was *really* uncomfortable. Squeezing the tubes, I mean.

It took me a while to will my hand to stop shaking. It felt stiff and awkward to hold the brush. A gesture or movement that had just a few months ago felt as secondary and natural to me as breathing suddenly felt cumbersome and out of joint so to speak.

"You've got this," Levi said, and Valory said, "I believe in you!"

I laughed out loud and took the plunge, dipping bristles into paint, and made the first stroke.

Levi and Valory jolted me, both bursting out into loud cheers and applause, and stepped back and laughed to keep from crying. It was nothing, just one little shaky brushstroke but it *felt so good*.

I'm afraid I wasn't good for very long, having to stop and stretch my cramping hand and shake it out *often*, Levi patiently listening to me and massaging my previously mangled and still healing hand regularly to keep me going. I wouldn't give up and I wouldn't surrender. Even though it took me probably two to three times longer than it would have before I'd been hurt, and even though my painting looked as though an older person with palsy or a starting-to-decline Parkinson's patient had attempted it, I'd painted something. It was imminently fixable with time, patience, and more sessions but most importantly, *you could tell what it was.*

It wasn't perfect, by any means, but it wasn't *awful* either.

I stood with my friends and cried happy tears as the light started to fail and we laughed and cried together in that cathartic and healing way that I just needed.

"I wish Zeke could see it," I said.

Levi sighed and said, "He can. Believe my pops sees everything I do. They're all knowing and all seeing now, Syn."

"Levi's right," Valory said, laying her head on my left shoulder.

"Hey!" We turned and one of the city officials in charge of locking up the gates called out to us from the nearest one.

"Sorry!" I called back, and he waved again. We quickly packed everything back up into my backpack and scurried out the gate so that he could lock it.

"Thank you," I said to him for being patient and kind while waiting for us.

"It's no problem," he said.

I said my farewells to my friends and we parted ways. I took a leisurely pace back to the mansion.

Synister still wasn't back yet, but Torment was and he made us all dinner, who was here, while we laughed and talked in the kitchen.

"So, where did you go?" Specter asked, finally.

I smiled and said, "To paint."

"Yeah?" Torment asked, flipping the stir fry he had going in a wok on the stove.

"Yeah," I said.

"How'd it go?" Spooky asked, and I felt my smile grow.

"Better than expected," I answered honestly.

"Right on!" Torment cheered and the topic was dropped for the time being.

That night, I took a hot bath and soaked my hand in the hot water laden with Epsom salts. It ached and it hurt fiercely. I would certainly rest it tomorrow, but at its core, I decided it was a good pain.

That night, I set my easel back up in the room so I would be greeted with it in the morning, leaving the painting of Colonial Park on it. One or two more sessions and I may be able to call it done, but it definitely needed refinement.

I went to bed feeling victorious that night. It was sometime in the wee hours of the morning that I woke to Synister coming to bed, freshly showered, and smelling divine.

I twisted in my semi-roused state to twine my arms around him and for my lips to find his in the dark. He was nude, and that was fine, so was I, waiting for him. Oh how I loved how his warm hands slid over my skin.

"Mm," he grunted in approval as I moved beneath him, and wrapped my legs around him, his chuckle low and deep as I pulled him down over the top of me. He settled his weight over me like I liked.

"Fuck me," I whispered into his ear, before catching his earlobe between my teeth, grazing it gently.

"Planned on it," he murmured back, sliding his hard cock against my folds, his mouth finding mine in the dark, as he plunged his tongue past my lips and teeth and devoured me from the mouth down. I arched, and he pressed down over the top of me, and *oh, how I loved that*. How I loved to be pressed into the bed under his muscular body, his pelvis grinding against mine under the soft caress of moonlight through the window.

"Please," I begged when he'd teased me for too long. "Please, please, oh, God, *please!*"

He chuckled, a sound deep and indicative of his namesake, as he rolled his hips. His cock slid in my wetness, before finding purchase and starting its slow and controlled slide into me.

Oh, yes! Like that. Just like that... I thought to myself, as he worked his thick length into my wet and waiting pussy. I bit gently along his shoulder and the side of his neck, his hair sable soft beneath one hand as I softly cradled his head and urged his mouth to the side of my neck. My other hand gripped his ass and tried to urge him in faster and harder, but he wasn't about that. No, he would do me in his own time, and he *loved* to drive me crazy.

It was as though sex was the last bastion of which he allowed himself to do so, and I was strangely addicted to his antagonistic brand of sex. Where he withheld, withheld, withheld until I was almost ready to throw him off the top of me in my maddened state of sheer frustration at which point, he would give me all that I could handle and then some!

"Hang on to me, baby," he urged. He withdrew only to plunge so deep inside me, I thought sure he aimed to split me right down the middle, but *oh God!* It felt so fucking *good*.

He rolled his hips, almost swishing his cock back and forth inside me and *oh shit*, the things that motion *did to me*. The way I felt that I would come right then and there. And how much and how hard I tried not to, but *shit, fuck, goddamn*, it was so close, but I knew if I just held off just a little bit longer...

"Mm, fuck, baby, that's it," he praised. I loved it when he dirty-talked me like that. Loved how he hooked an arm behind my leg and folded me damn near in half and loved even more how that made the angle of him inside me so fucking *deep* it almost hurt. He combined that deep, deep, angle with that roll to his hips, and I made these feral sounds, my body tightening under his like a cord stretched and about to snap. When it did, when I *did*, I cried, "Oh, yes!" and enjoyed that shining fall so much, knowing that he would still be atop me, he would still be fucking me, all the way through it to the very end.

What was different this time was when he finished, his thrusts becoming uneven, his body bucking him out of rhythm on a cry of, "God, I love you!" I froze, solid and uncertain beneath him, as he brought his mouth down to mine and kissed my suddenly cold still lips, stopping and drawing back to look at me.

"Kitten, what's wrong?" he asked me, and I reached up, capturing his face between my hands and asked, almost afraid the answer would be "no."

"Did you mean that?"

He pushed himself up off me further and searched my face. Hr said, "Would any man kill for a woman he didn't love?"

We stared at each other for so long, the moment something special and tenuous, stretching between us in the closed dark of his room, the moon outside high in the sky, the only witness to what felt like more of an exchanging of solemn vows than an exchange of I love yous. But those three little words pierced the heart and plunged soul deep when he'd uttered them to me. I hoped that mine had the same effect on him now, when I whispered through the dark, "I love you, too."

His mouth came crashing down on mine, and I felt myself go lax beneath him, the moment sealed with a kiss. I realized then that I had spent my entire life wishing, hoping, praying, and willing to *bleed* for anyone, if they would only hold me the right way, and Synister had. He held me perfectly, willingly, and seemingly effortlessly, and I held him back and would never let him go.

Epilogue

Synister...
One year later...

I watched from across the gallery as Madisyn laughed at something someone had said, her perfectly ruby red lipsticked lips wide in a genuine smile. Her white teeth sparkled like the diamonds that dripped from her lobes and throat, and her blue eyes sparkled like hard sapphires under the gallery lights as she entertained the guests of her very first showing.

She may have suspected that I had bought the gallery, and that the quote unquote gallery owner who had approached her as she had painted in Bonaventure had been paid handsomely to do so, but if she did, she was none the wiser.

Her hand still pained her, but she didn't let it keep her from painting. She was almost worlds beyond where she had been as an artist from before she'd been damaged.

She caught me watching from across the gallery floor, her paintings for the *Beauty Beyond Death* showing of her works, benefiting the Bonaventure Historical Society in the continued cemetery restoration and improvement efforts.

Reaper stood nearby, staring up at one of the pieces, his hands folded in front of him, his gaze wandering over the art before him as his lips curved in an appreciative smile. Grim stopped beside me, and I glanced over as he held two glasses of champagne which was on the house tonight.

"He's so proud of her," he said, and he had this tone that said that he was so proud of our strange brother who he'd known for quite a while.

"Sounds like you're proud of him."

He grinned and said, "I am," before he went up and handed Reaper one of the two glasses he'd been holding. I thought back fondly to the morning after we'd killed those two fucks. How he'd knocked on my door when he'd heard me and Madi talking the next morning. He'd been the first of the two of us to spot the difference, and had gone up to her easel and had stopped to look, his eyes roving the scene from Colonial Park. How he'd taken off his glasses and had turned slowly to Madi who had slipped from the bed wearing one of my shirts and had gone to stand next to him to look.

I don't think I'd ever seen so much emotion play over Reap's face before, nor did I expect him to hug her so tight and completely while she'd stood there and laughed with him. It was like I had caught just a glimpse of what Grim had seen in him – I don't know. It was burned into my brain, a new core memory. I didn't understand Reaper's friendship with my woman. All I knew was that it stopped at friendship and that there was nothing threatening about it to me. I couldn't explain that either.

It was almost a relief, honestly. Knowing that if something were to ever go sideways, that she would be taken care of.

She caught me watching from across the room and smiled, and I felt my heart swell in my chest.

"Ah, Señor Synister, a lovely evening," Castañeda purred by my elbow and I smiled, my eyes only for Madi.

"Indeed," I agreed.

"A lovely woman your Madisyn," he said, and I inclined my head in agreement.

"That she is," I said.

"And a talented artist, I must say," he said, looking around us. "I particularly like the one there with the fall foliage. It reminds me of the marigolds during our day of the dead festivals."

"I can see that," I agreed.

"I have put a handsome bid on it," he said with an appreciative smile for the piece.

"There seems to be some fierce competition," I said as Madi's parents approached her. She was on better terms with them, but they always seemed to remain on thin ice with Madi, which I understood.

"Were she my woman," he said. "I would not be able to resist."

"Oh," I said quietly. "I won't be."

He smiled, nodded, and moved across the room to his wife, who was equally a knockout in a crystal beaded crimson dress.

I went to Madi and placed my hand to her lower back, and said to the guest she was speaking with, "Terribly sorry, but would you mind if I steal her away for a moment?"

"Not at all!" they declared, and Madi let me lead her away, down the hall toward the restrooms.

"What's wrong?" she asked as I opened the door for her and she slipped inside.

"I can't hold out anymore," I said. Checking inside and out, I slipped in behind her and shut and locked the door behind us.

"Turn around," I ordered. "Leg up on the counter." She gave me a wicked smile, hiked up her short skirt and leaned over the counter, putting one knee on top of it, opening herself to me as I unzipped and brought my cock out.

I shoved into her with a grunt and very little preamble. I knew she'd been appreciating the view of me across the room as much as I had of her, her bald and naked pussy sopping wet and ready for me as I took her.

I watched her in the mirror above the sink as I fucked her over the counter, her guests just the other side of the door, appreciating her art, even as I painted the silvered glass with her panting breath. She tried to keep her moans down and her gorgeous breasts tried to free themselves out the top of her dress with every punishing thrust that I made.

I loved how absolutely feral her eyes looked as they stared back at me, demanding every inch. In the last year, she'd really grasped how much I loved her for her angelic ways in the streets but how the dirtier she got in the sheets, the more it fucking called to me and satisfied that evil fucking base and dirty longing I had.

She grinned savagely and demanded, "Harder. Love me harder," and to that, I couldn't say such a thing was possible. I could try and fuck her harder, sure – but love her? Love her harder than I already did?

Impossible.

The End

Also by A.J. Downey

The Sacred Hearts MC

1. Shattered & Scarred

2. Broken & Burned

3. Cracked & Crushed

3.5 Masked & Miserable (a novella)

4. Tattered & Torn

5. Fractured & Formidable

6. Damaged & Dangerous

The Virtues

1. Cutter's Hope

2. Marlin's Faith

3. Charity for Nothing

4. Stoker's Serenity

5. Justice for Radar

6. Lightning's Honor

The Sacred Brotherhood

1. Brother to Brother

2. Her Brother's Keeper

3. Brother In Arms

4. Between Brothers

5. A Brother's Secret

6. A Brother At My Back

7. A Brother's Salvation

Sacred Hearts MC Novella

Christmas with the Brotherhood

Indigo Knights

1. Her Thin Blue Lifeline

2. His Cold Blue Command

3. A Low Blue Flame

4. His Wild Blue Rose

5. Her Pained Blue Silence

6. A Cold Blue Call

7. Her Reluctant Blue Cavalier

8. Forged Under Fire

9. Under A Blue Moon

10. Sound of Blue Thunder

Sacred Hearts MC Pacific Northwest

1. Over the High Side

2. Wind Therapy

3. Apex of the Curve

4. Low Sided

5. Eating Asphalt

6. Hammer Down

7. Only Fool Riding

The Voodoo Bastards MC

1. Bourbon & Blood

2. Whiskey Shivers

3. Moonshine Lullabies

Paranormal Romance (with Ryan Kells)

1. I Am The Alpha

2. Omega's Run

3. Hunter's End

Indigo City Darker (with Jared KingPacal Lain)

1. Triple Threat

2. Double Shot

Standalones

Synchronicity

About A.J. Downey

A.J. Downey is a Pacific Northwest girl living in an East Tennessee world who finds inspiration from her surroundings, through the people she meets, and likely as a byproduct of way too much caffeine. She specializes in real and relatable romance stories featuring that real-life kind of love that everyone craves.

Stalker Information:

Website
www.ajdowney.com

Sign up for her newsletter at
http://eepurl.com/dkQiIH

Facebook Group - AJ's Sacred Circle
https://www.facebook.com/groups/authorajdowney/

f facebook.com/authorajdowney
🐦 twitter.com/authorajdowney
📷 instagram.com/ajdowney
BB bookbub.com/authors/a-j-downey